THE LOST KINGS

THE LOST KINGS

A NOVEL

Tyrell Johnson

ANCHOR BOOKS
A DIVISION OF PENGUIN RANDOM HOUSE LLC
NEW YORK

AN ANCHOR BOOKS ORIGINAL 2022

Copyright © 2022 by Tyrell Johnson

Library of Congress Cataloging-in-Publication Data
Name: Johnson, Tyrell, author.
Title: The lost kings : a novel / Tyrell Johnson.
Description: First edition. | New York : Anchor Books, 2022.
Identifiers: LCCN 2021047509 (print) | LCCN 2021047510 (ebook)
Subjects: GSAFD: Novels.
Classification: LCC PS3610.O38364 L37 2022 (print) |
LCC PS3610.O38364 (ebook) | DDC 813/.6—dc23
LC record available at https://lccn.loc.gov/2021047509
LC ebook record available at https://lccn.loc.gov/2021047510

Anchor Books Hardcover ISBN: 978-0-593-46686-5
eBook ISBN: 978-0-593-46687-2

Book design by Nicholas Alguire

anchorbooks.com

Printed in the United States of America
1st Printing

To Tessa. We made it.

The voices just can't worm through.

If I've killed one man, I've killed two—

—Sylvia Plath, "Daddy"

THE LOST KINGS

THEN

I'll never forget the color of the blood on his hands. Deep purple, like he was wearing gloves. The smell of ice-cold pennies. There was some in his beard as well, a thin slice of color striping his salt-and-pepper hair. In my memory, the moon shone silver through the window, sending a beam of metallic light into the cabin and onto his hands, making the pearlescent purple shimmer.

"This could be due to what we call memory bias," my therapist told me once.

It's possible that seeing any blood at all was such an emotional visual stimulus that I've since exaggerated the amount in my mind. It's possible that I only saw the barest glimpse of blood on his fingers, but in my memory, he's standing there, in the open doorway to the cabin, hands outstretched toward me as if for help, moonlight reflecting off his bloody palms. It's all frozen in time, a flash card I can call to mind over and over again, sometimes unbidden, unwanted.

I remember he spent what felt like hours in the bathroom,

the sound of water hissing violently from the sink. I don't remember if I sat on the couch and waited for him or if I stood outside the bathroom, but I do know that when he emerged, he was shirtless, with beads of water in his beard like river-trapped diamonds. He took my hand, which was a strange gesture on his part, and led me to Jamie's and my bedroom, shushing me even though I wasn't making a sound. I lay down and he ran his hand over my scalp. I sat frozen, both because it was oddly intimate of him and because I couldn't help worrying that he was getting blood in my hair. I imagined red streaks like ribbons spilling down the sides of my head.

"It's okay," he said.

On the top bunk, Jamie's breathing was slow but pronounced.

"It's all okay."

I woke in the night and saw him still sitting on the side of my bed, shirtless, his hands like trestles buttressing the framework of his head. In the morning, I found the piece of paper on the kitchen counter. It looked odd, that piece of notebook paper. I couldn't remember ever seeing paper in the house before. To this day, I don't know where Dad found it.

The note said—in hastily written, indelible scrawl—simply: *You're better off without me.*

When I went to show Jamie the note, I got this feeling in the pit of my stomach, like my spine was a rope and someone was pulling it, tugging me down, down, down. It was the feeling that life was about to change. As soon as I stepped into our room, I knew. Call it a twin thing. The cabin was shifting differently; it had hollowed out. The bare, dusty corners were deep and endless. If I'd called out, the sound would've bounced off the walls, echoing like an empty mine.

Jamie, like Dad, was gone.

If anyone were to read the script of my life and look for the catalyst, the moment I was set on a trajectory to becoming the woman I am today, this would be that moment. These would be the memories, etched onto my brain like an epitaph. Blood on my dad's hands. The single line of text across a large blank space. A little girl in a cold, empty cabin.

PART I
Oxford

CHAPTER 1

NOW

The elevator doors open and an old lady enters.

As she shuffles in, she doesn't see me leaning against the back wall. She's wearing a scratchy-looking purple sweater, purple sweatpants, and glasses with lenses as thick as my thumb. She turns to face the doors as they slide closed. I watch, waiting for her to press the button to her floor. As the elevator begins to move, I feel obliged to say something.

"Fifth floor?" I ask, nodding to the small white 5 on the panel, lit with golden light.

She turns, her eyes wide as if surprised to see me. "What's that?"

"Are you going to the fifth floor?" I ask a little louder.

"No, no, fourth," she says, turning back around. She still hasn't pressed a button, and now I have a social obligation. I don't know how to do this without making her feel stupid, so I lean forward and press the button for her. She says nothing. I look over at her white hair, which is sticking up at all angles as if she's just been electrocuted. She's got way too much hair spray on. It's pungent. Suffocating. A single flame in here and she'd light up like a Christmas tree. She's the type of old that doesn't really notice the world around her—I'm pretty sure she's already forgotten that I'm in the elevator. I could give her a heart attack if I wanted. Grab her shoulder, scream, and watch her drop like a fainting goat. That image shouldn't be funny to me, I know that, but I can't help myself. Bad thoughts find me; I don't go looking. The elevator stops and the doors open to the fourth floor. The woman gets off, and I have the small space, still fragrant with her hair spray, to myself.

Suddenly I feel the weight of all the decisions I've made leading to this point. It sits in my throat like bad acid reflux. My therapist tells me that we are the products of all the choices we've made in our lives, and each day is a new choice, a chance to reshape who and what we are. I will myself to step out of the elevator, to be someone different, to not do what I've come there for. Maybe I could join the old lady for a cup of tea, spray my own head with copious amounts of flammable chemicals. We could play bridge, become best friends. I'd call William, tell him it's over.

The doors begin to close, and I reach out a hand to press the OPEN button, my finger hovering over the plastic as I wait for myself to push forward, to watch the golden light fill the small white circle. But I don't. I lower my hand. The doors hum shut.

⬛

I knock on the door of flat 502. After a few seconds of silence, it snaps open. And there he is, William, smile on his face, slight stubble gracing his angular chin, eyebrows straight over pale blue eyes. His hair is unkempt and slightly graying around the ears, and he's wearing a white dress shirt tucked into jeans. On anyone else it would look ridiculous, but because he's attractive, because he's a brilliant professor, somehow it's endearing.

"Jeanie," he says. "There's my girl." He doesn't mind that I'm ten minutes late; he's just happy to see me. And his happiness is like measles—it's airborne, highly contagious.

"How's the conference?" I ask, stepping through the doorway. The room has a small living area, TV, kitchenette, and bedroom behind a partially closed door. From the window on the far side of the room, I can see the Thames and Saint Paul's Cathedral—I make a mental note to visit the latter. I'm not religious, but I like the small inward feeling I get when standing beneath those stone pillars, the ancient holy art, and the great dome, which seems to rise endlessly toward the heavens.

"Oh, you know," William says. "If you've been to one . . ." He waves a hand. He doesn't want to talk about the conference, or business, even though I know he presented an important paper to important people. He doesn't want to talk at all, actually. But I like to chitchat with him first, watch him squirm, wait for that moment when his patience is just tipping toward annoyance before I take my clothes off.

"Presentation went well?" I ask.

"It usually does," he says in that confident way he has, like he doesn't even know he's being confident, like it's this gut reaction he has to the world around him. Oddly enough, it's part of what attracted me to him in the first place. The way he looks at you over the top of his glasses. How his gaze travels to the pit of your stomach and tells you that you are not, in fact, better than him. We've been doing this for fifteen years now, and that gaze still gets me. I need it like a fix.

"So," he says, starting to move toward the bedroom.

"Tea?" I ask.

He pauses, deciding whether to force the issue or play my game. "Sure," he says, going along with it. He goes to the small kitchenette and fills the kettle with tap water and sets the lid down with a satisfying *tick*. I was never a tea drinker before moving to the UK. Now, God, that little *tick*—it's the sound of satisfaction, joy, hope.

"How long are you in London this time?" I ask.

He turns away from the kettle. He's got a weird little smile on his face, like he's copped to what I'm doing and won't let me play any longer.

"Does it matter?" he asks.

"I'd like to know when you'll be back home. Is there something wrong with that?"

"I don't think you give a fuck," he says. He's trying to bait me. To excite me.

"Maybe I don't," I say. Well, shit, I've lost my modicum of power; now we're playing *his* game. He has that skill. The ability to subvert expectations, to make you think you want one thing before revealing this other thing that, yes, oh, this other thing that you want so much more. Damn him. He reaches out and grabs my hand. I notice his wedding ring, and for the hundredth time—well, maybe not the hundredth—I picture his wife, Holly. I've met her a few times. She's blonde and beautiful and pristine like a porcelain figurine. She makes me wonder why he bothers with me. That damn ring. I wish he'd take the stupid thing off. How hard could it be to slip it somewhere I can't see before I arrive? But he never does. It's another power play. He thinks he can do anything he wants.

But what does it matter? I let myself be led, don't I? I'm even unzipping my jacket as we enter his bedroom. He closes the door and there's another *tick* as the metal tongue of the latch slides into place. It's a different sound this time, one with a more nefarious meaning. My sweater is up over my head now. Now his hands are on the back of my neck. Now my hands are on the brown belt holding up his light blue jeans. Before sliding into bed, I reach out and grab his hand and carefully slip the wedding ring off his ring finger. He looks at me, suspicious, but doesn't say a word. I heft the weight of it in my palm for half a second, feeling his nerves radiate from his pores. The room feels gravy-heavy. Then I slide the ring over my thumb, a near-perfect fit.

I'm in control now.

The bed creaks beneath us.

In the kitchenette, the kettle begins to scream.

That evening for dinner, I buy myself fish and chips and a pint of Guinness at the nearest pub. The fries are extra greasy, and I make a mental note to do some burpees in my hotel room that night to make up for the calories. I'd go for a run, but my hotel isn't near any parks and I don't like running in the city. I'm eating in silence while checking out the waiter. He's got a nice smile but is definitely shorter than me. It wouldn't be a deal breaker if not for his sideburns. Who has sideburns anymore? I astonish myself with the realization that I'm actually considering taking him back to my hotel room. But why not? William will be at some fancy party tonight celebrating his paper with his fellow professors. Why do I have to spend my evening alone? I take my time, drinking two more pints, listening to the Proclaimers bang away in the overhead speakers—five hundred miles plus five hundred miles equals one thousand miles. I decide not to sleep with the waiter. I can still feel William's body pressed against me, like his skin cells are commingling with mine in a microscopic dance: keratinocytes, melanocytes, Merkel cells, and Langerhans cells all having a party beneath a thin layer of cotton.

By the time I'm done eating, the city is suffocated in twilight. Traffic along the Thames has slowed to a steady crawl of serious drinkers, partiers, and the homeless. Most of the tourists are at shows or restaurants, or they've retired for the evening. I'm not a big-city person generally, but I do prefer the feel of European cities to American. It's the sound of heels on cobbled streets. The old stone, old wood, Gothic architecture, and history saturating every square inch. In old cities like London, especially at night, you feel as though you're walking with a horde of ghosts.

I buy one of the last tickets of the day for the London Eye and ride the giant Ferris wheel in its lazy circle. I do this almost every time I visit London. There's something relaxing about it. About watching the city descend beneath your feet, the Thames growing thin and the people small. I sit on the bench as, beside me, a beautiful East Indian couple snaps pictures, takes selfies, and records a video for their vlog, or Instagram, or Snapchat, or whatever people are using these days. Something about them annoys me. I think maybe it's the mere fact of their presence in a space I'd rather have to myself. As we're reaching the zenith of our circuit, they approach me and ask if I'd take their picture for them and I shake my head no as if punishing them for intruding on my solitude. At first they seem confused. Is it possible? they think. Can people actually deny this simple social nicety? I give them a smile to show I wish them no ill will, but the smile seems to confuse them even more. Eventually they walk away and ask a young man in a puffy vest, and he obliges them.

The carriage begins its slow descent, the moon rising as a counterbalance, cold and sharp and crescent. I reach inside my jacket, pull out a Snickers bar—drinking Guinness always makes me crave chocolate—and begin to eat in slow, methodical bites. Twenty more burpees when I get back to my hotel, I think. But I don't care; the sugar is luminescent on my tongue, as if I can taste in color.

CHAPTER 2

THEN

Before Dad uprooted us from the life we'd settled into, and well before he showed up at the cabin, his hands covered in purple blood, Jamie and I were living with Uncle Derek and Aunt Eileen in Santa Clara, California. They were nice enough. He was a high school English teacher, and she was a secretary at their Baptist church, which we attended every Sunday. They made us toast with homemade jam in the mornings and Uncle Derek would shoot hoops with us in the driveway in the afternoons. In the backyard, there was an orange tree that we picked from every spring, gorging ourselves on the sweet fruit until our mouths were sticky with sugary pulp and our fingertips stained and chalky from the peel.

We went to a nice school and made the friends you might expect, had our soccer teams, my stint in gymnastics, our school concerts, our barbecues with the neighbors, and, of course, Jamie's piano lessons. In the beginning, we both took lessons. I remember sitting at the bench first, plunking away at notes and realizing, for the first time, that you could be both bored and frustrated at once. Our teacher was a plump woman who always wore these long hippie dresses and had round fingers that weren't conducive to playing the piano, and yet she made them work nonetheless. She smelled of raspberries, and I didn't know if it was some weird perfume she wore, or if she was just constantly eating raspberries.

From the beginning of our lessons, two things were clear: I did not like the piano, and Jamie was a complete natural. His hands, small as they were back then, were already meant for subtle work: pressing keys, forming chords, making music. I quit after the first three weeks.

"You can't quit, Jeanie," Aunt Eileen told me. "You're so good."

"I'm not good. Jamie's good," I said.

"Jeanie, *you're* good."

But she couldn't talk me into it, and she wasn't about to force me. So I stopped. Jamie, on the other hand, practiced all the time. He even began to sleepwalk in the middle of the night, descending the steps to sit at the piano and play. Aunt Eileen didn't like the sleepwalking; she thought it had something to do with the trauma of losing our mom. So she invited their pastor over to pray for us. He prayed for all kinds of emotional healing and well-being and that Jamie would stop sleepwalking.

That night, Jamie played Beethoven's *Ode to Joy*, an easy enough piece, but impressive considering the small amount of time Jamie had been learning. It was strangely beautiful. The music echoed through the still house. It put me right to sleep.

But what did all that matter, anyway? The sugary tang of oranges, Jamie's piano playing. It was all about to disappear.

It was evening when Uncle Derek got the phone call. Jamie and I were watching a show with our dinner plates propped up on TV trays—a regular Friday tradition. During the rest of the week, dinnertime was "family time." That was how Aunt

Eileen and Uncle Derek put it. Even though they weren't our real parents, they liked to pretend they were, like kids playing dress-up.

Uncle Derek was quiet on the phone. Short responses: "Yes," "Of course," "Are you sure that's—"

Afterward, he and Aunt Eileen disappeared upstairs for a good long while as Jamie and I ate our pasta by the TV. I remember it taking a long time for them to come back—I know that because both Jamie and I had finished our meals, and normally when the meal was finished, we had to shut off the show. We didn't want to jinx anything, so we stayed quiet with our empty plates, spotted with flecks and smears of red sauce, while the show ran on and on.

When they did come back downstairs, Uncle Derek had this sad look on his face and Aunt Eileen's eyes were red and puffy.

"What happened?" Jamie asked. He was the more sensitive of the two of us.

"We need to talk to you about something," Uncle Derek said.

"About what?" Jamie again.

"About your dad."

They proceeded to tell us that Dad had been wounded on duty. "He's fine," Uncle Derek said quickly. "But he's coming home. For good this time."

Three years. Three years we'd lived with our aunt and uncle, seeing our father briefly between deployments. Even then he'd become something of a stranger to us—more of a concept than a person. An idea. A noun. Dad, Father, the patriarchal figurehead of our nonexistent household. It wasn't just that so much time had passed since we'd last seen him. It was that—slowly, between each mission—something began to change about him. He used to pick me up and toss me into the air when he'd first come home, and I'd laugh and laugh, flying above his head, weightless as an astronaut. Sometimes he'd let me ride on his shoulders. The world looked so much smaller from that vantage point, and I felt so much bigger. Eventually he stopped doing those things, though. I remember the first time he came home and didn't pick me up. I remember standing in front of him, not wanting to ask but hoping he'd remember, hoping he'd look at me with that smile on his face, lift me by my armpits, and everything would be the same. Only it wasn't the same. And, slowly, neither was he. His visits became brief. His hugs became perfunctory. His conversation became terse and aloof.

And now, now he was coming back to pluck us from our lives like flowers from a well-groomed garden.

"But will we still live here, with you?" Jamie asked. *What a stupid question.*

"No, honey," Aunt Eileen said.

"Idiot," I said.

"Jeanie," Aunt Eileen said, a mixture of sternness and pity on her face.

"He wants to take you to Washington state," Uncle Derek said. "You'll stay at the cabin on the coast."

We'd been to the cabin before. Half-remembered vacations when Mom was still alive. Small rooms, huge trees, the ocean as wide and impossible as the horizon. We'd played board games in that cabin—Candy Land, Trouble, Sorry—and roasted marshmallows outside while Mom made hot chocolate. They were vague, tenuous memories, but ones filled with a strange mixture of fear and joy.

"I don't want to go to Washington," Jamie said, already beginning to tear up. I remember wanting to punch him for those tears. I know that seems callous and insensitive, but maybe I'd wanted to cry, too. Maybe, for once, I'd wanted to be the weak one.

Dad came on a Tuesday morning. It was a bright, sunny

day. He had a long beard and smelled of a strange, musty deodorant. He was limping slightly, and he looked much older than when we'd last seen him. His face carried more lines, there was gray flecked in his beard, and his hands were rough and leathery. He was always a big man, six-four at least, with wide, imposing shoulders and anvil hands. He had dark brown hair and brown eyes like me. We hugged him like we were expected to, Jamie looking sheepish and scared.

Aunt Eileen, Dad's sister, kissed him on the cheek and tried to get him to stay a few days, but he wouldn't. He wanted to get to the cabin as soon as possible.

"At least stay for some lunch, Johnathan," Aunt Eileen said, her voice shaking with emotion. In the end, we did stay for lunch, but no one seemed very hungry despite the fact that lasagna soup was my and Jamie's favorite.

After, we said our goodbyes and hugged Uncle Derek and Aunt Eileen. I looked away when I thought I felt tears coming to my eyes, which I assumed were there only because Aunt Eileen and Jamie were openly crying, and even Uncle Derek looked a little misty.

Dad thanked them for everything, and we piled into his truck with our things tossed in the bed and took off down the road.

"You want music?" Dad asked.

"Sure," I said. Jamie sat silent with his hands on his lap. I figured anything would help drown out the horrible sound of our not-talking, of the engine grumbling, the wheels spinning on pavement, carrying us farther and farther away from the life we'd grown used to, the surrogate parents we'd come to love, and the friends we'd left behind. Dad turned on the radio and let it sit on some hip-hop song that I recognized from school. I twisted the dial, turning the volume way up. When that wasn't loud enough, I rolled down the window. No one asked me to roll it back up or stopped me when I stuck my hand out and kept it there until my skin felt vibrant, buzzing from the rush of the passing wind.

❖

Dad had purchased the cabin before being deployed. I think maybe he knew what was coming and so the cabin served as a weird sort of apology to the family. It wasn't even really a cabin. It's not like it was built of pine logs or anything. Really, it was a small one-story house with a fireplace, a kitchen that opened up into a dining room, and a narrow hallway that led to the bedrooms. But we all called it a cabin for some reason—we never questioned it as kids. We went there off and on the summer before Dad shipped out. Jamie and I played in the woods and caught sand crabs along the coast, letting their little claws pinch our fingers—at least I did, Jamie was too chicken. These were the years Jamie and I established ourselves as a team, separate from Mom and Dad. I remember things being better back then. Jamie would follow me around and do exactly as I said because, even though we were the same age, I always felt like his big sister, and he seemed to agree. And I liked having him with me; the world always seemed a little less frightening when Jamie was with me. Maybe I just felt brave because he was afraid of everything.

In the evenings, we roasted marshmallows by the fire and ate them with M&M's and Ritz crackers because Mom would always forget the graham crackers and Hershey's. Dad would keep busy with manual labor projects around the cabin, building a new countertop for the kitchen, erecting a woodshed, and fixing all kinds of things that had broken or sagged over the years. Once Dad was gone, though, we went only one time with Mom—the very last time. Mom drank a lot of white wine and read romance novels with women in big pink dresses on the cover. We didn't really have a bedtime in the cabin, but when we finally did slide between the sheets, Mom would have a rosy hue to her cheeks and be cuddly and happy.

"When's Daddy coming home?" Jamie asked one night as she was closing our door after tucking us in.

"Soon, baby, real soon," she said.

All parents lie to their kids.

I remember driving home from the cabin that last time on a long, winding trucking road. I remember that Mom didn't look good, which was unlike her. She was originally from London and had this posh accent and a way of keeping herself together that seemed infallible. Her silken blonde hair, diamond blue eyes. But now she looked tired, worn at the edges like a well-loved book. Jamie and I were in the back of the van, inventing a secret language that involved hand gestures and a lot of blinking. I'm sure it wasn't anything substantial, but with my memory-bias problem—thanks, Dr. Gardner—I recall being able to speak it fluently.

"Hey, look," Jamie said, pointing out the window. "Deer." I know now that they weren't deer. They were elk. But we didn't know the difference at the time. To us, they were the biggest deer we'd ever seen. I was about to point them out to Mom before Jamie could, when one of the giant deer jumped out onto the road. She saw the elk too late, swerved, and just barely missed the animal. Everything would have been fine then, except for the seventy-thousand-pound semitruck barreling down the road in the other direction. We just barely clipped it, but it was enough. It crunched the front left side of our car, folding it in on itself like an accordion. We went spinning off the road. It was then that I got that feeling for the first time. Life changing; a rope tugging me downward. I remember being hyperaware in that moment, like my conscious mind was logging everything away so that I wouldn't forget the feel of the car spinning, the chalk-white face of my brother, his hands gripping the armrest, the sound of the semi's brakes roaring like a T. rex, and the white tails of the elk spinning around us as they fled. I remember seeing my arms floating in front of me like they weren't attached to my body, like they were gliding slowly away and there was nothing I could do about it. I was separating from myself piece by piece. It felt like our car spun at least twenty times. Dr. Gardner told me that it was probably only a couple of spins. "But to you, I'm sure it felt like many more," he said.

And it did. Twenty. I swear. Twenty goddamned spins before we settled to a halt against a spruce tree on the side of the road. Mom turned around quickly, but it was clear she couldn't get out of her seat. The front of the car was folded over her lap like an extra seat belt.

"Are you okay?" she asked. She said one of our names then, but it slurred on her lips so I couldn't tell which it was. "Jeeeamie."

"I'm fine," I said.

"But you weren't fine, were you?" Dr. Gardner asked me.

But I was. I really was. The gravity of the situation hadn't settled on me yet. And while my limbs were my own again, it felt like my whole body was floating above the scene as I looked down at the ruined van like an amorphous spectator.

"Is Dad going to come home now?" Jamie asked, his voice shaking. It was such a random and stupid question, given our situation. I wanted to smack him and probably would have if not for the chalky paleness of Mom's cheeks. Looking back now, I realize Jamie was panicked, in shock, and was just latching on to an emotion he understood. He was trying to come to grips with his troubled reality.

"Yes, baby, he'll be home." Her voice was soft as she reached out a hand to comfort Jamie, but she couldn't turn her body far enough around. She shifted, grimacing as she did, trying desperately to reach him.

"And what was that like for you?" Dr. Gardner asked.

"What do you mean?"

"That she was reaching for him and not you."

"Are you okay, Mom?" I asked.

"I'm fine, sweetheart, we're fine," she said, twisting, twisting as Jamie started crying. Her voice was suddenly crisp, sharp as the glass scattered at our feet. "Everything is going to be just fine." She passed out then, and those were the last words she spoke to us.

See. All parents lie.

It was the middle of summer when Dad, Jamie, and I moved into the cabin again. Sunshine shone off the white bark of the alders, splintering through evergreen needles in the morning, creating fractured beams of light through evaporating mist. During the day, Dad would go deep into the woods with a case of beer and his guns and shoot, leaving Jamie and me to explore the area. Neither of us wanted to stay in the cabin and play board games, partially, I suppose, because they were for kids—we were eleven and considered ourselves basically grown up—and partially because they reminded us of Mom. But also, the forest around us was this wild and fantastical thing that we couldn't help but dive into. We'd gotten used to suburban life with our aunt and uncle; this was something altogether new. And while we were still heartsick over being torn from the world we'd come to know, we were, I have to say, a little appeased by our newfound freedom and space.

We were at that in-between age, where we weren't quite ready to stop playing pretend but we also knew it was childish; however, with no one around, we indulged ourselves. We climbed trees, decapitated sword ferns with sticks, and picked the caps off the bulbous heads of mushrooms to run our fingers along the gills beneath. We walked down to the ocean and tried to skip sand dollars and blue mussel shells across the roiling metallic waters. There was this small calm inlet where on extra-hot days we'd take off our clothes and swim in the water, jumping off craggy rocks into the salty brine. We were exploring the many vast mysteries of the world unfurling before us, testing ourselves against nature in order to learn both its boundaries and our own place within them. And if we returned to the cabin with sand between our fingernails, leaves in our hair, and salt on our skin, Dad never said anything about it. He was distant those first few months, drinking and shooting and, in the evenings, disappearing into town, which was only a few miles away. More than once he'd limped back into the cabin late, with a bruise on his face or his knuckles bleeding. The police showed up one night, and Jamie and I thought we were going to be taken back to our aunt and uncle's for sure. But they just talked to Dad outside for a while before driving away.

We made a lot of Chef Boyardee, packaged lunches, peanut butter and jam sandwiches, and a ton of crackers and cheese and salami. Sometimes Dad would make steaks or chicken, singing and drinking as he did. I remember those being the best days, when Dad seemed happy. He'd take our hands and dance around the front porch with us to some imagined song. Sometimes he'd spin me so fast, my legs would lift from the ground. Weightless. Astronaut. One time his bad leg, or the alcohol, got the best of him and he let me go. I went crashing into the kitchen table. It hurt, but we all laughed at the ridiculousness of it as well as the shock and relief of seeing Dad so totally out of character.

"What do you mean?" asked Dr. Gardner.

"Well, he was gone half the time. But when he was around, if he wasn't drinking, he'd be short with us. He'd stare out at the forest for hours, not moving. He'd punch the wall for no reason. I remember him yelling at Jamie a lot, too."

"Was he ever abusive?"

"He was just messed up," I said.

"There are all kinds of abuse," Dr. Gardner said.

I remember one night he woke us, barging into our bedroom and slamming the door behind him. He was definitely drunk, holding his rifle pressed to his chest.

"Under the bed. Now."

We rose slowly, scared and still bleary from sleep.

"Dammit, now now now!"

I remember sliding beneath the wooden slats of the bunk bed, breathing in dust and the smell of old wood, trying to keep my hands away from the stiffened husks of dead spiders. Jamie grabbed my arm and I let him squeeze it. The sound of Dad's ragged breaths, him sliding the bolt to chamber a cartridge, the snap of the safety.

"Fucking bastards," he was saying. "Fucking bastards. They think they'll get me. That's what they think. Well they got another thing coming, you hear me? They got another goddamned thing coming."

Jamie and I huddled beneath the bed while Dad sat against the door, his gun held ready. The crazy thing? I swear I heard footsteps outside the cabin. Soft voices whispering to one another like there really were people out there, looking for him.

"Fear manifests itself in peculiar ways," Dr. Gardner said.

"Felt so real, though."

Dad was quiet for a long time. Eventually Jamie fell asleep, his head resting against his arm.

"It's all wrong," Dad spoke up finally, his voice hoarse like he'd been screaming all night. "Supposed to be me, you know? God. A soldier's not supposed to come home to half a family. Not how it fucking works." He trailed off then; I think he fell asleep, and, eventually, so did I—head against my arm, same as Jamie.

I woke to the sound of a squirrel chittering anxiously in a tree outside as the golden glow of the early-morning sun speared through our window. Dad was gone.

◉

We met Maddox the day after a rainstorm. Everything was wet outside. The evergreen needles and the blooming green buds of the deciduous trees dripped so many tiny droplets of water that a fine mist sheeted over the forest like rain despite the clear skies overhead. Jamie and I were making our way down to the beach without having talked about what it was we were doing. Sometimes things happened like that with us. I don't know if it was a twin thing or if one of us was sub-consciously leading, but often we'd just be talking and mess-ing around in the woods and next thing we knew, we were building a fort, digging a moat, or making our way to the coast.

This time, as we reached the rocks, we saw a boy digging in the wet, gray mud as hard and as fast as he could with a small shovel. His whole body was caked in the sticky sand, his legs half buried as he knelt down and dumped the excess in mounds all around him. Above him, a line of seagulls like a pearl necklace hovered over the mudflats, eyeing the clams and mollusks beneath them.

"What's he digging for?" Jamie asked.

"Dunno," I said, walking toward him.

"What are you doing?" That was Jamie-code for: *I don't want to go over there.*

"Gonna go find out," I said, and Jamie went along quietly, just like always.

The boy was so focused on whatever it was he was digging for that we got within a few paces of him before he noticed us. He paused his digging, looking up and breathing hard.

"Hey," he said, like he'd been expecting us. I examined his face. His skin was a shade darker than ours, his hair black as night. His eyes were a bright brown that almost seemed golden against the silver light of the day.

"What are you doing?" I asked.

"Digging for geoducks," he said, wiping the sweat from his forehead with the crook of his elbow.

"What's a geoduck?" I repeated the word the way he'd said it—*gooey duck*—looking down at the hole in the mud, waiting to see a half-drowned duck come waddling out.

"They're like big clams," he said.

"What do you do with them?" I asked. Behind me, I could hear Jamie shifting around in the mud, looking back toward the rocks. A seagull screamed overhead.

"I think some people eat them," the boy said, looking back at his pit.

"But you don't?" I followed his gaze, unsure how he knew a geoduck was even down there.

"Nope."

"So this is just for fun?"

"Pretty much. You wanna help?"

I looked back at Jamie. He looked a little sick. "Sure," I said and knelt down next to the geoduck hole. "What do we do?" I asked as Jamie slowly lowered himself beside me.

"We just dig. I only have one shovel, though."

"That's okay. Hands work, too." I think I was waiting for him to be surprised. After all, I was a girl and willing to get down in the wet mud and dig with my bare hands. But he was completely nonplussed about the whole thing.

"Cool," he said, accepting both Jamie and me into his project without batting an eye or even introducing himself. "You dig on that side; I'll keep digging here. I think he's somewhere over there," he said, motioning with his shovel. "Ready?"

I was, Jamie wasn't.

We started to dig, fast and hard for some reason. I supposed geoducks could burrow deeper and deeper into the sand as soon as you disturbed their homes. So we went at it and slowly it became fun.

"I think I feel him over here . . . oh, there he goes," the boy said, his shovel scraping out more and more earth—that dense mixture of sand and mud and clay—until we'd dug a hole we could practically fit into. The bottom of it was a soup mixed with ocean water. Once Jamie was sufficiently dirty, I think even he got into the spirit of the thing.

"Is this it?" Jamie called out, revealing a small patch of shell beneath the wet mud.

"Yes!" the boy said. "Hold it there." He ran around the hole with his shovel and started scraping around the brown shell that Jamie was holding. I went with him and we slowly unearthed the ugliest creature I'd ever seen in my life. It was like someone had tried to stuff an elephant's trunk inside a clam. It had a long fat brown shell that squirted water out its backside, and on the other side, the wrinkly elephant trunk dangled like an old man's penis—I say this even though I hadn't seen a penis at that point in my life. But that's really what it was: a dickclam.

"Ew!" Jamie said, but he was laughing now. "That's it?"

"Yup," the boy said, holding it up triumphantly, sand covering his forearms and caked in the black strands of his hair.

"What's your name?" I asked.

"Maddox," he said, passing me the geoduck. I held it in my hands and even brushed its penis-trunk with my thumb and watched it recoil.

"I'm Jeanie King," I said, completely ignoring Jamie. He didn't volunteer his name, either.

"I know who you are. I've seen you around town with your dad."

"Oh," I said. I'd never noticed him before.

He looked at us now, his golden eyes flashing between us.

"So how do you find these things, anyway?" Jamie asked as I handed Maddox back the geoduck.

"You can see their little holes in the sand. If you step on them, they squirt water."

"Really?" Jamie said.

"Yeah, watch."

We walked around the beach for a while until Maddox found a row of small circular holes lined up along the sand. He ran across them, his bare feet stomping on top of each hole. As he went, fountains of varying heights shot up from the sand after him. One launched up his back and we all laughed. I'd never seen anything like it. I felt like we were aliens, and we'd stumbled onto a planet inhabited by a strange boy hunting for creatures of inexplicable wonder. I pictured their bodies submerged in the muck, surrounded by darkness in a mysterious, unexplored kingdom beneath our feet.

"I'm gonna go wash this sand off," Maddox said, turning toward the ocean.

"It'll be freezing," Jamie said.

"Yup." Maddox started to run for the water.

Jamie and I looked at each other. His eyes grew wide. "No way," he said.

I smiled, lifted my soaked, sandy sweatshirt over my head, and ran after Maddox. Eventually Jamie did the same.

From that moment on, the three of us were the best friends in the world.

CHAPTER 3

NOW

Every Tuesday at three thirty in the afternoon, I visit my therapist, Dr. Gardner. The Tuesday after my trip to London, he seemed to be in an extra-Zen type of mood. He looked placidly at me from behind thick glasses. His movements were slow, like the air around him was viscous. His voice was soft, carefully contained. Everything about him was sloth-like. But I knew it was an act, a suit he put on to affect the air of the perfect, understanding, calm therapist. It was enough to drive you insane.

"And what do you make of this?" he asked—a regular question of his, of any therapist, I suppose.

"Make of what?" I'd lost track of what we were talking about, lured in by his languid movements.

"You were telling me about this woman in the elevator. How she wore too much hair spray."

"Right," I said.

"And this bothered you?"

"Well, yeah."

"So why do you think that is?"

"Why do I think what is?" I didn't know why we were talking about this. I didn't really care. Sometimes I just came up with stuff to talk about so that Dr. Gardner felt like he was getting somewhere with me. I wondered at that phrase: *getting somewhere*. Where were we going, anyway? And who was steering the ship?

"Why do you think you felt this way?" he asked.

I stared at him.

"About the hair spray," he said.

"Because . . . I don't know. Because it's a confined space. If I'm not allowed to smoke indoors, no one should be allowed to wear that much hair spray. It's suffocating."

"Hair spray doesn't cause lung cancer," he said. "It's not dangerous."

"It's a fire hazard."

"Fire hazard?"

"Yeah, what if someone sets it on fire?"

"Someone?" He looked at me skeptically, his lip rising to his nose, which, for the briefest of moments, scrunched like a raisin. He quickly regained composure and adjusted his glasses as if that were the reason for his making the face.

I waved my hand. "I don't know." He nodded and I could see myself through his eyes: I was certifiable. I didn't like that look. "It's nothing," I said, backpedaling. "Forget about the old lady."

He stared, waiting for me to continue or change the subject. The clock on the wall had one of those smooth-moving hands, so there wasn't even a ticking noise to punctuate the silence, just the mute second hand sliding noiselessly over white space and black numbers.

"And how has your sleep been?" he asked.

"Same old," I said.

"Still waking up in the night?"

"Yup."

"Still having that dream?"

"Which one?" I knew which one.

"Of being lost in the woods."

"Some nights." Every night.

"Have you been writing it out like we talked about?"

"Yes." No.

"Good. And has that helped anything?"

"I'm not sure."

He nodded. He didn't carry a pen and notepad like therapists did on TV shows. Instead he recorded everything on his phone. But I kinda wished he would keep a notepad like a stereotypical therapist so that he wouldn't have this unbreakable eye contact with me for the whole forty-five. *God, I don't think I've seen him blink once. Blink. Blink, damn you!*

"So tell me about—"

"Listen," I said, leaning forward in my chair.

"Yes?"

"I'd never actually set a woman's hair on fire. It's just, with all that hair spray, I mean, can you imagine?" I started to chuckle but choked it down when his face changed. He looked perplexed. Is that something to be proud of? Perplexing your therapist?

"No, I can't," he said.

I leaned back in my seat. "Yeah, me neither."

❦

That weekend, to take my mind off William returning from his conference to his perfect home and his beautiful, posh wife, I decide to take the morning train to the Cotswolds. I like the fairy-tale feel of the place—the honey-colored stone, the gentle green hills, the quaint bridges and cottages. At least, I like it for a day or two. There's only so much walking around one can do.

I get a room at a small B&B run by an old man who is strict about the timing of the second *B* and very serious about the scarcity of his homemade bread.

"I only make a certain amount each morning and if the others get to it first then that's it, I'm afraid. So don't forget, seven thirty on the dot."

My room looks like Grandma exploded on the walls and the chairs and the heavy drapes pulled back off the windows. Bright blue floral patterns adorn nearly every surface, and there are fake flowers sitting on the nightstand. Despite being fake, they look droopy, their plastic spines bending from the weight of the polyester blue buds. During my stay, I do what everyone does in the Cotswolds. I roam the town, roam the hills, do some desultory shopping without buying anything, and then, when the sun is beginning to set and the shadows have grown cold on the cobblestones, I find the nearest pub and order a few pints. They don't have Guinness, so I order the darkest thing they have. It's smoky and thick with a nice brown head. I'm taking my first sip when I see two men walk into the pub, laughing together. They're roughly my age, I think. One is tall and lanky, the other shorter and a little pudgier but not too pudgy. They both have nice faces and confident demeanors that I find appealing—or maybe I just have Cotswold goggles on: Cotsgoggles. Doesn't matter; I like the look of them. I watch them out of the corner of my eye as they order light golden beers and sip together in a corner booth.

I'm on my second drink and they still haven't noticed me, though I've been giving them clear signs. Men aren't as forward in England as they are in the States. Screw it. I finish my pint and walk right up to their table and sit next to the shorter one.

"Hiya," he says, scooting over for me with a surprised look on his face. I've decided that he's actually the more attractive of the two.

"Are the two of you really going to make me pay for my next round?" I say, giving them a smile that says *I'm a dangerous Disney princess*, which, I've come to realize, is exactly what every man really wants: to be led sensually away by Cinderella and her glass high heels. Misogynistic? Yes. But very true.

"Of course not," the pudgier, more-attractive one says with a smile. Not gay then.

"I didn't think so," I say.

We end up sharing a bottle of scotch together. After, the shorter one comes back to the B&B with me, and we defile the hell out of the poor innocent grandma blossoms.

In the morning, I miss out on the owner's homemade bread. I bet it was delicious.

⊙

On the train back to Oxford, I think: I've never been on a train ride that was too long. There's something about sitting quietly and reading, sleeping, or—my favorite—watching the world spin by outside. Like time in fast-forward. The clack of the wheels on the tracks, the whoosh of the doors sliding open, the passengers all living their individual lives inside their individual bubbles, but existing—for a brief moment—inside our shared metal box. I like the bizarre mixture of solitude and community. It bothers me when people break protocol and try to engage me. I usually wait out their attentions by staring outside, focusing all my concentration on the colors zipping past my window. The grays, greens, browns. Small towns. Row houses. Rolling hills. I imagine all of it on a single thread. Someone pulling violently. I like this image for some reason. Something coming undone. The world irreparably unraveling.

☖

I live in a small neighborhood in Oxford called Summertown. It sits between the Cherwell and the Oxford Canal and is just a few miles away from the city center. It's what big-city people would probably call quaint, with its small shops, start-ups, cafés, and, for some reason, Oxford's branch of BBC studios. My house isn't anything special. A Victorian terraced house that I bought using the not-insignificant amount of money Jamie and I inherited from our dead mom. It wouldn't necessarily be considered old by Oxford's standards, but in comparison to most all of North America, it's pretty much ancient.

As I'm walking down my small street, along the rows of cars and blue recycle bins, I see Manda standing outside my house, waiting for me. I don't know if I have the patience to deal with her today. The whisky headache is knocking against my temples in an extraordinary way.

"Sorry to just pop in," she says, like she doesn't do it all the time. She's smiling, a hand on her pregnant belly in the manner of all pregnant women everywhere.

"No worries," I say, but I don't mean it. I'd dreamed of crawling back into bed or having a hot bath with a bottle of something and a handful of Advil. Manda and I are both thirty-three; we've known each other since university but have been neighbors for only five years. Sometimes I wonder why I decided it was a good idea to move in next to her. She comes over often enough when she needs to gab about something or to complain about her husband or how big her belly is. Her due date is in, like, a week. I have a weird relationship with her: as soon as I see her, I'd like her to leave, but as soon as she's gone, I wish she hadn't left. Another conundrum to tell my therapist about.

"Care for some tea?" she asks. I'm still standing at my door, and I realize that she's politely offering me my own tea. I don't know how to refuse an offer of something I already own.

"Sure," I say, giving her my best I-don't-have-a-hangover smile. She smiles back. Her teeth are shockingly straight given how British and old her family line is. Maybe that's just another stereotype. She's tall, like pushing six-foot tall, with dark near-black hair, long thin limbs, absolutely zero ass, but she has amazing boobs. Even though I've never actually seen them, they're the type of spectacular that you can't help but notice, even when she attempts to conceal them behind sports bras or baggy sweaters. And now that she's pregnant they've become nearly impossible to hide.

I unlock the door and we enter my house. It's nice inside, with floors that creak, clocks that make aggressive ticking noises, books piled on shelves—old textbooks that I've yet to sell back and the complete collections of Tana French, Sylvia Plath, and Maya Angelou—and, like most English housing, a ton of doors and walls and hallways that exist for no conceivable reason.

Manda lowers herself into her usual spot by the window, and I grab the kettle from the cupboard. When I go to fill it, I see Josephine—my obese gray British shorthair—curled up in the kitchen sink like a psychopath. Beside her is a bowl with old pasta stuck to the white porcelain; it's plastered on as if with superglue. When I start the faucet, Josephine lifts a lazy head, staring at me like how dare I inconvenience her, before laying back down. I have to hold the kettle at an angle so as not to disturb her tubby highness. She's a rescue and has been fat ever since I got her. I've put her on diets but, somehow, she just manages to get larger. The problem is—ironically—she's a brilliant mouser. I don't know where she gets the energy, let alone the speed.

"So," Manda says, "how was the weekend? You had a little holiday, yeah?"

"Sort of. Not really," I say.

"That's two in as many weekends. First London, and now . . ."

"Cotswolds," I say.

"Oh, lovely," she says with an excitement that sounds, oddly, genuine. "How was it?"

I can still feel a hand pressed against my back, the weight of him against me, the nebulous feeling of being both inside and outside my body.

"Quiet. Peaceful," I say, pressing my palm to the side of the kettle, feeling the stainless steel grow hot against my fingers, grounding me in place.

"I love it out there, I haven't been in ages. Not since the honeymoon," Manda says, her hand patting her belly as if to illustrate the sudden passage of time.

"That's right," I say. "I forgot that's where you guys went."

"Course I would've loved to have gone somewhere more exotic, but on Donald's salary, I mean . . ."

And here we are, complaining about Donald already. She's made it there in record time this go-around.

"God, can you imagine Hawaii?" she says. "Course I'd look like a beached whale right now. But I mean, Cabo or, I dunno, the Maldives. Good Lord, the Maldives." She sighs.

"Never been," I say as the kettle begins to hum, testing out the pitch of its forthcoming scream.

"Has anybody?" she asks. "Has anybody ever actually been to the Maldives, or is it just some fantasy that the world has cooked up to make people like us feel miserable." She likes to do this, Manda, include you on her misery as if you're in the exact same shoes she is and can completely relate to everything she's saying even if you can't or, perhaps more accurately, don't want to.

"I'm sure they exist," I say, pulling the now-screaming pot from the stovetop. "They exist so that rich people have pictures to show us just how rich they are." And there I go, mimicking her, using *us* to confirm my inclusion in her little sad-club. I can be a bit of a chameleon at times, adapting to my surroundings, feeding off another's personality and appropriating it as my own. What does that say about me? *Dear Dr. Gardner, who am I?*

I pour us each a cup of tea and then, deciding I don't give a shit anymore, go to the liquor cabinet and produce a bottle of Laphroaig. It's expensive scotch, but I need something to take the edge off. I pour it into my tea as Manda laughs. "Good Lord, a very good weekend, I guess," she says.

Without asking, I reach across the table and splash a bit into her cup. "Oh no, I'm—" she starts, but I completely ignore her. "Okay," she says. I'm not sure if the "okay" means *I'm okay*, as in *please don't pour whisky into a pregnant lady's tea*, or if it's an *okay, I guess I'm imbibing whether I like it or not*. I suppose I don't really care one way or another. Manda looks down at her drink as if expecting it to turn some unnatural shade of blue. I take a sip and am surprised at how delicious it is. Smoky and strong.

Something clicks inside me then. Some existential part of me comes alive and suddenly everything feels ridiculous. The balance the two of us are maintaining within our lives, our conversation, our posture at the table, how we hold our tea and sip just so, how my eyes are probably bloodshot and puffy, how her belly is so distended it looks like at any moment it might slide down her legs onto the floor and roll straight out the door—it's all so pointless. She doesn't ever say how uncomfortable she is. Maintain the charade, the balance. I want to upset that balance.

I don't want to hear about how disappointing Donald is today. The truth is, I think she loves being married to Donald. I think she loves being disappointed. I think she gets off by complaining and feeling like a saint for staying with him. But really, he's doing her a favor. By staying with her, he's allowing her to dream about all the better lives she might have had, all the Cabos and Maldives she might have visited when, in reality, she was always going to end up with a Donald in a small English suburb sipping tea and dreaming and complaining. It makes me want to shock her out of her pity party. Or maybe it makes me want to roll back the curtain, just slightly, and reveal to her the person that she's complaining to, let her see a bit more of me and let her run away screaming. "You ever been fucked in the ass?" I ask her.

"What?" she asks, holding her cup of tea, not having taken a drink yet.

"Fucked in the ass," I repeat, bolder and louder this time. "Have you ever done it?"

"Jesus, Jeanie," Manda says, looking around as if microphones directly wired to the queen herself might be hidden in the multitudinous hallways.

"It hurts, I'll tell you that. And, to be honest, it's not that enjoyable. Some women get off on it, I guess. But not me. I learned that the hard way." I take another sip of my tea-whisky—a larger one. "That's how my weekend in the Cotswolds was."

Manda surprises me by taking a sip of her own drink. She sets the cup down carefully, the porcelain clacking pleasantly against the white wooden tabletop.

"Once," she says in a half whisper.

"What's that?" I ask.

"I did it once, in college. My boyfriend, he, well, he was much more experienced and, I dunno, I guess he sort of talked me into it."

I can't help the smile from forming on my face.

"Why are you smiling? It was awful."

Now I'm laughing, and Manda is taking another drink. She sets the cup down again, the same clacking noise. I'm still laughing. Now Manda is laughing, too. I've forgotten my headache and, for the first time since college, I feel like Manda and I are actually friends.

⬤

I work as a cashier at a small shop in Summertown that serves whole family-size dinners, ready to eat. Just plop them in the oven for a few minutes, and voilà, dinner is served—lasagna, fettucine, shepherd's pie, all kinds of soups. It's not necessarily hard work, what I do. I'm not logging hours behind a desk, slinging concrete, or slogging through slow, endless department meetings as my soul disintegrates inside me. I'm either pressing buttons on a screen to complete a dinner purchase or recommending dinners to customers who are looking for something specific.

I work an evening shift that night at the shop, entering just as my boss, Deloris, is leaving.

"Oh good," she says, grabbing her jacket as if she's been waiting for me to arrive. The store is empty except for Mr. Hannigan, who's examining the casseroles like he does every Monday night. "I've got to get out of here, dear, you're fine to help Mr. Hannigan, I'm sure."

"No problem," I say. "Big date tonight?" I ask. Weirdly, Deloris is always off on another date. She's fiftysomething, maybe early sixties, I can't tell, to be honest. She's got silver hair and a fairly plump figure but a kind face and a heart of gold—one of *those* people. Her husband died something like ten years ago and she's recently discovered the dating scene.

"Yes, actually, and it's our third date in a row." She's patting her jacket for something.

"Ah, third date," I say. "You know what that means."

"I don't," she says, looking up from her coat to meet my eyes. "What does it mean?"

I laugh. "Come on, Deloris. Third date. That's the sex date."

"Oh, nonsense. He's not getting anywhere near my Mary tonight."

"Your what?"

"Not until the fifth date, at least." She winks at me and I laugh again. "Ah, there it is." She hustles around the counter, grabs her bus pass, and stuffs it in her coat.

"And where did you meet Mr. Wonderful?" I ask as she's heading toward the door. I don't want her to go quite yet. I'd rather catch up, if only for a minute or two. I like Deloris. She looks almost put out by the question. In the corner of the shop, Mr. Hannigan has moved on to the soups. He won't choose soup, though, he never does. He's the type who likes to peruse all his options, imagining all his possible evenings before choosing the beef-and-cheddar casserole like he always does.

"Oh, you wouldn't believe me if I told you," Deloris says, nearly reaching for the door handle.

"Try me," I say, leaning against the counter and crossing my arms beneath my chest.

Deloris looks at Mr. Hannigan, then back to me. "Online," she says, nearly whispering.

"Deloris," I say in mock scandal.

"I know, I know, but Andrea got me on this site. Made me a . . . what is it? Portfolio? Profile? Anyway, I liked the look of his picture and he liked that I was a businesswoman and we got to talking. Texting? Emailing? Oh, whatever it is."

I shake my head, still smiling. "He sounds wonderful."

"We'll see. I like him well enough so far."

She's still standing by the door, waiting for me to release her.

"You know," she starts, "this online thing, you might—"

"Well, you enjoy your night, Deloris," I say.

She nods. "Yes, of course. You as well, my dear." She shuffles out the door to a slate sky already trending toward darkness. A few college students pass the shop, followed by a woman pushing a pram filled with groceries. I'm about to sit down in the chair behind the counter when Mr. Hannigan finally trundles up to the register.

"I've decided," he says as if he's accomplished some great task for which I should be congratulating him.

"Excellent choice," I say, then ring up his beef-and-cheddar casserole.

When the place is empty and quiet again, I can hear the buzzing of the freezers keeping the dishes cold and fresh and ready to cook. I open the drawer to my left to pull out the Margaret Atwood novel I've been reading, but I don't see it. I open up the drawer below it, thinking maybe I put it in a different drawer by mistake. Nope, nothing. Did I take it home? I kneel down and open the bottom drawer, sifting through duct tape, an old binder, a stapler, rolls of receipt paper, and scissors. The bell chimes again and I stand up.

When I see who's at the door, my feet cement themselves to the floor. Somehow, I've become more solid than the objects around me: the counter, the card reader, the cash register, the cup full of pens. Everything is flimsy, insubstantial, ethereal compared with the density of my own skin and bones. I feel that rope pulling my insides downward.

"Jeanie King?" the man who just entered says.

"Fuck me," I say.

Standing in the doorway, looking at me from the blaze of his golden eyes, is Maddox.

CHAPTER 4

THEN

It wasn't until the leaves had gone from green to yellow and red that Jamie and I realized that we were probably supposed to be in school. We had conflicting emotions about this. On one hand, not having to go to school as a kid was like being told you could have as much candy as you wanted any time you wanted it. But on the other hand, we were just kids, and not going to school was weird. Besides, we felt like some kind of authority figure would find out and track us down. We carried all the guilt our father didn't.

"We have to tell him we want to go to school," Jamie said one day, in an uncharacteristically assertive tone.

I just shrugged, surprising even myself. "Fine."

We found Dad in front of the cabin, sharpening one of his knives on the Adirondack chair.

"Jamie and I want to go to school," I told him, my back straight, my head lifted like I was more confident than I felt.

"Both of you, huh?" He looked between us like he couldn't quite believe our mutual consensus. "You're serious?"

"Yes," I said.

"And what do you think they have to teach you that I don't?"

"Uh, math," I said.

"What do you need math for?" he asked, his blade making a metallic shushing sound as it slid across the square white whetstone.

"So other kids don't think we're stupid." I must have said something right, because he laughed.

"Well, that's the most honest reason I've ever heard." He set the knife down and looked at the both of us. Jamie kept his eyes glued to his feet. "Fine," he said. "I'll talk to somebody."

And he actually did. By the following week, we were enrolled.

Being thrust into a new school after a whole summer of just Jamie and me alone in the cabin with Dad was jarring. We felt like suddenly we were experiencing the wider universe again. Somehow, we'd completely forgotten what it was like to be around other children. In that summer of freedom and zero structure, we'd grown wild. My hair was matted and unkempt, Jamie's face constantly had a smudge of brown dirt across his cheeks. The other kids at school were alien to us— pristine little planets unto themselves, absorbed in their own worlds, drifting through outer space, looking for other planets that were part of the same solar system. It was dangerous and chaotic, and there were collisions: supernovas bright and red as blood.

Dad took us to school each day in his truck, grumbling about how it was all a waste of our time and his gas. But to his credit, he took us, every single day, even when it snowed and the roads to the cabin became treacherous with slippery rocks and frozen ruts.

"Can we skip today?" I asked him once. "We wanna play in the snow."

"No," he'd said. "You asked for this. Now it's your responsibility to see it through."

He even began to make us peanut butter and jam sandwiches and bought ziplock bags at the corner store to put them in. It was strange, seeing him up in the morning—bloodshot eyes—spreading jam on bread. He didn't have any type of job to go to, partly because he got money from the government for his service in the military, but also because of the money he probably got from Mom.

At school, we rarely saw Maddox because he was a grade ahead. So Jamie and I were glued together, both in class and out. We were so lost in our own world that we became outcasts. Everyone assumed we didn't want any part of their games, and I suppose Jamie and I assumed that about each other as well. I would never have told Jamie this, but I remember watching the other girls in a circle, playing some sort of hand-slapping chanting game and wishing I could join them. Instead, I said to Jamie: "That looks so boring."

I was pretty sure, though, that Jamie genuinely didn't want to hang out with the other boys. There was this boy named Daylen in our class. He was a big kid who had jet-black hair and constantly wore sweatpants. He sat behind Jamie and had begun to prod him with a pencil during class. Jamie ignored it, hunkering down in his seat like it was a shell. I thought maybe this was how boys joked around. I thought maybe Jamie didn't mind so much. But then Daylen started making verbal jabs. "Why are you so small?" he'd ask. "Is your brain the same size?" Stupid shit that didn't even make sense. But Jamie just ignored it, so I ignored it, and the teacher, Mrs. Everson, didn't notice. It wasn't until Jamie told Dad that he didn't want to go to school anymore that I realized Daylen was actually getting to Jamie.

"Why not?" Dad asked.

"I just don't want to. It's stupid. You were right."

He looked to me for approval, but I didn't know what to say. I was beginning to like school. There was this girl, Samantha, who shared her dessert with me, and I thought maybe we were becoming friends. So, that day, after Dad forced a tearful Jamie into the truck, I waited and watched Daylen from the corner of my eye. Sure enough, little Mr. Sweatpants had a straw in his hand, and he was chewing a small bit of paper. "Hey, little girl," he said to Jamie. Then: *splat*, he shot the wet ball of paper through the straw and it struck Jamie's neck. Jamie swatted it away like it was a fly but kept his eyes glued to the teacher. I could see the tears already building. How long had Jamie felt so miserable? When had Daylen's attentions finally broken my brother? And how had I not noticed? He was my twin, after all. Had I not really cared? Didn't matter. I cared now. I cared about staying in school, about Samantha and her mom's delicious chocolate cookies, about Jamie and the look of defiant terror in his eyes. So I rose, in the middle of class, and walked behind Daylen. Reaching down, I pulled his chair out from underneath him. He toppled to the floor, and when he did, I lifted the chair and threw it on top of him as hard as I could. He brought his hands up to block most of the impact, but a part of the leg struck him against the chin and split his skin open. It was a small cut, but there was enough blood that he screamed as if I'd slit his throat. I didn't say a word; I just walked back to my seat and sat down to the sound of the teacher's screaming rebuke. Didn't matter, Daylen got the message. He never bothered us again.

Dad was called into school that day, and we all took a trip to the office. Daylen cried and accused me of trying to kill him. I wouldn't say a word. I was suspended for the rest of the week and had to write a letter of apology. *Dear Daylen, I'm sorry for throwing a chair on your head.* Dad let Jamie take the week off as well, and so the two of us got to disappear into the snowy forest and build igloos and stockpile snowballs filled with rocks in case Daylen and his friends ever came to attack us.

One evening, while Jamie was in the bathroom and Dad and I were sitting by the fire, Dad said, "Tell me what really happened." His face never left the dancing flames, his hand around the neck of a beer bottle. I told him everything. After, I figured he'd lecture me about talking it out, making nice, about being kind to everyone, even losers, even bullies. That's what Uncle Derek and Aunt Eileen would have said, using pithy Presbyterian catchphrases.

Instead, Dad nodded, took another drink of his beer, and said: "Good girl."

◉

It was around this time that Dad began to take us out with him on the weekends to go shooting. He'd rigged up a platform between two trees where he shot beer cans, Coke cans, milk jugs, and whatever else we had lying around. He had his Remington .308 rifle that decimated cans and left large gouges in the body of an old stump. He let us shoot his .22 bolt-action Marlin Model 60 with his box of Winchester Super-Xs. It hurt my shoulder at first, but eventually I got used to it.

Jamie, on the other hand, did not. He put on a brave face, but it was clear: he didn't like the loud noise, the snap of the stock against his shoulder, or the way Dad would smack him in the back of the head when he missed. They weren't gentle smacks, either. "What the hell was that?" he'd say. "Not even close."

Jamie missed the target more often than not. But not me. Or, at least, I rarely did.

"Inhale," Dad would tell me as I sighted through the scope. "That's it. Line up the target. Exhale. Pause . . . now squeeze the trigger, don't pull."

And the aluminum can would split and tumble to the grass.

"Hell ya!" Dad would yell. "That's my girl." He'd place a hand on my shoulder and shake it, and I have to admit, there wasn't anything better in the whole world.

It soon became a regular thing that we'd do after school or on weekends. But after the first two or three outings, Jamie stopped coming.

Dad and I developed a strange sort of bond over shooting. He still wasn't the dad I remembered from before his deployment, the dad who'd play dolls with me, have tea parties, and tickle both Jamie and me to tears before Mom would yell at us to go to bed. Now he was distant, resigned, always with a can or bottle of something close by. Since moving to the cabin, I'd felt, to be honest, slightly scared of him. Of the dark, deep-river looks he'd get on his face; of the way he'd yell at nothing in the middle of the night; of how he'd rub his wounded leg with dead, lifeless eyes; or of how he'd tell Jamie to "Buck the hell up," "Stop your blubbering," "Don't be such a fucking girl." Sometimes I'd see bruises on Jamie's neck or arms, pale blue like spilled ink. But now, now that we had our little time in the woods murdering beer cans and jugs of milk, something was germinating between us. Not something old, from the before-dad, but something new, something fresh and green, with soft leaves unfurling. He put his hand on my shoulder more, smiled at me from time to time, and I began to feel something like love for him. I even liked the special treatment he gave me over Jamie.

"It sounds like you were competitive with Jamie," Dr. Gardner said.

"Me? I dunno. Aren't all siblings?"

"Was Jamie competitive with you?"

"No, he couldn't care less," I told him.

"And why do you think that is?"

I shook my head. "I think Jamie just wanted to survive Dad."

"Do you think that's why he left?"

❧

I remember one time, there was this lightning storm. Dad had been brought home by the police again. He had a welt under his eye and was listing slightly in the wind, which sent sheets of rain pounding on our windows and rooftop. The trees were swaying madly, their limbs gesticulating like they were trying desperately to warn us of something. And every few seconds there'd be a flash of lighting and *bang*, the monumental report of thunder.

Jamie was practically shaking with fear. Dad had a fire burning hot in the hearth and was especially drunk. He kept glancing over at Jamie, who was staring out the window, ashen faced.

"Just ignore it," Dad said to Jamie. "It's fucking fine."

"Can trees snap in half?" Jamie asked.

"No," Dad said. He was sipping from a bottle of Jack Daniel's, sitting too close to the fire and wiping his swollen eye. His head drooped lazily every once in a while. He was somehow about to pass out despite the cacophony outside. I was sitting at the kitchen table, practicing bridging a deck of cards over and over again. The soft tapping of the cards against the scuffed wooden table was barely audible over the machine-gun rain on our windows.

A flash of light lit the cabin in iridescent silver, followed only a second later by a tumbling roar of thunder. Jamie let out an ear-piercing shriek, which jolted Dad from his half doze.

"Goddammit," he said, standing sluggishly to his feet. "I said get away from that fucking window, didn't I?"

He charged for Jamie, who cowered deeper into the couch, scared as much of Dad as he was the storm. Dad grabbed him roughly by the arm and practically threw him across the room. He landed hard on the floor.

"Stop being such a goddamned baby all the time, huh?" Dad said.

Jamie burst into tears. It was too much for him. Any other time, I would have stood up to Dad; I would have fought for Jamie, protected my brother. We were a team, him and I, always had been. Dad was the outsider, and it was my duty to do or say something. Anything. Only, I didn't. I didn't because Dad was beginning to show an interest in me. We were bonding over our skill and love for shooting. I didn't want to ruin whatever it was that we were building together. It was like this precious glass figurine that I had to stuff with cotton and build walls around or else it would shatter into a million pieces. So I said nothing. I sat at the kitchen table, shuffling my deck of cards over and over again, my eyes fixed on the interchanging black and white faces as if they were the most mesmerizing thing in the world.

Somehow, Dad softened. Maybe he saw what he had become, maybe he felt bad for how hard he'd thrown Jamie, or maybe Jamie's tears finally got to him. Either way, he knelt down in front of Jamie, the fire lighting half of his face in maleficent, flickering orange.

"Sometimes," he said, "you have to face your fears head-on. Look them in the eye and laugh." He stood. "Come on."

"What?" Jamie asked, his eyes puffy, his nose filled with snot.

"Come with me." Then he turned and looked at me. "Let's go, Jeanie."

I set my cards down and stood, eager to please, eager to

show I wasn't scared like Jamie. It was a sort of betrayal, how acquiescent I was, a treachery I felt in my stomach. Earlier that day, Jamie and Maddox and I had thrown starfish into the low tide, laughing together at how their little bodies spun like pinwheels in the air before crashing down into the water with a sloppy splash. I'd liked the way Jamie's laugh had sounded, so carefree, so light. But now I was standing on the other side of something that I'd placed between us. A stone wall, with Dad in the middle, looking down in judgment.

Dad led us outside. Jamie tried to protest, but Dad grabbed his hand and forced him out the door. Our clothes were soaked almost instantly as the howling wind stung our eyes.

I was already freezing, goose bumps rising along my arms, water dripping from my hair.

A flash of light split the sky, and in the following chorus of thunder, Dad lifted his hands into the air and screamed as loud as he could. It was a deep-belly, lion roar. I know it couldn't have been louder than the thunder, but to my ears, with Dad that close to me, it was.

"You too," Dad yelled to both Jamie and me, grabbing our hands. Our palms were wet and slippery against one another, but Dad held on tight. We waited, watching the rain fall down in waving sheets. It wasn't long before the next flash. Dad gripped our hands tight, lifted them into the air, and when the thunder sounded, he screamed again. And beneath his scream was another sound. I looked around him and saw Jamie, mouth open, tears or rain or both wetting his face, veins bulging in his neck and forehead. He was screaming at the thunder, just like Dad. I was so amazed at seeing Jamie like that that I forgot to scream myself. I just watched him, entranced by this deep well of emotion spilling out of my brother. The thunder tapered off and with it, I realized, the rain. Even the wind died down, though the trees somehow still trembled. All around us was this sudden, strange calm, as if we were encased in some invisible bubble, the three of us standing still while the world shuddered around us. When the next flash and thunder cracked, we all screamed. And our scream became one. Loud and strong and long. We were still screaming when the tall pine tree in front of us exploded.

That's what it seemed like. No one saw the bolt of lightning strike the tree. All we saw was an eruption of fire spurt down the spine of the great evergreen accompanied by the loudest bang I'd ever heard. It sounded like two semitrucks colliding at full speed. Even Dad jumped, but none of us rushed back to the cabin, not just yet. We'd been filled with something, something impossibly strong, and it still radiated in our bones. And so we watched as a part of the tree splintered and crashed to the ground, maybe only twenty yards from our cabin. That's when Dad started laughing. Loud, crazy belly laughs that had him doubled over. Then Jamie started laughing, too, though I'm pretty sure he was crying as well. It was so absurd, so fantastical that I couldn't help but laugh along with them, if only to feel that same connection between the three of us, staring down the broken, smoking tree as the rain began to fall once more.

It's probably memory bias—I know, I know, shut up, Dr. Gardner—but at the time, I would have put a hand on a Bible and sworn that the three of us, with our screams and the power of our connection, had called down that bolt of lightning ourselves.

⬛

When Jamie and I weren't in school, we spent a lot of time with Maddox at the beach. We'd dig up geoducks, stomp the globular heads of bull kelp to see who could make the loudest pop, and chase seagulls and herons and cormorants across the mudflats. We'd build oblong walls of sand around us and fight against the oncoming tide to see how long we could maintain our fort. Sometimes Maddox would bring a few bucks and we'd walk along the rocks to the burger place by the pier and buy a basket of fries and share them while a horde of seagulls eyeballed us. Other times, we'd just run across the soft sand as fountains of geoduck spray exploded behind us like mortars. To this day, I remember the feeling of running, full tilt, across the beach, the yawning ocean stretching out to infinity. It seemed impossible that the water had an end, or that our days together would ever cease to exist.

Maddox was fascinating to me, from his wild, golden eyes, to the way he ate steaming hot fries without burning his mouth. Sometimes he had this crazy intensity and focus, like when our sand fort was being systematically dissolved by the irascible force of the tide; other times he displayed a sort of blasé lack of awareness that came across as confidence—the way he'd walk up to the counter at the corner store, his hands and face covered in mud, and buy us a bag of chips while Mrs. Whitaker gave him a disapproving look from behind the cash register.

"You all right, Maddox?" she'd ask, her eyes drowning beneath the giant glasses that didn't fit her face.

"Yeah, why?" he'd ask, completely oblivious.

I didn't know much about his homelife at the time, other than the fact that he was a child of freedom. Like us, he was used to the unstructured routine provided by parents like my dad. We'd meet him at the beach at any time of day—or night, in one instance. He'd gotten this crazy idea involving a tennis ball, a golf club, and a jerrican of gasoline. We met along the rocky promontory on the south end of the beach and watched as he soaked the tennis ball in gasoline and began fumbling with a matchbook.

"What's the goal here exactly?" Jamie asked.

"Oh, you'll see." Maddox smiled like he had this great secret.

"It's pretty obvious," I said, always a smart aleck. "You're going to light the tennis ball on fire."

"And then what?" Jamie asked. He sounded nervous, like he knew we were doing something we weren't supposed to be doing but was secretly excited about it all the same.

"I'm guessing," I said, "judging from the golf club—"

"Don't ruin it!" Maddox said.

Eventually he managed to light the match and bring it to the neon hairs of the tennis ball. It lit on fire with a glorious *whoosh* that made us all laugh. Jamie even clapped his hands as Maddox jumped back to avoid being burned.

"See?" Maddox said, smiling as if his efforts had already paid off.

Then, swinging the golf club with surprising speed and accuracy, Maddox hit the flaming tennis ball with a hollow *thwop*, sending it careening into the ocean. It was pretty magical, I'll give him that—as if a fiery meteorite had descended right in front of us and landed in the water with a hissing puff of smoke. But he'd brought only the one ball, and the joy quickly faded. So we sat on the rocks and watched the stars above us turn in their unpredictable patterns.

I wasn't unaware of the draw of boys at the time—both Jamie and I had turned twelve at this point, our birthday had been in June—I just didn't quite know what to do with it, this strange attraction. The other girls seemed so confident, so sure in the way they laughed at the boys. I remember seeing Maddox in the hallway, talking to a girl from his grade. I felt strange emotions riffle through me, both at seeing him outside of the beach, and at him talking to someone who wasn't me or Jamie, somebody who was, in fact, a pretty blonde girl named Shelley Evans. When I approached the two of them, I didn't really know what I was doing, just like I didn't really understand the emotions buzzing inside me.

"Wanna meet at the beach today after school?" I asked Maddox, interrupting whatever they'd been talking about. Shelley Evans looked at me like I was an ant she wanted to dig her heel into. I kinda hoped she'd try.

"Yeah, sure," Maddox said, completely unflustered.

"Sounds good," I said, and twirled around, my brown tangle of hair swinging behind my back. I realize now I was laying claim to Maddox, whatever claim I thought I had over him. I didn't want to date him or kiss him or anything like that, not then, anyway, but I did want him to like me the most. To not want to talk to any girls but me. I suppose it was why I didn't invite or even tell Jamie I was heading to the beach after school. Jamie was reading in his room, Dad was God knew where, so I slipped quietly outside and down the path toward the beach. It was weird being out without Jamie. It wasn't like we were together all the time. I did things on my own. Only, I was going to meet Maddox, and that was always a thing Jamie and I did together. It was another small betrayal; I'd begun to stack them, one on top of the other, collecting them like trading cards.

I found Maddox by the dead log we often met at. He was eating a bag of peanuts, tossing one casually every once in a while to a seagull that stood a few feet away from him, patiently waiting for its next treat.

"Hey," he said, glancing over my shoulder like he was looking for Jamie. "Check this out," he said—no preamble, no small talk with Maddox. He stood up from the log. The seagull, sensing his movement, launched into the air but flew only a few feet away before landing once again on the wet sand and looking back at Maddox or, rather, at the bag of peanuts he'd set on the log beside me.

Maddox took a few steps, then lowered his hands to the

sand and lifted his feet into the air. For a full five seconds
he stood like that, hands planted on the sand, feet lifted
toward the sky, arms shaking and shifting to keep his balance. I laughed and clapped like the perfect audience, and I
was genuinely impressed. Slowly, Maddox's feet began to tilt,
then spin to one side. He tried to correct it, but gravity got the
best of him, and he flopped backward, his backside striking
the sand with a hard slap. Sand, flattened out against a body
and hardened by saltwater and sun, was solid as concrete.
Maddox grunted as all the air rushed out of his body. I could
practically see it, a gray puff escaping his lips as his lungs
shrank like raisins.

He gasped and made this horrible sucking sound. I rushed
to him as if there was anything I could do.

"Are you okay?" I asked.

Maddox, of course, couldn't answer; he was too busy gulp-
ing air. He nodded, though, closing his eyes, which were filling
with tears. I felt so embarrassed for him. And it was weird,
seeing him like this. He was always so confident and carefree.
To see him wounded, vulnerable, to see the child in him broke
something in me. I knelt down in the sand next to him and
put a hand on his shoulder as if that might do something.
Slowly, he got his breath back.

"That's not how it was supposed to go," he said in a stran-
gled voice.

I laughed and he managed a pained smile.

"Wanna go get some fries?" I asked.

He nodded and I helped him to his feet. For a brief second,
I kept my hand on his arm. God, we were just kids then, not
even pubescent, but I still felt a strange thrill at the base of
my stomach. A stirring I didn't understand but loved desperately. I let go of him as we started walking along the beach,
but as my hand slid off his arm, he reached out and grabbed
my fingers, holding tight to my palm. I looked down at our

fingers, skin and bone interlacing one into the other to the point where, if not for the darker shade of his skin, I wouldn't have been able to tell whose fingers were whose. We walked hand in hand along the beach all the way into town, the bag of peanuts left on the log behind us, an offering to the seagull.

"Is that when you began to fall in love with him?" Dr. Gardner asked.

"I never said I was in love with him," I said.

"Oh . . . I see."

"But yes," I said. "I guess that would be the moment."

CHAPTER 5

NOW

"So how's work going?" This was one of Dr. Gardner's regular questions during the first few weeks of our sessions.

"Same old same old. I think Deloris is sleeping with someone." I sank deeper into my chair. This was a safe subject for me. No hidden land mines.

"And you enjoy the work?" he asked.

"I dunno. I don't mind it; let's say that."

"You know, a little bird told me you did quite well at Oxford," he said. "Your professors were very impressed."

Uh-oh. Land mine. "Were they?" I said, sighing to show him that he was treading on dangerous ground. Or, rather, not dangerous, just tired. I didn't need or want a pep talk from my therapist. I wasn't paying him for this.

"I heard rumors you've turned down research grants and scholarships."

"Right," I said. "Well, I don't know if you heard, but my mom was fairly rich. She left me a good chunk of change."

"So what I'm hearing is that you've got the resources, the

education, and the skills to do pretty much anything you want."

I could feel my jaw clenching. I leaned my head to the side and heard a small pop. I used to be scared that if I cracked my neck too many times or too hard, I'd snap it in half. Now I kind of wonder what that would feel like.

"Any reason you didn't pursue something more . . . academic?" he asked. But he meant more *fulfilling*, more *challenging*, more *interesting*, more *anything*.

"Maybe I wanted to go into food services," I said.

"Earlier you said you don't mind your job, not that you like it or pursued it."

He was trying to bait me. It was working. "And how do you like *your* job?" I asked.

"It's challenging at times, but I find it very rewarding."

"Well, good for you. You're the top one percent of people in this world who feel that way. Everyone else is like me. We show up, punch our hours, have a few laughs here and there, sometimes we're bored out of our minds, sometimes we're frustrated, sometimes we want to toss a plate of spaghetti and meatballs in Mrs. Holloway's face if she brings it back one more time for not being meaty enough. But it's a job. I do it. Just like everyone else. And maybe I like being just like everyone else sometimes."

He stared at me. I could see the look in his eyes. *Yes*, he thought, *yes, more, more.*

"And what do you feel like other times?" he asked.

"What do you mean?"

"You said you like feeling like everyone else sometimes. That implies, most of the time, you feel like something else. What do you feel like most times?"

A victim. A psycho. A maniac.

"I don't know what I meant," I said. "I'm completely normal."

"No one is completely normal. Normal is a relative term."

"Well," I said, "I'm a relative kind of girl." He gave me a confused look. Even I didn't know what I meant. I smiled wide at him in the most normal way I could manage.

❦

Maddox always had this way about him. An aura, you might say. Like anything he did or wore or said was exactly the right thing. It wasn't quite confidence; rather, it was a lack of self-doubt, self-scrutiny, which is different from confidence, I think. Either way, everything about him always seemed so solid, like he was real in a way that others weren't. People envied him for that. Wanted to be like him no matter what he wore or said. It's like those models in fashion magazines; they could be wearing a modulated garbage can and somehow you'd stare at their pretty faces, glossy legs, and white teeth and think, *I should just see how much those garbage cans cost.*

Standing in the doorway to the dinner shop, Maddox wears a navy-colored jean jacket over a dark green hoodie, black jeans, and brown shoes. His hair is cut shorter than when he was a kid. There are more lines around his eyes and forehead, but they're the distinguished kind, not the catcher's mitt kind. He looks, if I'm honest with myself, absolutely gorgeous. A more mature version of the boy I used to know. The angles and corners of his face chiseled into something more concrete. His eyebrows caterpillar-thick and perfect, his golden eyes both sharp and endless. It's been nearly a decade and a half since I've seen him.

"Maddox," I say, frozen, suddenly unsure of the mechanics of my own body. I stuff my hands in my pockets to prevent them from doing something weird.

"Jeanie, wow, it's great to see you."

"Yeah," I say like an idiot. "What are you doing here?"

"Uh, well, getting some dinner for one," he says.

"No," I say, then forget how to continue the rest of my sentence.

"No?" he says, looking back at the door. "Are you closed?"

"Oh, no, I mean, we're definitely open."

"And you work here, huh?" he asks, but not in a condescending way. He looks around the shop as if just discovering it. He nods in approval of this fantastic profession I've chosen for myself.

"No," I say. "I just like standing behind this counter." I venture a hand from my pocket and rest it on the countertop. "I'm a big fan of counters." It's meant to be a joke, to lighten the mood, but instead, he shifts awkwardly.

"Duh, right, sorry. How do you like it? Working here, I mean."

"It's a job," I say. "And you, what are you doing these days?" Such terrible conversation. Such stiff small talk. I want to vomit. I want him to leave and never come back. I want him to stay forever. To throw me down on the unswept floors.

"I'm a journalist, actually."

I smile. "So you did become a writer."

"Of sorts."

"And what brings you to Oxford?" I ask.

"Yeah," he says, as if agreeing with the question. He takes a step toward the counter, some of his surety coming back to his posture, his movement. "I've actually, I mean, I'm here to see you, Jeanie." I laugh. I can't help myself, it sounds so ridiculous. I'd meant it to come out as a sort of isn't-life-odd kind of laugh, but instead it comes out like the I-see-fairies kind.

"You're here to see me." I mean it as a question but forget to raise my voice at the end of the sentence.

"I'm in town for a few days," he says. "Would you wanna

grab dinner or something tomorrow? We could catch up for
real."

"Tomorrow?" I'm stalling, though I don't know why. *Yes*,
that's my answer, of course it is, just say it. "Yes," I say. "As
long as it's not . . ." I look around at the freezers, the frozen
meals.

"No, no," Maddox says, laughing. "We'll go somewhere,
if that's okay with you."

"Yeah," I say.

He pulls out his phone and takes down my number. "Seven
o'clock okay?" he asks.

"Yeah," I say.

"Great," he says.

I'm nodding. "Yeah, great," I say, then try to mentally calculate the number of times I've said *yeah* in the last two minutes. He came here to see me? What does that even mean?

"I'll text you." He waves his phone at me as if to say *this,
this is the thing I'll be using to contact you.* "It's great to see
you again, Jeanie." He says my name, testing it, as though to
confirm that this is reality, that I'm right in front of him. Am
I really here? Is he? Or are we still on that beach, feeding fries
to seagulls, young and immortal?

"You too," I manage. He leaves, and the little bell chimes
overhead, somehow giving off a different pitch than normal.
Or perhaps my ears have changed. Maybe my entire perception of the world has shifted.

It's only a few minutes later, when my blood has a chance
to cool and I sit down on the chair behind the counter, that I
realize that Maddox didn't, in fact, buy anything.

That night, I open a bottle of wine and settle into a rerun of
The Graham Norton Show with Josephine snoring in my lap

and a light rain falling on the small square patio out back. I'm trying to pretend like everything is normal. This is just a usual end to my evening. A glass of wine or whisky and a show on the telly. I'm very content on my own. Having anything like a steady partner gives me hives. That's why William is so great. He's like a relationship that isn't a relationship at all. He has his wife to make happy and a job that keeps him busy, so I end a lot of evenings on my own, drinking, watching shows, listening to Josephine snore. *The Graham Norton Show* is just starting—Tom Cruise and some actress I don't recognize. They're promoting his latest movie in which he does a lot of running away from various people and objects chasing him. I lose the thread of their conversation, unable to focus with the specter of Maddox hovering over my shoulder. I go to the kitchen and pull out a half-drunk bottle of scotch—the wine is already gone and I'm not nearly as drunk as I should be.

I take my glass of scotch and a cigarette out to the back patio. Leaning up against a support beam, I drink and smoke while Josephine stalks something in the bushes. The rain has a calming effect, or maybe I'm drunker than I thought I was. I alternate between sips of scotch and inhales of smoke—the cigarette balancing out the peatiness of the scotch, bringing out its sweeter flavors. The falling rain looks bright, crystalline in the darkness of the evening.

By the time I make it back inside, I know sleep will take me like a train wreck in maybe another hour. I don't want to watch any more TV, to see all the beautiful people smiling, solving murders, chatting, singing, dancing, or whatever show that'll be on after Graham Norton, so I open my computer to write a note to Jamie. I still write letters to him from time to time, but I never send them, of course. I haven't told Dr. Gardner this, though I suppose I should. But I like to keep some things from him, some secrets that are just for me.

Dear Jamie, I start. *You'll never believe who I just ran into.*

I reach for my glass of whisky and realize it's empty. I set the glass down. I shouldn't be drinking anyway. I can barely focus my eyes on the cursor, which is blinking at me in anticipation. *Well?* it says. *What else?*

I stare at the screen a moment longer. The letters are becoming blurry. My eyes unfocused.

Do you think Dad did it? I type. It's not the first time I've asked him this question.

Where are you? I type next—another regular one.

The words hover over blank white space as though any moment they'll fall, unprotected, down the page into oblivion. I stare at the question, expecting him to answer somehow. To write back to me from beyond the Matrix. *Knock, knock, Jeanie.* I move the cursor over to the right-hand side of the document and click the little X. *Save changes to your file?* the computer asks me.

No.

I manage to make it to the couch before I pass out.

I don't sleep well. I dream of sitting down with Maddox at a restaurant where they don't have any cutlery, so we have to eat with our hands. I dream that I've lost my shoes, so I have to go barefoot. I dream I can't find the restaurant and Maddox abandons me for some other friends. I dream I show up and Maddox is standing with Jamie and they're both telling me that they know about my pregnancy. Weird, stress-filled dreams that have me waking up with my jaw clenched tight.

"You're a grinder," my dentist once said to me.

"Excuse me?" I said, imagining all kinds of sexual connotations.

"Your teeth. You grind them a lot at night."

"Oh," I said. I hate the dentist.

I wake up in the morning with a first-place, blue-ribbon, Oscar-gold kind of hangover. My head is pounding, my mouth is chalky, and there's a weight on my stomach that I think is probably a churning ball of alcohol until I realize it's Josephine, curled on top of me and snoring like an old lady.

I stand up and she tumbles to the floor, landing on her side with a thump—so much for the whole landing on their feet myth. When she rights herself, she's all protracted claws and raised hackles, looking at me with this shocked expression as if she can't believe the audacity of what I've done to her, or perhaps she can't quite remember who I am. She's always struck me as a cat teetering on the edge of a pleasant, oblivious drunk.

I make my way to the kitchen, turn on the tap, and set a glass of water beneath the hissing faucet. The sun is incandescent through the haze of my windows, and I lower my head onto my forearm to hide my eyes. It's not until I feel cold water splashing over my fingers that I realize I've overfilled my glass. I turn off the tap and take a few big gulps. Luckily, I don't work today, so I've got enough time to recover before meeting with Maddox. I call Dr. Gardner and he doesn't pick up, so I leave a message telling him I won't be able to make our Tuesday meeting. I can't handle talking about my feelings right now. I take a few Advil and make my slow way up the stairs to my bed. There's nothing better than crawling into bed after sleeping all night on a lumpy couch. That is, there would be nothing better if not for the poison currently working its way through my body. Still, I'm asleep practically as soon as my head hits the pillow.

⬤

When I finally do peel myself out of bed, I settle for looking quasi-presentable as opposed to actually public-ready, and take a bus to the Ashmolean Museum. I like going to the museum when I'm hungover, which is often enough that I've become a member. It's quiet and cool and there's something relaxing about the ancient art. The pots in glass displays, the old tools, gilded knives, plates, paintings, and white Greek and Roman heads. I read somewhere that the ancient Greeks painted their sculptures elaborate colors, but time has made all the paint fade away, leaving only the white marble. I picture rooms full of colorful sculptures, so lifelike you'd think they were about to turn to you and ask for an olive.

I pass a man in his sixties, leaning over a fifth-century gold necklace fashioned into a string of acorns. I feel my phone buzzing against my jeans and look at the screen to see William's number. The alcohol in my stomach takes a right-hand turn toward my intestines. I don't want to pick up. But I also *do* want to pick up. I shouldn't pick up; I really shouldn't— I'm in a museum for God's sake.

"Hey," I say quietly into the phone. The old man examining the necklace doesn't look up. I imagine he's picturing the necklace around his own neck, that he harbors a secret desire to be beautiful and covered in golden acorns. I smile at this, relaxing slightly.

"Jeanie, hi. I didn't think you'd answer," William says. He sounds tired.

"Why?" I ask.

"Oh, nothing, I just—"

"Did you not want me to? I can hang up and you could call back." I'm joking, but also not really joking.

"No, it's fine. I'm glad you did."

"Okay," I say. The old man has moved on to one of the white sculptures. I work my way around the room, maintaining my distance from him—partly because of my hangover and partly because I don't want to disturb him. I know the importance of museum time.

"Listen," William says. "I was wondering if I might come over tonight?"

This is odd. He's been to my house only a handful of times in the years we've known each other. I feel a small thrill at the idea of him coming over. "Sorry," I say. "I can't. I'm going out tonight." *With Maddox.* Good Lord. The alcohol in my stomach is doing somersaults now.

"Out?" he says, the word popping from his lips. He doesn't like me going out, doesn't like the idea that I've got other men in my life. Hypocrite.

"Yes," I say. "I'm going out." I could elaborate, tell him about Maddox. It'd make him jealous, too, but leaving him in the dark is so much crueler.

"Where are you going?" he asks. He's feeling extra bold today.

"I'm not your whore, William," I say. I'm thinking about punctuating the power of my statement by hanging up the phone.

"Jesus, Jeanie. It's fine, have a great evening." He could hang up now, too, but he doesn't. Both of us sit in the buzzing quiet between our devices' electronic signals, traveling to space and back, from one phone to the next—so much distance for silence to travel. I can't hear him breathing, but I know he is. Maybe he's rubbing the line across his forehead like he does when he's thinking.

"You have a great evening yourself," I say, finally.

"Dunno what I'll do without you." His voice has taken on a playful, flirtatious tone. It makes me mad for some reason.

"I'll tell you what to do," I say, suddenly emboldened. "You go get a bottle of champagne, maybe some chocolates or flowers, you bring them home, you give them to your wife, the two of you get good and buzzed, not drunk, but buzzed enough to be nice and loose. You give her a long massage, I mean a half hour at least, feet and everything, then you take her upstairs, you peel her clothes off, and you fuck her until she comes twice. You hear me? I'm serious, William. Twice."

Silence. Judgmental stares from centuries-old marble eyes.

"Jeanie—"

"Good luck," I say, and hang up the phone.

I don't know if he'll do what I say, but even if he gets those chocolates, flowers, champagne, even if he does fuck Holly, he'll be thinking of me when he does, and for some reason, that's almost better than him coming over.

I stuff the phone back into my pocket and turn to see the old man, barely two steps away from me, staring, eyes owl-wide like I've shaken his old British bones to the core.

I smile at him as he opens his mouth to say something, but I beat him to it. "I'm a sex therapist," I say. "Jeanie King. Look me up if you're having any issues." Before he has a chance to respond, I turn around as confidently as I can, marching away from the goggling eyes of the old man and all the colorless, white marble heads.

I go home and smoke on the back patio again, still trying to calm my nerves. It's only one o'clock and my date with Maddox, if you can call it a date, isn't until seven. The clouds overhead are a single plate of white. I scan through the assortment of bushes and weeds in my garden that's not really a garden. Morning glory. Couch grass. The green alkanet, whose small blue flowers I actually find pretty. My non-garden is a travesty next to Manda's just over the stone wall: her towering foxgloves like painted bells, her rambling rose, peonies, hollyhocks. Suddenly the smoking isn't doing the trick; I want out of my garden, or weed patch, whatever you want to call it. I put on my trainers and go for a run. I take Banbury down past the shops, the red and brown brick homes, Wycliffe Hall, and into University Park. Running takes my mind off the world. That, and it helps me sweat the alcohol out of my body. I focus on my breathing. I take in the reds and yellows of the deciduous leaves and realize that I don't like the changing seasons. The transitory nature of fall and spring makes me feel untethered, like everything is tumbling. It makes me desperate for something more substantial. Give me extremes. Give me summer or give me cold. Give me the harshness of winter over the soft gestures of fall. Winter is an exclamation mark—obvious, almost violent in its finality—while fall is a comma, uncertain, asking the one question that vexes humanity more than anything else in the world: What happens next? What happens tomorrow? Next week? Next winter? When we die? How does this not drive more people insane? Perhaps it does, and we carry on quietly in our madness.

There's a group of young kids playing football—soccer—on the green and I watch them for a while between the passing trees. A woman is shushing her yappy white dog on the park bench. Farther down, a group of crew members are rowing their canoe in the Cherwell with easy, practiced strokes. It's been awhile since I've been running. And, as often happens to me during the changing seasons, my thoughts turn extreme: maybe I should become a personal trainer. I could start by sharing workout videos on the internet, build a following, contact the gym, and start taking clients. It feels so good to run. My feet move faster as the soles of my trainers crunch against the gravel beneath me. I duck under a stray branch of a maple tree, which is reaching out its long arm over the path. By the time I've run the whole loop of the park I'm sweating, my lungs are full of cold air, my hands are pressed into my hips, and I've made a seven-step plan on how I'm going to change my life and become a fitness coach. I'm going to have a nice chat with Maddox tonight, he's going to tell me that he just wanted to catch up after all these years, we'll part pretending that we'll keep in touch, and then I'm going to change everything about myself.

However, by the time I've reached my house, the endorphins have faded, and I've reverted once again. I'm panicked and shaky and I'm never going to quit my job at the dinner shop or step foot outside of Oxford, maybe not even Summertown.

My mind is a violent pendulum. I blame the changing seasons.

⬤

"Jeanie, hi!" Manda says through the phone.

"Hey," I say. "Can you come over?" I ask.

"Now? Sure," she says, overeager. God, Manda's great, how had I not realized this before?

"I just, I've got this thing tonight and I—" I'm a teenager who doesn't know what to wear. Am I really doing this? Calling up a friend to help dress me? Is it the clothes I'm worried about, or do I just need a pat on the hand? Reassurance. Confidence. "I just need some help getting ready."

"Getting ready?" she asks. She doesn't know what I mean.

"It's fine if you're busy. It's not a big deal." I backpedal, regret calling.

"No, of course, of course. I'll be there, glad to help. Give me twenty, okay?"

"Sure, yeah, that's great. Thanks," I say.

"Not a problem."

We hang up the phone and I feel a little better. It's five thirty and Maddox has already texted me the location and the time: The Eagle and Child at seven o'clock. Two and a half hours. How long does one need to get ready for something like this? How much makeup does it take to bury the child inside you? What clothes do you wear when you're attempting to rewrite the past?

CHAPTER 6

THEN

Jamie and I turned thirteen that summer. Our limbs were growing longer, mine especially. I remember standing in front of the mirror, my legs looking like overlong vanilla stalks sprouting from a midsection not yet fully developed, my arms hanging apelike down my sides. I was a thing half formed, like a caterpillar pupating in its chrysalis. Only, I didn't think I was turning into a butterfly. I didn't know what I was becoming. Jamie, on the other hand, was experiencing just as drastic a transformation, but his was into something entirely different. His face was taking on these perfect angles, his hair was a golden blond, his eyes were settling into a deeper shade of blue. His features were just like Mom's; he was, as weird as it is for me to say as his sister, becoming beautiful.

I spent more and more time with Dad at the shooting range. We'd moved on to other guns. His .308 rifle; his Browning 12-gauge shotgun, which bruised my shoulder, but I enjoyed, nonetheless; and handguns. He had a Nighthawk pistol, the first I ever shot. He showed me how to hold it two-handed, how to aim, reload, set my feet. I loved it all: the pop of the bullet being jettisoned from its casing; the jerk of the recoil against my wrists instead of my shoulder; the snap of the can splitting as the hot bullet burrowed into its bright aluminum body. Turns out I was just as deadly with handguns as I was with rifles.

"My girl," Dad kept saying over and over again, and each time, something wonderful came alive in me. A memory blossoming: Mom smiling at me while Dad was away those early years. "You're so much like him," she'd say. "Guess that's why you're such a daddy's girl." And I had been. I remembered. He was big and strong and could toss me in the air as if my whole body were made of feathers. I'd said *Daddy* before I'd said *Mommy*. He used to do this thing where he'd kiss me on the nose. "I love that little nose," he'd say. One day when he asked for a nose kiss, I brought my face to his and made our noses touch. He laughed, and from then on, when he asked for a nose kiss, that's what we'd do: touch our noses together as if they were the ones kissing, not us. I'd always laugh.

One day when we got to the shooting range, we saw a crow on the ground, picking at one of the pop cans. Maybe it could taste the leftover sugar. Dad stopped and watched the crow for a minute before telling me to load the .22.

"Some real practice today," he said, eyes still on the crow. I knew what he meant, but I pretended I didn't as I loaded the gun, my hands feeling clumsy as I fumbled with the cartridge.

"Aim for the chest," he said.

"Dad, I don't want to."

"They're pests," he said. "A complete nuisance."

"Dad."

"You're fine," he said. "Time to grow up." It was something he'd say to Jamie, not to me. I didn't like it. But I did as I was told. I brought the crosshairs over the bird's heart. I took a deep breath. I tried to pull the trigger. The bird looked up, its beak lifted to the air. Another crow landed in the tree above him, cawing as if in warning.

"Now," Dad said. And I shot. I was barely aiming; my hands were shaking. I'd never killed anything before. I was sure I'd missed, sure the bird was going to launch from the ground and join its friend in the treetops. But, somehow, my bullet struck the bird right in the chest, right where I'd been aiming, right where Dad told me to.

Dad let out a raucous laugh, then started across the field for the bird. "Come on," he said when I didn't follow. I started moving toward him slowly. My limbs felt weird, and the gun was heavy in my hands.

The bird was lying on its side, black feathers glistening as if they were wet. It was still breathing, little chest rising and falling in rapid succession.

"Watch this," Dad said, leaning over the animal. "I'll teach you a trick."

He picked up the bird. It flapped violently in his hands as Dad lifted its black body in front of him. It was still clinging to life, still desperate to be free. I wanted to cry.

"You pinch behind the wings just here." He brought his hands behind the bird, his big palms cupping the little black body. "Hold tight and watch. See, it suffocates him."

The bird's head was upright, eyes wide and panicked. But, slowly, it began to droop, beak lowering toward the ground, until it was still and lifeless. I felt a burning in my stomach, a pain as if I was going to be sick. I'd seen it all before. The way the head lolled forward, the way the life left the eyes. Mom had done the same thing in the car. Her pale face slowly falling, her eyes going glassy. I pictured Dad pinching the back of her neck.

I thought I was going to throw up in the grass.

"Jesus, look at that," Dad said. "Right in the chest. Nice shot, girl."

"What are we going to do with him?" I asked, doing my best to keep my voice from shaking.

"Eh, nothing," he said. "They're not good eating." He turned the bird as if to get one last look at it, then he tossed the body into the bushes. "Coyote will get it," he said. "Circle of life."

Is that what happened with Mom? I wondered. The circle of life?

He put a hand on my shoulder and led me back across the field. "Beautiful shot," he said again, the weight of his hand on my own neck, fingers pressing into my skin. I felt so small then. So tiny. The size of the bird.

I realized then that pride, fear, sadness, and nausea can be the same feeling, can coagulate into a single element, fusing together so tightly you can't tell one from the other.

That night, Dad came home later than usual, drunker than usual. Jamie was asleep when Dad collapsed in the chair by the fireplace and passed out. I got a blanket from the closet in the hallway and draped it over his shoulders. I don't know what made me do it, but I brought my face to his—his mouth was open, beard long and wiry. He smelled of alcohol and the faintest scent of something else—cardamom or cinnamon, something earthy, spicy. I brought my nose to his, just the barest touch. *Nose kiss, Daddy*. His head lifted suddenly, his eyes peeling open, staring at me.

He yelled, a horrified shriek I'd never heard from him before. As he did, he shoved me off him so hard I tumbled to the floor, smacking the back of my head on the ground. I saw a flash of red and yellow, and when it cleared, there was Dad's face, large and angry. In his hands was his pocketknife, held over my eye.

"Dad!" My voice was high, sharp, desperate. "It's me. Stop!"

He brought the blade toward my face, the tip of it touching the skin just to the right of my eyelid. I grabbed his arm.

"Dad!"

But Dad wasn't there, not really. He was breathing hard now, big puffing sounds as his cheeks inflated like bellows. I felt the tip of his knife pop through my skin, felt a teardrop of blood race down the side of my head into my hair.

"Dad, stop!" I pushed against his arm, but he was so big, so strong.

The blade lifted suddenly, his arm rising. I looked up at him; my left eye was blurry. He had a confused look on his face, and his eyes darted from me to the knife, which he lowered slowly.

"Fuck," he said on an exhale. He stood, making his lumbering way back to the fireplace and his chair, the blanket discarded on the floor. He fell back onto the chair, his knife still in his hand. He closed his eyes. "Fuck," he said again, even softer.

My heart was alive in my chest, tearing into the seams of my ribs. I lay there, unable to move, afraid that if I did, he'd wake again and attack me. I don't know how long I stayed there. Long enough for the fire to die to embers and the room to grow cold.

I heard Jamie's footsteps before I saw him above me. His blond hair stuck up on the side of his head where it had been pressed against his pillow. He leaned over and grabbed my hand.

"Come on, Jeanie," he said. His words broke whatever spell had been cast over me. I let myself be helped from the floor, following him to our room. Holding Jamie's hand, I looked over my shoulder once and saw Dad, snoring slightly.

He licked his lips and turned his head. I knew, in the morning, he wouldn't remember a thing. I was glad for it.

Maddox, Jamie, and I began to expand our horizons beyond our regular spot by the beach. Maddox had grown up in Washington, and he showed us all his secret places. Jamie and I followed him around like he was the leader of our own little Lost Boys' club. He showed us this secluded cove along the north side of the coast that you had to climb down a steep promontory to get to. Two trees had fallen across either side of the cove's rocky walls, and Maddox had strung up a makeshift swing from the bottom log—you couldn't really swing all that much, but you could sit on it, which we did. He took us deep into the forest and showed us his favorite climbing tree, a tall Douglas fir. Thick branches sprouted from the trunk, growing thinner as you reached the top and emerged into a world of green needles and rough bark that pulled at the skin of your arms. The heavy scent of sap hung in the air. Looking around, you could almost imagine the tree went on forever, that there wasn't a ground at all, or that you had gone so high that when you got back down, you'd find everything had changed; that it was no longer the world you'd left.

Maddox and I continued to spend a few afternoons alone, just the two of us. It began to take on a dangerous feel, as if we were sneaking around, getting into trouble. I suppose that was part of the excitement. We'd walk the beach, go on hikes together, sometimes go to the cove with the fallen logs and talk or just sit and read. Maddox liked to read these science fiction magazines. They had pictures of spaceships, plants with mechanical arms, and busty alien women with six eyes on the cover.

"This is what I'm gonna do someday," he told me once, his legs dangling over the log, rocking back and forth.

"You're gonna be an astronaut?" I asked.

"No, I'm gonna be a writer."

"Oh," I said. "Like, write about aliens?" I leaned over the log I was on to get a better look at the magazine.

"Maybe. Or, just, anything really. Dad wants me to be an athlete like he was. But that's not me," he said.

"An athlete?" I asked.

"Yeah. I'm fast, just like him. But I don't like to run. I like to write. One day I'll move to a big city and give talks about my books and go to writing conventions and everything."

"Sounds cool," I said, even though I had no idea if it was cool or not. It was the first time I heard him mention his parents. I wanted him to elaborate but I also didn't want to pry. I looked down at the log beneath me and began to absentmindedly pick away the blue-green moss on its surface.

"You wanna come with me?" he asked.

"To a big city?"

"Yeah." He looked up at me. I could feel his eyes, his expectant stare. He wanted me to say yes; he wanted me to agree to go wherever he was going, to tell him that we would always be together, that things would never change.

I picked up a piece of moss, examined it carefully in my hands, letting the moment stretch on and on, his longing making the space between us electric, while, in my belly, petals of joy unfurled.

❦

Love must've been a sporal thing that summer, floating thick in the breeze, because it was around this time that Dad began to bring Stacy home. Stacy had dreadlocks and a nose ring. She had freckles on her cheeks and eyes that constantly seemed to be half closed. She wore tube tops and ripped jeans and skirts that were so short you could see the pink of her panties when she sat on the couch. She smoked inside the cabin and laughed like a pig. *Snort snort snort*. She and Dad had ugly, noisy sex in the evenings, and sometimes not in the evenings.

Both Jamie and I hated her with a red-hot passion. She treated us like inconveniences that didn't have permission to occupy the same space as her. She was high a lot of the time and laughed way too much. I even began to imitate her pig-like snicker, to her extreme annoyance.

"Did you hate Stacy because she wasn't your mom?" Dr. Gardner asked.

"No," I said. "We hated Stacy because she was a bitch."

Actually, the real problem with Stacy was that she wasn't our mom *and* she was a bitch. She didn't love Dad, and we both knew, deep down, that he didn't love her, either.

It was because of Stacy that we first found our way onto the roof. We discovered that if you shimmied up this alder—which was leaning just over our cabin as if it couldn't quite be bothered to fall on top of it—you could make your way onto the roof. We'd go up when we heard Dad's truck or when we knew Stacy was coming. We'd hear them laughing or yelling at each other or having sex. Sometimes we'd sneak up there at night and watch the stars.

"Say it," Stacy would tell Dad as the rocking bed clapped against the wall. *Snap snap snap snap*. "Say it!"

"I love you," Dad would mumble, voice breathless and deep. *Snap snap snap*. But he didn't. Not really. No one did. Fucking Stacy.

Sometimes Jamie and I would knock on the roof when they were done sexing, and we'd laugh when Dad freaked out. One time he told Stacy to get under the bed, and we heard the slide and click of a bolt-action rifle as Dad kicked the screen door open, screaming into the empty forest. Looking back, I know it wasn't funny, not really, but Jamie and I nearly peed ourselves trying not to laugh.

I remember this one time, Stacy and Dad were sitting by the fire while Jamie and I were playing a stupid board game in the kitchen. It was midday, but Dad was already mostly drunk, and Stacy was high on something.

"Where's my cigarettes?" she asked no one in particular. I saw the packet at the end of the table. Jamie saw it, too, but neither of us said anything.

"I can never find those damn things," she said, her eyes darting around the room as if she couldn't quite control them. Eventually they settled on the packet on the table.

"Jeanie," she said, "bring me my smokes."

"Get them yourself," I said.

"Excuse me?" Stacy said.

"I said, get them yourself."

"You kidding me?" she asked, looking from me to Dad, who was staring into his beer bottle like he was searching for a fly. "They're right next to you, just bring 'em to me."

"No," I said, turning back to the board game in front of me. I picked up a card.

"You gonna let her talk like that to me?" Stacy said, raising a hand to my dad like she was holding something out for him to inspect.

"Jeanie," Dad said. "Come on."

He clearly didn't even know what he was asking. "Fine." I reached for the pack and threw it at her. Stacy yelped like I'd thrown a knife. The packet bounced off the couch and landed on the floor.

"Jesus Christ," Dad said, sitting up now, startled by Stacy's scream. He glared at me, his eyes unfocused, his lids drooping like old curtains. "What's wrong with you?"

"I gave her the cigarettes," I said.

Stacy glared at me, her chest heaving. The anger was heavy

on her face, weighing her features down. "Pick 'em up," she said slowly.

"They're right in front of you." I looked over at Jamie for approval. He shrugged. Chickenshit.

"Pick 'em up," she said again, emphasizing each word.

I looked at Dad. "Just pick them up, Jeanie." He leaned back in his chair, taking a gulp of beer. "Fucking women."

I stood as slowly as I could, walking across the room toward the cigarettes. They were barely a foot away from Stacy. She stared at me the whole time. I leaned over, picked up the pack, and brought it to her. She didn't reach for it at first, just stared at me like she was trying to figure out how else to punish me. Finally she took the pack, but before I could turn away, she reached out and flicked me hard on the forehead.

"See," she said. "How easy was that?"

The skin on my forehead vibrated. It took everything I had not to punch her right in the throat. But I knew how that would play out. I knew that Dad would get involved. It was then that I realized that if Dad had ever been on Jamie's and my side, he wasn't anymore. He was on Stacy's side.

My jaw was clenched as I walked back to the table. Behind me, I heard the *flick flick flick*ing of Stacy's lighter.

As a result of Stacy's intrusion into our lives, Dad and I stopped shooting together as much, and Jamie and I spent more and more time with Maddox. But soon, we were back in school and the weather was changing. The ocean took on a metallic sheen, cold radiating from the water in rivulets of steam. Even though we were back to both caring and not caring about class and homework and the other kids, Jamie, Maddox, and I still existed in this small microcosm we'd created for ourselves. The weirdest thing was seeing Maddox in school with the older kids; it was like he was part of this other club that existed within the walls of our school, one I knew nothing about. It was this feeling, I think, this exclusion from a part of his life, that made me kiss him for the first time.

It was the beginning of spring and Maddox and I were at the beach, feeding fries to seagulls. He liked to rile them up by running at them and then throwing a fry into the air to watch as they swarmed and dived to be the first to catch the food midflight.

As the sun began to set, we took off our shoes and rolled up our pantlegs. We walked along the mudflats closer to the ocean, the still pools of water surprisingly warm between our toes. We stuck our fingers into the shallow water and poked sea anemones and sponges as crabs and small fish swam around our palms in a panic. We found a log to sit on and tossed rocks and the hollowed halves of white shells across the beach as the sky turned a crazy shade of purple-blue. My feet were beginning to freeze, but they were too wet for me to put my socks back on.

I don't remember what we'd been talking about, but I remember a silence stretching and my heart jumping in my chest when I said: "Have you ever been kissed?"

"Me? No," he said, like the question hadn't taken him off guard.

"Really?"

"Nope, you?"

"No," I said.

Another silence, punctuated by the cry of the last remaining seagull. I turned and saw it, wings outstretched to ride high currents of wind toward wherever it was seagulls went at night.

"If you had to kiss someone," Maddox said, "who would it be?"

"I don't know," I said.

"Ya, you do," he said like we were playing a game. "You'd kiss Daniel Mason."

"Daniel?" I laughed. "Uh, no thanks. You know his dad owns the tannery, right? He always smells like cowhide."

Maddox laughed. "No he doesn't."

"Why'd you think Daniel?" I asked.

"I dunno," Maddox tossed a rock across the mudflats; it skipped twice before sinking into a small pool. "I saw you and him talking in the hallway."

I tried to think of a time I'd been talking to Daniel in the hallway. I pictured Maddox watching me and felt a thrill of excitement. "Well, I don't know," I said. "But not Daniel. What about you?" I asked. "Who'd you choose?"

He picked up another rock and looked down at it. It fit the palm of his hand perfectly. It was circular apart from a jagged edge at the top. "I don't know either," he said.

"Maybe we should be each other's first kiss." The words jumped out of my mouth, and my bones felt like they'd snapped into place. Frozen, locked at the joints.

"What? Like you and me?" he asked, lifting his gaze from the rock and turning to meet my eyes. "Like kiss now?"

"Sure," I said shrugging, the perfect picture of nonchalance. "Why not?"

He stuffed his hands into his pockets. "Okay," he said. We were thirteen and fourteen now, at the budding cusp of teenagehood, nearly adults in our preadolescent minds. Why wouldn't we kiss? Why wouldn't we try it out? I already smoked cigarettes for God's sake.

We sat in silence for a moment longer. The contract had been signed, but neither of us knew how to move forward.

"Okay," he said again as he turned to face me. I did the same, and slowly, awkwardly, we brought our faces together, then our lips. They touched. His were surprisingly warm despite the cool air, and there was a wetness to the kiss that I wasn't sure was coming from him or me. But there was also something electric. Some struck cord vibrating from my lips down to my pelvis. I wanted to bottle that feeling and keep it with me at all times. Is that what I'm searching for now? I wonder. All the men in my life, always coming and going. All the sex I've had. Maybe what I really want is that struck chord. That first kiss. I want it to last forever.

But as quickly as it happened, it was over, and he was pulling away from me.

We looked at each other for half a second, and the serious looks on both our faces made us laugh. And just like that, we were back to ourselves again, friends out at the beach, having conducted an experiment that we both knew was important but weren't really sure why yet.

"Well, I guess now I've been kissed," Maddox said.

Above us, passing clouds looked silver in the starlight. Our toes froze in the chill night air.

I laughed. "Yeah, me too."

CHAPTER 7

NOW

"Tell me more about Maddox," Dr. Gardner said the first day I'd told him about our kiss on the beach.

I felt my fingernails dig into the sides of the armrest and did my best to relax my grip. "There's not much to tell. What do you want to know?"

"What do you feel when you think about him? After everything that happened?"

I shook my head. "Nothing much. I haven't seen him in so long."

"Not since high school, right?"

"Right?"

"Were the two of you intimate?"

He wasn't smiling, but I could tell he wanted to. I wanted him to as well, so that I could stand up and wipe that damn smile off his face. "I don't think I should be talking about this with you," I said.

"Who would you rather talk to?" he asked.

"I don't know. Anyone."

"Is it the subject matter that makes you uncomfortable or me?"

"I never slept with him," I said, hoping that would be the end of it.

"But you'd have liked to." He made it a statement, not a question. I sat in silence. I didn't have to answer statements. But then he did that thing where he was silent for so long, and I began to feel my hands starting to squeeze my chair. My palms were growing clammy.

"Do you regret how things ended?" he asked, trying a different tack.

"My dad once told me that regret was for assholes and time travelers."

"That's interesting," Dr. Gardner said in the most uninterested tone I'd ever heard.

"I'm not even sure it makes sense," I said.

"Do you wish you could go back in time?" he asked.

I was growing tired of the verbal sparring. "Yes," I said, giving in.

"And what would you do differently?"

I shook my head, turned my gaze to the window. Raindrops were racing down the glass. As kids, Jamie and I would sit by the window and pick two raindrops and bet on which one would make it to the bottom first.

"Everything," I said. "I'd do everything differently."

"Let's see what we're working with," Manda says, and flings open my closet. She looks from one wall to the next. "Okay," she says, lingering on the vowels slightly too long. The o and the a stretch out into exaggerated judgment.

"I know," I say. I don't keep the nicest clothes in stock. I work at a damn dinner shop, what do I need date clothes for? Not that this is a date.

"So is this a date?" Manda asks.

Dammit. "No, no," I say. "Just catching up with an old friend." Is it, though? Why is he really here? What does he want with me? Why now?

She gives me a conspiratorial look. "A friend you'd like to impress?"

A friend I'd like goggling over me like a drooling puppy dog. "I guess so. At least a little, you know."

She laughs. "Oh, I know." She spends a few minutes sifting through my shirts and pants and sweaters. She picks an outfit and lays it on the bed. "Try that on," she says, already turning back to the closet. I can hear the hangers sliding against the metal rail like hissing snakes.

For the next hour, we dissect my entire wardrobe, and I come to the inevitable realization that I hate absolutely every item of clothing I own. Maybe every item of clothing I've ever owned—except for this one shirt that I had in high school with a pink guitar on it; it fit me perfectly, looked absolutely fabulous, and was the one and only shirt I've ever loved. I don't think I'll ever love again.

"That's it," Manda says, looking me up and down. I'm wearing black leggings with one of the only dresses I have. It's casual as far as dresses go. Navy blue and just low-cut enough to see some cleavage without screaming *look at my tits!* "You can pair it with a scarf and a sweater, but I think this is what you're after. Classic sexy."

I smile. "Classic sexy sounds good."

"It does, doesn't it?"

"I wish I had your boobs, though," I say.

"No you don't. That's a whole world of back problems you're asking for. And now with my belly, look, look how I have to walk." She models her walk across the room. She's leaning back with each step, belly leading the way, to make up for the weight of both her stomach and her breasts. "I look like the wind is constantly, and very slowly, blowing me over."

I laugh; it's a genuine laugh that comes from somewhere deep. It feels good.

"You don't think it's too much?" I ask, looking back down at my dress.

"No way," Manda says. "You look so Dench."

"Dench?"

"Yeah," she says. "Like Judi Dench."

"Do I want to look like Judi Dench? Because if you're trying to dress me like Judi Dench—"

"No," she says. "It just means excellent. You know, 'That's so Dench.'"

I've lived here over a decade, and I've still not fully adjusted to the language. It took me a year to realize that trainers actually meant shoes, not people who train.

"So it's a good thing?" I say.

"Super good," she says, eyeing me up and down. "Super Dench."

◉

I'm a little late to meet Maddox, but I'd rather be a little late than early. Early implies an eagerness I'm not ready to convey. The Eagle and Child—or The Bird and Baby, as some call it—is a relatively small pub on St. Giles' Street, just past the World War I memorial, a cross rising out of a small turret. The pub's claim to fame is that it was one of the meeting places for authors J. R. R. Tolkien and C. S. Lewis in their little writers' club that they called the Inklings. It's a fantasy nerd's paradise. I remember Maddox and his science fiction magazines and wonder if that's why he suggested this pub. The beer is typical, the food is fairly average, and as far as ambiance goes, there are better Oxford pubs—The Turf with its outdoor beer garden, or riverside pubs like The Trout—but The Eagle and Child is old and classic with a basement sort of feel to it. You can practically sense mythical worlds seeping from the old wooden beams and tables. It's easy to understand why two fantasy authors might have found inspiration within its walls.

It's fairly busy inside, and I have to shoulder my way past the bar. It's loud in a murmuring sort of British way, and has that old carpet, old wood, dark beer smell to it that is both comforting and a little bit off-putting.

"He's got a weighty pair on him, I'll tell you that much," one drunk college student is saying to another drunk college student in that loud, I-want-the-whole-room-to-hear-me-make-sentences way some people talk when they're drunk.

I'm surprised when I see Maddox sitting at a table in the corner of the room with an amber pint and some fries in front of him. Across from him is a table with two blonde girls who are giving him hump-me eyes.

"Jeanie," he says, smiling and half standing like some sort of fifties gentleman.

"Hey," I say, pulling out the chair.

"I'd have grabbed you a beer, but I didn't know what you'd want."

"That's fine," I say. "What are you drinking?"

"Honestly, I don't remember the name," he says. "Something weird like pigs-head ale."

"Sounds delicious."

"I'll get you one."

He's already moving to the bar before I can tell him that I can get my own beer. But I decide to let him. He can buy me one beer. As he leaves, I can't resist looking over my shoulder at the blonde women who are—yup—staring at me. Their eyes snap away as soon as mine meet theirs.

While he's gone, I stuff a few fries into my mouth as daintily as I can. Maddox returns with my drink a minute later. There's a cream-colored head on my beer. He sets it down in front of me and I thank him.

"So," he says. He's smiling and I can't help but smile back. It's the ridiculousness of the situation. Of the two of us here in this pub in Oxford after the ocean of distance and time between us. He lifts his pint, reaches it out across the table. I lift my own drink and we touch glasses, toasting the randomness of the universe. "It's so weird seeing you again," he says after he's taken a sip.

I laugh, setting my glass down. "I know," I say.

"Whoa, you gotta drink after you touch glasses," he says, eyeing my pint like I've spilled it all over the table.

"What?" I say.

"You can't toast and then set your glass down without drinking. It totally negates the toast."

I laugh. "Says who?"

"Says everyone," he says. "Now you gotta take two drinks to make up for it." He's kind of joking but he's also a little serious. He's the type of guy who takes stupid rituals like this at face value. It's the kind of thing that starts out endearing and ends up being infuriating.

"You've got issues, you know that?" I say, but my voice is light. I feel light.

"Bottoms up, Jeanie King." My name on his lips again. An absurd thing.

I lift my glass and chug nearly half of the pint, then wipe my mouth and set it back on the table with a satisfying clacking noise.

Maddox has a suspicious smile as he watches. "You trying to impress me?" he asks.

I shake my head. "If I was trying to impress you, I'd show you my handstand."

His mouth opens, his eyes searching mine as if to confirm the memory.

"Oh my God," he says, lifting a hand to his forehead. "I forgot about that." No he didn't.

"You fell flat on your ass." We both laugh at the memory. I'm thinking of how he held my hand afterward.

"I was trying to impress you," he says. I want him to say it again.

"I was very impressed."

"Ha, no you weren't."

"You bought me fries afterward to make up for it."

"Oh man," he says. "Those were good fries."

"That's one thing I miss about America," I say, lifting one of the fries from the plate between us. "They do fries better there."

"So why are you here?" he asks. "I mean, if it's not for the fries. How'd you end up in Oxford?" He sits back and sips his beer, ready for a story. And I give it to him. A version, anyway. How I wanted to get out of the country, go on an adventure of sorts. I tell him that Oxford is where my mom went to school. He didn't know that little detail and finds it fascinating. I like the feeling. I like the fact that he finds me fascinating. It's the same feeling I get with William, only better, less tainted.

We finish our beers and Maddox goes to the bar for the next round. Again, I don't stop him. Maybe I do want this to be a date. I watch him as he's walking back through the small crowd. How unreal he seems. How strangely happy I feel in this moment. Is life really like this? I wonder. Is the world this small? Something is turning inside me now. Something I hadn't wanted to look at but is now bubbling to the surface. He's walking toward me so casually, he's practically dripping with existential nonchalance. He sits, smiles at me as he slides my pint across the table.

"So how did you find me?" I ask. At the bar, a chorus of laughter. Jealous eyes behind me. Maddox's eyes in front of me, golden as a harvest moon.

He looks down at his drink and one corner of his mouth turns upward. "You know, you don't make it easy. No social media or online footprint of any kind. Couldn't find your employer, email, phone number, nothing. If you were trying to disappear, you did a good job, and I would know."

Suddenly I don't like the way my skin feels. The angles of the chair legs press against my ankle. My dress pinches my chest. I don't say anything. I let him talk.

"I told you I was a journalist," he says. "I'm an investigative journalist." He pauses as if to gauge my reaction.

"Sounds very adult," I say, taking the pint glass between my fingers and bringing it to my lips.

"Yeah, well, it means I've got a number of connections."

"I see. And how did that lead you to me?"

"I was able to track down a paper written by a professor at Oxford. I think you know him."

I can feel my face fall. Gravity grabbing my cheeks and pulling them downward. William's paper. The conference in London. Goddamn William.

Maddox is looking into my face, seeing my reaction. "I take it you know about it?" he asks.

"Yes," I say.

"He didn't use your name, but I recognized the bones of the story." He's twisting his pint around in a circle. The fries look like they've taken a turn from lukewarm to lukecold. I wonder how long he's been here waiting for me, and how long he's been planning this evening, thinking about how it would go, what he'd say, what I'd say. I feel ambushed.

"I see," I say.

"Do you know what the paper says? Have you read it?" he asks.

"No," I say. "But I can imagine what it says."

"So you know what he says about . . . Jamie?"

"Yes, probably."

He's nodding now. I can feel his eyes on me, but I'm not looking at him. I'm staring at my beer—a bubble of foam pops in the thick brown head.

"Jeanie, why didn't you—"

"I don't want to talk about it. Please." My hands clench at my sides.

"Of course. I'm sorry." He spins his pint glass again, the beer inside swirling ever so slightly. "Anyway, the paper led me to Oxford, and then it was pretty simple to track you from there."

I take another drink from my pint, looking around the room as if something more interesting has caught my attention. He waits for me to swallow. "And so here you are," I say.

"Yeah, I know. It's a bit weird. Sorry, but it's not like you gave me any other way to reach you." He doesn't sound annoyed or put out. He's stating facts, laying his cards on the table.

"Maybe that was for a reason," I say.

If he's hurt, he doesn't show it. "I'm sorry—"

"It's fine," I say. "But why? Why look for me?"

He takes a deep breath. We've gotten to the meat of the conversation sooner than he'd expected. But I've never been one to beat around the bush. I burn bushes like Moses. Didn't he burn a bush? Called it God? Just like a man to set something on fire and then assume his creation is divine.

"I think I found your dad," he says.

Our table somehow becomes unmoored from reality. We're drifting in empty space, the bar and people around us a black void.

"What?" I manage, realizing I'm somehow angry. Angry at him? Angry at the words he just said? Or maybe just angry at myself for thinking that this might have been about him wanting to see me. Wanting me. It's so stupid I want to scream. And that word. *Dad*. It drains the blood from my veins. I'm bloodless. Strings of cells and flesh and bone about to collapse on the chair in a heap.

"I've been looking for a long time. I know, I'm sorry—"

"Stop apologizing."

"I've, well, in college, while studying journalism, I chose to do a paper on what happened to your dad. Since then, I've sort of been obsessed with it. It's kind of a hobby. And, listen, they found the body."

"Dad's body?" I ask, not sure if I want it to be true or not.

"No, God, sorry. No, they found her body. Stacy."

"Jesus," I say. "So he did it. He killed her."

"No one knows for sure. As a journalist, I've got my sources, but even then, I only got glimpses into the investigation. But I can say it looks that way. They've reopened your dad's case. It's no longer a missing persons. It's a murder investigation."

"Jesus," I say again. It's not that I'm surprised. How could I be? It's just that hearing the words out loud has a calcifying effect.

"They found the body on a remote section of the Oregon coast," Maddox says. "Some kids came across it. Can you imagine?"

I can't help but picture Maddox, Jamie, and me wandering the beach and finding a body as kids. We probably would have loved it.

"Anyway," Maddox says, "the body was bloated and unrecognizable, but they matched her DNA and dental records. It's definitely her."

"But they think he killed her?" I ask.

"They don't know. At least not for sure. But her wounds seem to point in that direction. She sustained a blunt force injury to the skull."

I look down at the fries in front of us, wondering how it was possible that just a minute ago they'd looked so appetizing.

"Sorry," he says. "Anyway, look, I did some more digging. I found several of your dad's closest friends from the military that I thought might be housing him. I've looked into them all. I don't know for a hundred percent, but, look . . . it's basically a hundred percent."

"What are you talking about?"

"One of his army buddies owns a lot of property in the Catskills, just northwest of New York City. He wasn't exactly forthright when I talked to him, but I'm telling you, Jeanie, your dad is living on his property. I can almost guarantee it. I talked to a bunch of people in the area, showed them a picture of your dad and several of them admitted to seeing him in the past year or two. Then I used Google Earth and found a cabin up the hill from the man's house. I'd bet my retirement fund your dad is living there."

"Is he . . . alone?"

Maddox's look of confusion turns quickly to sympathy. He knows what I'm asking. *Jamie.* "I don't know. But I think so."

A haze of sounds from the bar, the blackness around us. I think I hear someone say my name. *Jeanie, you're . . .* It's Jamie's voice. The last thing he said to me. *You're?* Had he said *you're? You're* what? The women at the table behind us laugh. Their jealousy has evaporated, and they've moved on to making fun of me, talking about how out of my league Maddox is.

"Why didn't you go to the police?" I ask.

Maddox shrugs. "The police have already been there. Apparently they searched the place years ago. But I think your dad was on the move then. I think he's only settled there in the past few years. I was going to go to them, and I will, but"—he taps a fingernail against the scarred wooden table—"I wanted to go to you first. The guy wouldn't admit to hiding your dad, and I wasn't about to trespass, but I bet he'd tell you. Family, you know?"

I'm shaking my head, a slow, steady motion I can't seem to stop. Maddox flew across an ocean to give me this information. He's always been like this. I can picture him running into the sea on a cold day because it seemed like a good idea in that moment, the wind in his hair, the sand stretching out before him. He never looked more alive or himself. The problem is, in his impulsiveness, he doesn't stop to consider the ramifications of his actions, the freezing cold he'll feel after. This idea, it's the same thing. He hasn't thought it through—how it might hurt.

"And you thought, what? That I still want to see him? That I'd just hop on over there and he and I would have a nice chat and a cup of tea?"

Maddox looks hurt and confused at the same time. "No, Jeanie, I just thought you should know. If you want to find him, I can drive you, we could—"

"Why? So you can get your story? Is that what this is about?" I sound angry, but I don't know if I really am. Desperate. That's a better word. I'm desperate. I wish I could go back to the quiet life I'd created before Maddox showed up at the dinner shop.

"Yes, Jeanie. I want to get the story. But if that's all I wanted, I wouldn't be here. I want to do what's right for you.

I want to give you a chance to see him before the police get to him. They *will* search that place again, Jeanie, whether I tell them about it or not. It might be a while before they get another warrant, but they will get there."

"You want me to pull him out of hiding, that's all you want. You want to be the one to find him." There *is* anger now. It's piling on top of my desperation.

"I do, of course I do," he says. "I care about what happened. I care about this story. But I only care about this story because of you. Because I've always cared about you. That's why I'm here." He looks genuine. He probably is. But does it matter? Do I care? No, I don't. It's all too much. Seeing Maddox had already been too much, but now, suddenly confronted with my dad, with the possibility of answers, with even a hope of understanding what happened to Jamie—I can't take it. The room is elongating. My limbs are beginning to separate from my body. I feel weightless, like in the car accident. I can't breathe.

My hand is gripping my pint glass as if to keep my arm in place. I can't seem to release it. My legs are burrowing into the floor, if I wait any longer, my body will split at the seams.

"Great seeing you again, Maddox," I manage.

I head for the door. I can hear Maddox saying my name. He might even be chasing after me. I move fast through the crowd, spilling a little beer on my fingers. But I'm slim, I can squeeze through the gathered shoulders. The night is over, just like that. The room is heavy. Heavy with people, heavy with the smells of beer, aftershave, old wood. The walls seep with memory, pouring forth tales of rings of power and talking lions. My legs are wobbly things about to give out beneath me. Somehow, I reach the door and head into the cool night, beer still in hand. It's not the first time I've stolen a pint glass. Probably won't be the last.

CHAPTER 8

THEN

It was in the middle of our eighth-grade year when Jamie first made his appearance in the music room at school. I remember walking down the hallway and hearing the sounds of a piano trickling through the walls. A crowd of maybe ten or so students had gathered by the door. Among them was the band teacher, Mrs. Magnuson, who stood watching with her hands folded across her chest. The familiar sound of the song grew louder as I approached. When I looked over the shoulders of the students, I saw Jamie. His blond hair swayed back and forth as his fingers danced over the keys. I'd almost forgotten, in our time in the woods, his skill with the piano. And, somehow, he'd gotten better. The song he was playing was familiar, and yet I would have sworn I'd never heard him play it before. It was as if his skill had been growing, germinating inside him all this time without the need for any real practice.

I watched him, mesmerized like everyone else as the song sped up. His fingers moved so fast I couldn't imagine how he could calculate each individual note. They danced and twirled over the keys in a seamless flow, the music like something out of a Regency ballroom—giant dresses, men in wigs, horse-drawn carriages. It filled the music room and rose over the students. Jamie was something out of time. Something I could barely grasp. Something beyond me. I realized in that moment that he'd outgrown me. He had removed himself from my orbit and was sailing toward distant solar systems. Fancy parties. Brightly lit stages. The upper echelon of society.

When the music finally did come to an end, in a flurry of notes that grew quickly softer, when he lifted his hands from the piano, a strand of hair dangling from his forehead, the students erupted into applause as if Jamie had just scored a touchdown. I watched as the kids looked back at Mrs. Magnuson in amazement, their eyes sparkling with ecclesiastic wonder as if Jamie had led them all to the divine. Jamie looked up from the piano at the crowd as if shocked that anyone else in the world still existed.

Something was stirring inside me, and I didn't know it was pride until I saw Mrs. Magnuson work her way through the crowd and put a hand on Jamie's shoulder. I saw the look of hunger on her face. She had found something special, something she could attach her name to and put out into the world. But it was more than pride that I felt. It was also sorrow. A deep, penetrating, cut-glass kind of sorrow. I saw Jamie's beauty, his skill, his smile, the way everyone looked at him. I saw how I was drawing closer to our drunk of a father, shooting defenseless birds in the woods, eager to be praised and loved over Jamie. In that moment, I didn't just see what everyone else saw: a star being born. I saw the supernova, a cataclysmic solar event that obliterated the progenitor in complete totality, after which, the resulting object became one of two things: a neutron star, or a black hole.

Jamie, or Jeanie King.

On a sunny Sunday afternoon, Maddox broke the protocol that he, Jamie, and I had set in place for ourselves. We were walking the north side of the beach where there were large sandstone rocks with honeycomb weathering that made them easy and fun to climb. We spent hours alternating between scaling the rocks and sitting and watching the water and the birds. Maddox and I would glance at each other from time to time like we had this great secret. Jamie must've noticed something, because he seemed quieter than usual.

"Wanna come over for dinner sometime?" Maddox asked us.

"Like, to your house?" I realized it was a stupid question as soon as it was out of my mouth, but I couldn't help myself. Maddox's home life was such a mystery, I could almost be convinced that it didn't exist, that Maddox lived among the rocks and kelp and came out only to join Jamie and me or to attend school.

"Yeah, Dad says he wants to see 'whoever the hell you've been running around with all day.'" He said the last part in a deep, mocking voice.

Maddox gave us directions to his house, and we agreed to meet him there that Saturday evening. Before we left for his place, Jamie and I escaped into the woods and smoked one of Stacy's old cigarettes—well, *I* smoked; he watched. After the instance with Stacy's cigarette packet, I found one of her half-smoked cigarettes in the journal I kept, where I'd write out my thoughts, draft stupid poems, or draw random pictures that weren't very good. The cigarette had burned through several pages and left black gossamer patches blooming across the journal. I was so mad, not just that she had burned my journal, but that she had taken it, and read it probably. It was an intrusion. I felt violated. I almost wanted to tell Dad, but I knew whose side he'd take. So instead, Jamie and I had started stealing her cigarettes. At first we just hid them around the cabin—under couches, beneath cushions, in random drawers in the kitchen. Then we started taking them outside and burning them in a small makeshift firepit. Eventually we tried smoking them. Jamie coughed and passed the cigarette to me, refusing to try again. "That's disgusting," he said through tight breaths. When I took a puff, I coughed, too, but forced myself to keep smoking until my throat felt dry, my chest warm, and my head light.

Now I'd gotten used to the feel and I liked it. The cigarette between my fingers, the warmth in my lungs. It calmed me down. I didn't know if it was the nicotine so much as the practice. The slow breath in, breath out, watching the smoke gather in front of my face. Jamie wouldn't try after that first time.

"You're gonna smell like smoke. Maddox is gonna know," he said.

"I'll brush my teeth," I said.

"Your clothes will smell like it," Jamie said.

"So. Who cares?" I said. Jamie shrugged, like *your funeral*, but I knew what he meant. We were, the both of us—whether we admitted it or not—a little nervous about going to Maddox's house. It'd been a long time since we'd been in any kind of home with two adults, dinner on the table, maybe something playing on TV. We were going to be as out of place as wild wolves in a restaurant. Though we knew Maddox's parents let him do most anything he wanted, we also knew that sometimes he had to be home for dinner or he had to get back to do chores or he couldn't come out today because his mom was sick—she struggled with occasional seizures—and he had to help take care of her, things like that, things we didn't have with Dad.

I remember standing in front of the mirror before leaving

for Maddox's placc. I was trying to get my tangles of brown hair into something like a braid but was failing miserably. When was the last time I'd washed it? Combed it? I couldn't remember. Mom had always taken fastidious care of my hair. She used to put it in french braids, ponytails, pigtails, side ponies, and buns. She did it partially because she liked the way it looked and partially, I think, because she liked doing it. I can still feel her confident hands. The way my hair pulled tight at the sides of my scalp, how it hurt a little but I didn't cry out because I was sure Mom knew what she was doing. I trusted her. She'd let me watch shows while she did it, too.

"I wish she hadn't let me, though," I told Dr. Gardner.

"Let you watch TV while she did your hair?" he asked.

"Yes."

"And why's that?"

"I dunno . . . it's like, sometimes I feel like I should have looked at her more. Memorized her face. I remember looking at an old photograph of her because I couldn't remember what her neck looked like. I know that sounds stupid, but . . . anyway, I saw this mole on her neck and was like, what? Did she always have a mole there?"

"And how did that make you feel?" he asked. It was a cliché question. Therapists shouldn't be allowed to ask it.

I shook my head. "It's just a mole, you know. It shouldn't make me feel anything."

"Grief manifests in all kinds of ways we find peculiar. It doesn't matter if it should or shouldn't make you feel a certain way; what matters is what you felt."

I bit the inside of my lip. My knee was tapping. "It was just a mole."

I didn't want to talk about Mom anymore. Mom had always been a delicate figure in my memory. Maybe to offset Dad's roughness—the jagged, harsh way he moved through life. Or maybe it was the fact that my memories of her were so distant now that she'd become dreamlike, wispy, and ethereal, as if a strong wind might blow her away forever. A dream half remembered. A hand on my cheek soft as goose down. I held her in my head like that, careful of her delicacy, her transience, barely daring to look too long at her or to breathe too deeply.

Standing in front of the mirror, I ran my useless hands through my hair, trying to twist it around and around like Mom used to do, trying to tie it into something that would stay, but no matter how hard I tried, it was like a frayed rope. I pulled and pulled and twisted and wrapped everything into my hair tie, and when it all fell loose, I pulled more. I pulled so hard my eyes started to water and my face went red. My scalp was throbbing from the pain. I looked down at my hand and saw a clump of hair resting on my palm. The strands looked like fingers, curled and lifeless. My hands started to shake.

"Ready?" Jamie asked as I stepped out of the bathroom, my hair pulled back into a haphazard ponytail. I resented Jamie for his perfect blond hair, his blue eyes. The way he looked so much like Mom.

"Let's go," I said.

It was starting to rain as we made our way down the rutted dirt road toward the main drive.

"You don't want to bring a coat?" Jamie asked.

"No," I said.

It was the beginning of spring and there was new warmth to the air. The ferns were reaching their arms over the gravel. Green buds were sprouting, animals emerging, insects skittering; the whole world was moving in a buzz of activity that you could almost hear if you were quiet enough.

Maddox's place was just past town along the main drive. It was a small two-story with chipped white paint and the remains of a fence falling apart on the front lawn. By the time

Jamie and I approached the driveway, the rain had turned into large fat drops.

"Shoulda brought a coat," Jamie said as we stepped over the fence and onto the yard. As we did, we heard a crash like furniture falling over from inside the house. Then there were raised voices. Jamie and I froze, unsure whether we should continue toward the door and knock, wait for things to calm down inside, or turn and leave. My hair was growing heavy with rainwater, and I could feel my jeans beginning to stick to my thighs. I looked at Jamie and he shrugged. Neither of us knew how to continue. I took a cautious step forward just as the door swung open.

"See how it fucking turns out, huh?" Maddox's dad was yelling at him in the doorway. He was thin with bony arms that dangled from a loose-fitting gray shirt that had a picture of a naked woman holding a guitar over her crotch. His skin was pale white, which was an odd contrast to Maddox's soft brown complexion. "You just fucking see how it all goes down, Mr. Know-it-all! Wait and fucking see!" Maddox attempted to get past him, but his dad grabbed Maddox's arm, jerking him roughly. "Hey. I'm talking to you." For a brief moment, a wild, animal fear flashed across Maddox's face; it was quickly replaced by rage as he ripped his arm away from his dad and bounded down the front step. Maddox's dad gave a strained laugh before he slammed the front door. He hadn't so much as glanced at me and Jamie.

"Come on," Maddox said, storming past us toward the road. Jamie and I followed him, practically jogging to keep up with his long strides.

"What happened?" Jamie asked.

"Nothing," Maddox said. And we let the matter drop. He stormed ahead, wiping his eyes from either rain, sweat, or tears, I couldn't tell.

As we made our way down the street, marching swiftly to

put as much distance as possible between ourselves and Maddox's house, I felt a growing need to make things right. To fix Maddox's pain. I didn't like his quiet strides, the furrowed look on his face.

"How about you come over to the cabin?" I asked.

"Jeanie," Jamie said. I could hear it in his voice. *Not a good idea.*

"Yeah," Maddox said, surprising the both of us. "Let's go."

I could feel Jamie's gaze on me, but I refused to look at him. I knew what I would see there. Eyes wide. Eyebrows raised. An expression that read, clear as anything: *What if Dad's home?*

He wasn't, as it turned out. On the section of dirt where he usually parked his truck, I could see the empty lines of tire marks, the flattened dirt, grass, and pine straw. The sun was a good hour before setting, but because of the tall evergreens standing sentinel around the cabin, there was a mock twilight settling in the forest. We made our way inside and Jamie and I stoked the fire.

"You hungry?" I asked Maddox.

"Sure," he said.

There wasn't much to eat, so we made peanut butter and jam sandwiches with thick slices of cheddar cheese on the side. I wanted to ask Maddox about what had happened back at his place with his dad, but also didn't want to pry, and he didn't seem particularly talkative, either. His usual jovial demeanor was subdued as we ate.

I don't know if it was because of this, because I didn't like the way his eyes stuck to his plate, but after we'd eaten, I asked: "You want a beer?"

Maddox and Jamie both looked at me. Maddox curious, Jamie panicked.

"Your dad lets you drink beer?" he asked.

I shrugged. "He's never said not to, and I know he's got a six-pack in the fridge."

"Jeanie," Jamie said.

"Come on," I said. "What's a couple beers? He probably won't even notice, I swear. He'll think he drank them." And it was true. He came home drunk most nights anyway. There was no way he kept track of the beers he had or hadn't drunk.

"This is a bad idea," Jamie said at the same time that Maddox smiled and said, "Yeah, sure."

I went to the fridge with a growing sense of excitement. I pulled out two beers—I was sure Jamie wouldn't have one. They were Heineken, their green bodies cool and smooth to the touch. I set the beers down on the kitchen table then rummaged around in the drawers for the bottle opener. I couldn't find one, so I used the side of a can opener to pop the caps like I'd seen Dad do before. There was a satisfying snapping sound as each cap broke free from the bottle.

"I'm not having one. You're on your own," Jamie said, even though he could clearly see I'd only taken out two.

"Even if you don't, you think he really won't be mad at the both of us?" It wasn't fair of me to say, to use the strained relationship between Jamie and Dad. To play up on his fears like that. Except, it was the truth. In fact, Dad would probably find some way to take it out on Jamie, even though it had all been my idea.

Maddox and I took a sip.

"Ugh," Maddox said. "Tastes like pop gone bad."

I laughed, but he was right. It was pretty gross. I didn't care, though; I was going to drink it anyway. We kept sipping as we made our way outside to sit on the Adirondack chairs and watch the stars poke their heads out from between the sharpened tips of the evergreens. There was a small breeze, funneled down the old road, but it was warm, hinting at the summer to come.

"So where is your dad?" Maddox asked.

"Who knows," I said. "He's not home that often."

Jamie mumbled something that might have been *good riddance.*

"I like your house," Maddox said.

"It's a dump." I wasn't sure why I was ragging on the cabin, maybe because it didn't seem like a proper house out here in the woods. I suppose I wanted him to know that my standards were higher than this, that I was better than my circumstances.

"So where's your mom?" Maddox asked. It was odd that he'd never asked about her. But that was one of the rules the three of us had set, unspoken, into place. We never asked about family. Somehow, the fact that he was at our house changed things.

"She died," Jamie chimed in. I looked over at him. He was staring out at the trees. "Car accident, years ago," he said.

"Oh," Maddox said. "I'm sorry."

I took another drink of my beer, realizing that I'd finished half of it. My head was already starting to feel a little bit light.

"Sometimes I wish something like that would happen to my dad," Maddox said.

"What?" I asked. "Like die in a car accident?"

Maddox brought the beer bottle to his lips and blew over the top, making a low whistling. "Yeah," he said. "I know that sounds really bad, and probably I don't mean it. But, you know, just sometimes."

I leaned my head back against the hard wood of the Adirondack chair. "I get it," I said.

Jamie nodded.

We were silent again for a long while, listening to crickets singing in the bushes. An owl somewhere asked his existential questions: *Who? Who? Who?* And in that silence, another noise, as grating as nails on chalk: Dad's car driving down the rutted road.

"Shit," Jamie said, turning to Maddox. "You gotta go."

"You're fine," I said to Maddox, taking another drink of beer. Maddox started to stand. "You're fine," I said again, grabbing his arm and guiding him back down to the seat.

"Jeanie, toss the beer," Jamie said.

I took another drink. I wanted to prove something to Maddox, like I was grown up, that I wasn't afraid. I wanted to challenge my dad. So I kept that beer bottle in one hand, and my other resting on Maddox's arm as Dad's headlights split through the darkness, nodding up and down along the old road. We all watched in silence as the truck pulled up to its spot and Dad killed the engine. The door snapped open and he half tumbled out—drunk. How he'd managed to get home in the state he was in was a mystery.

It took him the first step onto the front porch to notice the three of us sitting in the chairs. His eyes scanned us and settled on Maddox. He frowned, confusion written on his face. I could practically feel every atom in Jamie's body thrumming, electric with the desire to flee.

"Who the fuck is this?" he asked.

"A friend," I said. "Maddox, this is my dad."

"Nice to meet you, sir," Maddox said, confident, but not daring to hold out a hand.

Dad laughed. "So you just go ahead and bring anybody over, huh?" Dad asked. He was swaying slightly, as if a good gust of wind could knock him over. This was a dangerous type of drunk—his silliness could quickly turn to anger and I knew it. So did Jamie, who sat silent in the seat beside me, practically shaking.

"You Iraqi?" Dad asked.

"Dad!" I said, desperate for him to stop talking.

"Gotta be Mexican," Dad said.

"Half Filipino," Maddox said.

"You all fucking each other?" Dad said, his eyes resting on each of us. "That's what kids your age are doing." He said it like it was something that had been bothering him for a long time, like it wasn't just the alcohol talking. He was amusing himself at this point. He didn't really care what he was saying. "Every generation starts younger. Soon it'll be goddamn babies doing it. Your parents know you're here?" Dad asked Maddox.

"Yes, sir," Maddox said. "But I should probably get going." He wasn't rising yet, though; it was almost as if he needed permission first.

"You're fine," I said.

"Are you drinking my goddamned beer?" Dad asked, pointing at the bottle in my hand.

"Yes," I said. The courage and the fight I'd had inside me were slowly melting away, replaced by the fear that was radiating off Jamie in waves.

"Good Lord, you've got a set of balls on you," he said. "How about you, son?" He looked at Maddox, a smile on his stupid drunk face. "You got a heavy pair as well?"

"I'll go," Maddox said.

"No," Dad said. "Where you going? Come on, it's fine. Listen to your girlfriend. I'm just getting to know ya, that's all. I'm the dad here, it's my job. I'm fucking Dad."

"That's okay," I said to Maddox. "You can go." I'd had enough. I didn't want Maddox to see any more.

Maddox looked from me to Jamie, as if unsure if we were going to be okay. I felt anger rising in my throat. None of this was okay. It wasn't fair. I wished Dad was gone more than ever then. I wished he was someone different. I wished he'd never gone to the war, had stayed the dad who loved us and played with us. I wished he'd never come home from Iraq. Anything other than what he was now. "See you tomorrow," Maddox said over his shoulder as he moved past Dad, but as he did, Dad grabbed his arm. Surprisingly, Maddox jerked away, roughly.

"I tell you to go yet?" Dad said.

"Leave him alone!" I yelled, standing now, the beer gripped hard in my palm.

But Dad had a hold of Maddox. I could practically feel his iron grasp on Maddox's arm. And in Maddox's face, that same wild-animal look he'd gotten when his own dad had grabbed him. *Don't touch me, don't grab me, don't force me.*

"Dad!" I yelled again. I felt a growing desperation in my gut. This was all my fault.

Dad was pulling Maddox toward him, grumbling nonsense. "It's my fucking house. My goddamn family." He'd turned the sharp corner toward angry now as Maddox twisted his body, pulling, trying to be free of my father.

I watched as Dad yanked on Maddox's arm again, pulling him in close. My insides clenched into a burning ball.

"Jeanie," I heard Jamie say from beside me, but I never found out what he wanted because the beer bottle was out of my hands before I'd really thought it through. Maybe this was what it was like to feel drunk. I wasn't sure. I'd meant to just hit Dad in the chest or shoulder, to startle him for long enough that he'd let go and Maddox could run. Instead, the bottle slammed into the side of Dad's head with a solid, heavy crack, and Dad dropped like his legs had been cut from under him. Jamie gasped as I said, "Shit."

For a single breath, the three of us stared at Dad, his body motionless in the grass. Then he groaned and rose slowly to his elbows.

"Go," I said to Maddox. Maddox looked from me to

Jamie, then back to Dad, as if reluctant to leave. "We'll be fine," I said. "Get out of here."

"Is he okay?" Maddox asked, looking from Dad to me, unsure what to do.

Dad made it to his knees, put a hand on his face. I could see the blood on his cheek, a dark stream, falling from his eyebrow to his beard. I ran down the porch and raced over to Maddox. I put my hands on his chest and shoved hard. "Go!" I yelled.

"Jeanie," Maddox said.

"He won't do shit to us, but I don't know about you. Please. Go!" I shoved him again, harder this time. As if I'd launched him into movement, he turned and ran through the trees, his legs kicking, arms pumping, and for half a second, I watched him go, amazed that anyone could move that fast.

When Dad made it to his feet, instead of lashing out at me, he started toward his truck. I knew that he'd get back in, he'd drive down the road and find Maddox. I had to stop it. I lowered my shoulder and ran into Dad as hard and as fast as I could. I heard Jamie yell "Jeanie!" the same time I heard Dad grunt from the impact of my body. At any normal time, had Dad not been drunk and probably concussed, my whole weight against him wouldn't have done a thing, but now, he lost his balance and all six feet four inches of him fell back onto the grass, me on top of him. He looked up, searching my face as if just remembering who I was. Anger flashed across his eyes, his mouth twisted, and suddenly my body was twirling. The trees somersaulted through my vision until I landed on my back, Dad's heavy body weighing me down. And then I couldn't breathe. At first, I thought maybe the wind had been knocked out of me, but then I felt the incredible pressure against my throat. I reached a hand to Dad's knuckles, his fingers taut as ropes around my neck. Behind him, Jamie appeared, his face contorted, tears on his cheeks, his little fists slamming into Dad's back and shoulders. But Dad didn't even register Jamie or the blows he was landing. His lip was twitching, his fingers were gripping tighter and tighter. I began to see red and gold lights at the edges of my vision. The lights grew brighter as darkness pooled around them. Was this what it felt like to die? I wondered. I pulled on Dad's hands at my neck and was able to lift my chin and get out a single, choked word: "Dad." It was all I could manage, and honestly, I didn't know what I was trying to say. But it's what I said, and it was enough. As if released from a spell, Dad's face fell. His grip loosened. He sat back slowly, looking down at my body as I gasped for air. Jamie was at my side, blubbering something. He helped me to my feet and led me back into the cabin as Dad collapsed onto the grass, unmoving. For a horrible second, I wanted to run back to him, to tell him I was sorry, to hug him tight, to ask him to lift me onto his shoulders like he used to do when I was a kid. I wanted him to come inside, to have a tea party with my stuffed animals, to run his hand through my hair and tell me everything was going to be all right. To not be this person who drank, who disappeared, who hurt me. Instead, Jamie and I made our way into our room. The air slowly came back into my lungs, though my throat was still raw and pulsating. Together, Jamie and I moved the bunk bed up against the door so that Dad couldn't get in. I was pretty sure he still could if he really wanted to, but we had to do something to help us feel safe. Safe from Dad. It didn't feel right. *Mom would have killed him,* I thought. *She'd fucking kill him.*

We crawled into the bottom bunk together that night, our shoulders touching. The warmth of our bodies, Jamie's silent tears. I was glad for Jamie then. Glad he was with me. Glad I wasn't alone.

"It's fine," I told him as he cried. My words were raw,

choked, but I said them anyway. I comforted my brother and pictured Maddox running away into the night, wondering where he was, if he was all right, how far away he'd gotten, wishing I'd gone with him. "Everything's going to be fine," I said, and leaned my head against Jamie's shoulder.

CHAPTER 9

NOW

"When was the last time you cried?" Dr. Gardner asked me during one of our very first Tuesday sessions.

"Cried?"

"Yes." Dr. Gardner waited for my response, eyes staring at me over the rims of his glasses.

"I don't know," I said, genuinely unsure.

"When your father left?"

I shook my head. "No,"

"When your mother died?"

I tried to think back. I remembered there'd been this constant ringing in my ears after the accident. The doctors said that head trauma could have all kinds of effects, but I knew it had nothing to do with the accident. It was the hollow echo of Mom's absence. There were no tears, just the constant, empty ringing. I must have cried. I'm sure I did. But every time I thought back to the days after the accident, it was always Jamie crying, not me. I'd held it all in.

"Jamie cried," I said. And he had. He'd cried buckets.

Cried every single day for at least a month. Mostly at night, but sometimes it would be random. Aunt Eileen pushing him on the swing and he'd just burst into tears.

"But I'm wondering about you," Dr. Gardner said.

I flip through my memory bank like a Rolodex, back further, deeper. "My doll broke when I was a kid. I think maybe Jamie broke it because I'd done something to him, I don't know. But I cried. I was so mad."

"This was before your mom died?"

"Yes," I said.

"That's a long time ago."

"I know."

"Nothing in school? University? Bad breakups?"

I shook my head.

"And why do you think that is?"

I was still shaking my head.

"Jeanie?"

"Yes?"

I stared at the laces of his shoes. One of them was loosened and would surely come undone the next time he stood up. I thought about crossing the room and doing them up for him.

"Why do you think that is?" he asked again.

They wouldn't even need to be redone, just pulled tight.

"Jeanie? You still with me?"

"I don't know," I said.

"You don't know what?" he asked. "If you're still with me, or why you haven't cried in so long?"

I shook my head again. "I don't know," I said.

⬛

The bell chimes above me as I enter the dinner shop. Deloris is in the back, pulling out a dish that, from the looks of it, is shepherd's pie. A young couple watches her, eyeballing the dish as if afraid she might drop it.

"Jeanie, hi honey, mind ringing this up?" she asks. She's off on another date tonight. I can tell. She's got the excited, rosy cheeks of an elderly woman about to get laid. Or maybe that's just my own overcharged sexuality rearing its head again. I want to ask her about it but can't bring myself to talk about dating after the debacle with Maddox. He's continued to call and text: all apologies and explanations, which I don't respond to.

"Sure," I say, stepping behind the counter. Deloris sets the dish on the counter and I ring it up.

"How's your night going?" I ask the couple, pulling forth the fake-enthusiastic part of me. It's like another personality I keep locked away until I'm at work.

The man looks away, but the woman smiles, clearly used to being the conversational one. "Just surviving the kids, you know?"

I give her a customary laugh. "Nope, I genuinely don't."

"No kids?" the woman asks. She's got red hair with really red lipstick and a thick scarf that looks more itchy than comfortable.

"God, no," I say. The woman's face falls; she looks taken aback. "Not that kids are a bad thing," I say quickly. "I just . . . not for me."

"I totally get it," she replies in a tone that says she doesn't get it at all, that she can't fathom a woman who doesn't want to fulfill her purpose: procreation. "Not everyone can handle them." Her husband pulls out his card and slides it into the reader.

I wonder if she even knows how she sounds. She's got the blissfully contented look of a woman who is living the exact life she expected and is 100 percent confident in her choices. *Oh, I could handle it*, I want to say but don't. The only thing is, I don't want to be responsible for fucking up another life like every other parent in the history of the world.

The machine vomits their receipt and I hand it to them with a smile. "Well, good luck with the kidpocalypse," I say.

"The what?" she asks as her husband turns toward the door.

"You said you were surviving . . . never mind," I say with an awkward laugh and a wave.

"Okay, thanks," the woman says, following her husband out the door.

The little chime rings and I watch them through the glass, walking down the street, shepherd's pie in hand. "Good Lord," I say for no one reason in particular.

"Everything all right?" Deloris says. She's already donned her coat and gloves.

"Yeah," I say. "Everything's fine."

"Good." She's patting her coat pockets for the bus pass she can't ever keep track of.

"Deloris?" I ask.

"Yes, dear?" Her head swivels on her neck, searching the floor as if she might have dropped the pass earlier.

"You ever feel like everyone else understands something that you don't? You know, something important that some-one was supposed to tell you but never did, and everyone just assumes that you know it, too, and when you do or say some-thing that proves you don't know this really important thing, then you become this, I don't know, pariah?"

Deloris pauses her bus-pass search to look at me, concern tugging her eyebrows like a fishhook. "Jeanie," she says, reaching toward me. I look at her gloved hand grasping the top of my pale, naked one, and I think I should feel something in this moment, this show of affection should do something to me. I should be emotional. This is human contact, genu-ine empathy and concern, more than just hands, one on top of the other. "No one has everything worked out," she says. "Everyone is just pretending they do; I can promise you that. And the better you get at pretending, the further you get from yourself." She must've read that somewhere. It's good.

I give her a little laugh like *I know, I know, it's fine, I'm fine, don't worry, really, it's fine.* "You're a wise woman, Deloris."

She winks at me. "I know, dear. And I don't even have to pretend."

I laugh again, a real one this time. "Another date tonight?"

"Yup, fifth one and don't you say a word about it."

I mime zipping my lips and throwing away the key.

"If only I could find my—"

"It's on the counter," I say, pointing. It's always on the counter—the most obvious place to look.

"Oh, right, of course. Thanks, dear." She swipes the pass and heads toward the door. "You know, if my head wasn't attached at my neck, or however that saying goes. See? Nobody's got it all together."

"Even in all your wisdom," I say.

She laughs. "A good night to you."

"Night," I say.

❒

Between my bus stop and the dinner shop, there's a music store with a large piano in the window. I always look at it as I pass. Sometimes I even stop and stare, marvel at the simplicity of the interlacing white and black keys. And, of course, I think of Jamie, his delicate fingers poised over the instrument. That moment of silence before he began to play. He was a marvel. All his teachers told him, told Aunt Eileen, too. *He could play anywhere,* they said, licking their greedy lips, throwing the word *prodigy* around like they'd invented it. They wanted to be the ones to push his talent into the world.

The door to the shop opens and a bald old man with tiny spectacles emerges. "Wanna come in and have a go?" he asks in a heavy Scottish brogue, his face wrinkling into a kind smile.

"Me? Oh, no, thank you," I say.

"Seen you peeking in every once in a while. I don't mind if you'd like to give it a tinker."

"No, I really can't," I say. "I don't play. My brother did." My brother *did*, as in, he can't anymore. I picture him now, in that music room while a small crowd gathered to watch, fingers dancing over the keys.

"I teach lessons as well," the man says. "I can give you a quick one if you like. A sort of sample." He smiles and I let myself be led into the shop.

He takes me straight to the piano. I sit down at the bench, the black varnished wood uncomfortable beneath me. I stare at the keys. *Beethoven's Moonlight Sonata. Clara Schumann's Piano Concerto. Nocturne in E-flat Major by Chopin.* I can hear them all still. Jamie's fingers moving as if he's simply told them to play and they play. Why can't everything in life be as simple as music?

"Name's Billie," the man says as he sits next to me on the stool.

"Jeanie," I say.

"Jeanie. Good. Now, I want you to lift your hands over the keys but don't touch them. Keep them nice and loose, see, like you're holding two squishy tennis balls in your hands. Relax the wrists. There ye go."

I watch my hands respond to his commands, lifting in front of me as if some spirit moves them.

"Good. Now place your thumbs here, and each finger like this, yes. Now we should probably start by learning to read music, eh? That's what all the books say. But since this isn't a proper lesson, let me teach you a few chords. Sometimes it's better to hear how your fingers can make music first. That's what I think, anyway."

The white keys feel cool and smooth beneath my fingertips.

"Now press down your thumbs, middle fingers, and pinkie fingers at the same time. That there's a D chord."

I do so without thinking and hear the piano respond. It's not music, but it's the beginning of music. Notes ringing in harmony, hammers pressing down on strings inside the black wooden body. They say your olfactory sense has the strongest link to memory, but I disagree. It's auditory. But not just any sound will trigger it. Music. Music grinds at one's memory more than any smell in the world.

I lift my fingers suddenly as if they've been pressing against hot coals. I stand up. If the old man hadn't been sitting beside me, I would have toppled the bench with the backs of my legs.

"Thanks for the lesson," I say.

He looks flustered but nods nonetheless. "Anytime, lass." He smiles like he knows exactly what I'm thinking and feeling. I wonder if he does, if he understands the grip music can have over one's heart and soul and throat. Going to sleep to the sound of Jamie practicing. Songs ringing through my aunt and uncle's house.

Clair de Lune, Rhapsody in Blue, The Well-Tempered Clavier.

I hurry out the door.

In the brisk autumn air, standing outside the music shop, I look at my phone. Another text from Maddox.

I imagine Dad now, living his life in New York, having no idea about my fucked-up existence. I wonder if he even cares. He shouldn't be allowed to not care. Does he even know that Jamie played the piano? He shouldn't get to live on in ignorance. He owes me something. He owes me everything. Answers. I deserve answers. Why did he kill Stacy? What happened to Jamie? Why did he leave me behind?

Shit. I do want to see him. I do want to track him down and drag him out of the hole he's crawled into. I want to look him in the eye and tell him how terrible of a person he is. I want to see the look of regret on his face and bask in it. The look of pure despair for what he's done. For how he treated us. For how he abandoned us. For whatever he did to Stacy. For whatever he did to Jamie. And if there's any chance he might be with Jamie, or be able to lead me to Jamie, isn't it worth it? Of course it is.

Ignoring Maddox's newest message, I write back. Three words. Three little words is all it takes for a life to change.

OK, I text. *I'll go.*

CHAPTER 10

THEN

I've never been one of those girls who got into BDSM. I can handle a lot of weird stuff during sex, but pain doesn't do it for me. Probably, if I brought this up with Dr. Gardner, he'd trace it back to the day that Dad choked me. But it's not that. It's that sex is for feeling good, and choking feels like shit. All that next day after Dad's confrontation with Maddox, my throat felt tight and uncomfortable and scratchy like I'd swallowed a starfish.

We didn't see Dad until the afternoon that day. I wasn't sure where he'd been because his truck was parked in its spot and his guns were still inside. Probably at Stacy's. Her trailer was more or less within walking distance. When he did show up, he didn't look or sound drunk, but he did look haggard, with a red, jagged line across his forehead where the beer bottle had struck him. He'd washed the blood from his face, but I could still see a pink stream of skin where he'd rubbed it raw. He limped through the door and looked from Jamie to me.

"Jeanie," he said, my heart slamming in my chest. "Come here." He headed down the hallway toward the back room. I followed. His room was littered with clothes, old bottles, small pieces of machinery by the window that looked like they might have been a clock at one point. Dad was rustling in a large bin in his closet. When he emerged, he had a small blue box in his hand.

"I meant to give this to you," he said.

I took the box; it was light like nothing was in it. I resisted the urge to shake it.

"Open it," he said. I snapped the lid open. Inside was a golden necklace with a small pendant. At first glance, it looked like the letter *K*, but then I noticed the distinct outline of feathers and a beak. It was a bird. A heron. I'd seen them along the beach, heads bobbing into the water in search of small fish and crabs and mollusks.

"It belonged to Mom," he said.

"I never saw her wear it."

"She got it from Grandma. She only wore it on special occasions."

I lifted the necklace from the box, turning it back and forth, watching the sunlight flash through the window and reflect off the golden surface. I tried to picture it dangling around Mom's neck but couldn't. I couldn't even remember what her neck looked like. This bothered me. Suddenly there was a tunnel opening in my stomach. *What's wrong with me?* I thought. *I should be able to picture my mom's neck.*

"What's the matter?" Dad asked. "You don't like it?"

I shook my head. "I love it."

He exhaled. "Good," he said. He patted my shoulder once, twice. "You know I love you, right, Jeanie?"

I nodded, wondering what Jamie was doing right now.

When I looked in his eyes, I saw they were red. I didn't know if it was actually because of tears, or just the hangover.

"It won't happen again, girl." His hand reached around the back of my neck, resting there, gentle but heavy.

Later, I stole an old picture of Mom from Dad's room. I mounted the frame carefully on his bed. It showed Mom holding an apple and laughing. Her vibrant red lips perfectly matched the color of the peel, which was offset by the pale brightness of her golden hair and her eyes, which were ocean blue. I wondered what she was laughing about. What had made her so happy? Had Dad told her a joke? I stared at her neck, small and slender and long like a swan—or a heron. Then I put the necklace on over my head, lifting my hand like I was holding an apple. I smiled wide, turned my jaw just so, and pretended I was looking in a mirror.

☙

Jamie and I found Maddox later that day by the beach. He was skipping sand dollars across the flat expanse of water. I wondered if he'd been waiting there for us all day—it was Saturday—hoping we'd find him there.

"What happened last night?" Maddox asked.

"Nothing," I said, giving Jamie a look to keep his mouth shut. "He yelled some more then passed out. Sorry about that."

"It's fine," Maddox said, shrugging.

"He can be a dick sometimes," I said.

"Sometimes?" Jamie kicked divots into the sand with his shoes. I raised a hand to my neck and felt where the skin was sore, then traced it down to the outline of the necklace under my shirt.

"Sorry I ran," Maddox said.

"I told you to," I said.

"Yeah, but—"

"It's fine," I said. "I'm glad you did."

"I probably shouldn't come over again, I guess." Maddox looked out across the water as if trying to locate the last sand dollar he'd thrown.

"Yeah, probably not. Dad gets drunk sometimes and—"

"Sometimes?" Jamie said.

"Come on," I said, starting to walk along the beach with no destination in particular in mind. Jamie and Maddox followed me. The sea air was cool on my face, salty in my mouth. A seagull screamed beneath the reaching white clouds.

☉

Later that day, Maddox had to go back home for some reason, so Jamie and I walked along the pier. Weirdly, it was nice to be alone with him. Maddox and I had been spending more and more time together, and Jamie had been taking private piano lessons with Mrs. Magnuson and practicing as much as he could. It's not like we didn't still see each other all the time, but there was something familiar about being out on the pier, just the two of us, something nostalgic and comforting.

We sat along the edge of the pier, watching the water. A rain cloud was passing over the bay, a mile or so out. We could see the pebbled surface of the water, disturbed from the torrent of rain. From this distance, the raindrops looked like millions of gossamer tentacles dangling from a jellyfish cloud.

"We gotta get out of here," Jamie said, apropos of nothing.

"Because it's gonna rain?" I asked.

Jamie was picking at a bit of loose wood along the edge of the pier. Our feet were dangling over the water. Beside us was a grouping of rotting wooden pilings—all that was left from an older version of the pier. The wood looked like soggy cigars, and the barnacles growing along the sides like some sort of disease.

"No," Jamie said, a sliver of the dock breaking free between his fingers. "We have to leave the cabin. We can't stay with Dad."

I swallowed. I could still feel the raw tightness in my throat.

"He was just drunk," I said.

"He could have killed you."

"No he couldn't." I wanted to believe it. To feel, deep down, that no matter how drunk or out of his mind with rage, he'd never go so far. But I'd seen the dead look in his eyes as his giant hands squeezed. I could still feel them. If I wasn't wearing my hair down, you could have seen the bruises on the sides of my neck. "Besides, where would we go?"

Jamie looked at me, energized. He was acting as if I were taking him seriously now, which I wasn't. "Aunt Eileen's. She'd take us back."

"What? We're gonna walk all the way to Santa Clara? Don't be stupid," I said.

"We'll hitchhike or something." Jamie tossed the splinter of wood into the water, where it floated for a few moments before the waves carried it beneath the dock.

"And then what? Dad's got custody. You think he'd just let us stay in California? You think that's how it would end?"

Jamie shrugged, started picking at the dock again. He was going to tear the whole thing down, one tiny sliver at a time. "Maybe."

No, not maybe, and he knew it. He hadn't thought it through. Dad would come get us, drag us back to the cabin by our ears.

"We can't stay here," he said.

"I'm not leaving," I said. Was I scared of Dad, too? Scared of how mad he'd get when he realized we'd left him? Did I not want to leave Maddox? Did I not want to start life all over again?

"We can't stay," Jamie said again, but it was different this time. A subtle change. I only heard it because I knew him so well. This time, when he said *we*, what he meant was *I*. Jamie couldn't stay here. I did feel fear then, a needle in my stomach, sharp and deep.

"You can't leave," I said.

He didn't respond, just kept picking at the stupid dock.

"You can't leave me," I said again.

This time he nodded. "I know."

A mother and her child joined us at the edge of the pier, the kid climbing along the rails to get a better look at the ocean. The mother scolded him and had to grab his arm and pull before he finally relented. She apologized to us for some reason, as if the sight and the tranquility of the pier somehow belonged to us. I suppose, in some way, it did. Or it least it felt like that. In the same way all the special places of your childhood feel like yours and yours alone.

We sat in silence for a long while after the mother left and the rain cloud had floated its way across the bay and into deeper, more dangerous waters. The sky was growing dark when we saw something huge and shiny slide above the surface before splashing back below the ocean.

"What was that?" Jamie asked, sitting up straight.

"I don't know," I said, still staring at the water, hoping whatever it was would come back. "Dolphin?"

"That was way too big to be a dolphin." I knew he was right.

"A whale I guess," I said.

"Do we get whales here?" he asked.

"It's the ocean, isn't it."

"Geez," he said, eyes as fixed as mine on the silver, undulating waters. "Did you know that no one knows where blue whales go to mate?"

"That can't be true," I said.

"It is, I read it in a book in the library."

There was another, much smaller splash that caught our

attention, but after staring at the blur of blue water beneath the swiftly darkening sky, we decided it was just a bird this time.

"Maybe that's where we should go, then," I said.

"Where?"

"Wherever the blue whales go."

Jamie shook his head because he knew I wasn't serious, but he had a smile on his face. He was picturing some lost, undersea world where we could escape and live out our lives in blissful, aquatic peace. Far away from Dad and everything else. Maybe Mom was waiting for us there.

"Come on," Jamie said, standing. "Let's go."

But I didn't move. Long after Jamie had given up waiting for me and left, I stayed and watched the water, afraid to look away, knowing that the moment I did the whale, and all his secrets, would surface again.

●

When I finally made my way home, it was late, and I saw someone moving around in the cabin. The door groaned like an old man as I slid it open and stepped inside. I saw Stacy before she saw me. She was kneeling on the floor, her head practically buried in the couch cushion.

"What are you doing?" I asked.

She jolted upright, spinning toward me, a look of pure terror on her face. "Goddammit," she said, breathing hard. "Don't you knock?"

"It's my house," I said.

She tugged on one of her ugly dreadlocks like it was a nervous habit. She was wearing sweatpants and a red robe that was partially undone to reveal her black bra and concave stomach. "It's your dad's house."

"I live here, too," I said. I should have ignored her, gone

straight to bed, but something about that desperate look on her face made me feisty.

"For now," she said.

"You looking for something?" I asked, knowing perfectly well what she was looking for.

"Yeah," she said. "My damn cigarettes." Her eyes narrowed on me, on the smirk on my face, as if just now realizing that she hadn't been misplacing them all this time. "You know where they are, don't you?"

I shook my head. "Why would I?"

Her eyes didn't leave mine. I stared right back. "You been hiding my cigarettes, you little bitch?" She stood, walking toward me, her dreadlocks swinging like the tentacles of some poisonous sea creature.

"No," I said.

"You—"

"I've been smoking them," I said, emboldened by some surge of energy, of anger at her implications that this wasn't my home or that, somehow, she was going to evict me from it. Like Jamie, she wanted us gone. Well fuck her.

Her face went blank. "Excuse me?" She took another step forward.

"I've been smoking them," I said, more clearly this time.

Her hand shot out faster than I'd have given her credit for. She pinched my jaw between her fingers, squeezing hard.

"Listen to me, you fucking—" She'd probably done this before, gripped a kid's jaw, gotten their attention and made her point. It probably usually worked. It would've worked on Jamie; he'd have been silent and cowed as a kicked dog. But I wasn't Jamie. So she never got to finish her sentence. I punched her right in the nose. Something cracked against my knuckles and sent a painful vibration through my entire forearm.

She didn't scream like I expected she would. She staggered

back, letting go of my jaw, a look of shock and crystalized fury on her face. From her nose, two twin streams of blood spilled down to her lips. She lifted her hands and touched her nostrils gingerly, then eyed the spots of blood dotting her fingers.

"Bitch!" she screamed this time as she ran toward me. I tried to punch her in the face again, thinking it might be as easy as the first time, but she batted my hand away and threw the weight of her whole body into me. She had the slight build and brittle bones of an addict, but she still had me in height and weight. I was only thirteen, after all. So when I went crashing to the floor, her body pressing into mine, I lost all the air from my lungs. I managed to get my hands up over my face, but her fists still found my jaw and my ears, flashing ribbons of red erupting every time one of her blows connected. I must have bit my tongue or my cheek because I tasted the warm, coppery tang of blood. Stacy was saying something to me with each strike, but I couldn't make out what it was.

Eventually I managed to turn and wriggle away from her, sending a wild kick at her midsection as I did. It connected, but not very well.

"I'll fucking kill you!" she yelled. I realized then that I'd underestimated her. Her mania. Her drug-addled puddle of a brain. Stacy wasn't just a bitch; she was psychotic.

Footsteps in the hallway, the sound of Jamie's voice: "Dad!"

Stacy ignored him, grabbing the chair by the fire and tossing it at me. It struck my hip, but I barely felt it. I scampered to my feet just as she came at me again, blood smeared from her nose across her cheek. She looked like something out of a horror movie. I threw another punch at her, but it was desperate, weak, glancing off her collarbone. She reached out and managed to get a grip on my chin again. She pushed my head upward, my neck stretching and bending unnaturally. I, honest to God, thought she was actually going to rip my head off until I heard Dad's voice from behind her.

"Stacy!"

Stacy let go of me as both of us turned to see Dad standing in the hall in his boxers, his face puffy like he hadn't fully slept off the evening's drinking.

I put a hand to my neck to make sure the skin, still tender from Dad's squeezing hands, hadn't torn. I felt warm wetness streaking my left ear—one of her blows must've cut me.

"Your little shit of a daughter," Stacy said, "she's been stealing my cigarettes, and she just fucking punched me."

Dad's gaze was fixed on me now, his eyes bloodshot, his nostrils flared. I opened my mouth to try to explain, to tell him that the cigarette thing had been a joke, that I only punched Stacy because she'd grabbed my jaw, but Dad was moving now. He closed the gap between us in a few long strides. I started to step away from him, remembering the feel of his hands around my throat, waiting for him to reinstate his grip, to finish what he'd started. "Dad," I managed to say. But he didn't come for me; he grabbed a fistful of Stacy's dreadlocks and yanked hard. He was big and strong and her feet went limp as she screamed, but Dad didn't stop. He dragged her across the floor of the cabin, threw open the door, and tossed her onto the gravel like a bag of meat.

"Fuck you, Johnathan King!" Stacy said. "Fuck you and your slut daughter!"

"Get off my property," Dad said, then closed and locked the door behind him.

Stacy was screaming now. I looked over my shoulder and noticed Jamie in the hallway for the first time, staring at me, face pallid like he was about to pass out.

"Bed. Now," Dad said.

Just as Jamie and I turned toward our room, we heard the rock crash through the window. Jamie let out a pathetic little yelp, and I ducked as if Stacy had come crashing through the window herself. Dad took one look at the rock and the shattered glass, unlatched the door, and stormed out.

Stacy shrieked and ran. I could see her pale limbs flailing in the moonlight before she disappeared into the darkness of the surrounding evergreens. Dad got into his truck, the headlights cutting through the darkness like twin blades. He drove after her.

I can picture her now, sprinting through the trees, robe flapping in the wind, blood smeared across her face. The bottoms of her pink feet flashing in the headlights of Dad's truck. Was she terrified? Furious? Were there tears streaming down her face, joining the blood smeared over her lips? What did she feel in those last moments? I guess no one will ever know. As far as I've heard, Stacy was never seen again.

CHAPTER 11

NOW

"And what happened after that?" Dr. Gardner asked when I'd finished telling him my story.

I took a deep breath. "The next time I saw Dad, his hands were covered in blood." I was silent for a long time, focusing on not chewing my lip.

Sometimes I pictured Dr. Gardner cracking me open like an egg. Snapping my ribs, splitting my hips, wrenching my skull apart, and wading through the gooey center of me. I wanted him to find the rot, the thing that made me the way I was, and then I wanted him to carefully remove it like a tapeworm. Then he'd sew me up. *There*, he'd say. *You're all better*. If only I could manifest my sorrows into something physical enough to be excised.

"And that's when he left, wasn't it?"

"Correct," I said. "He and Jamie."

"Do you blame yourself? For what happened?"

"No." *Yes*. "I was just a kid. I didn't murder anyone."

"No, you didn't," Dr. Gardner said. He leaned forward in his seat. "Jeanie, you didn't kill anyone. Your father did."

"I know," I said, biting my lip. "I know he did."

☻

"What made you change your mind?" Maddox asks. We're at his gate at Heathrow. We hadn't gotten the same flight, and mine isn't for another hour, but I'm sitting with him to kill the time. We're sipping our respective beverages, me an earl grey and him a black coffee. The terminal is busy with that subdued level of mumbling and foot traffic that combines into a humming white noise; it smells clean, like a freshly vacuumed doctor's office. I've never liked airports. They've got all the annoyances of a shopping mall with all the stress of travel and deadlines. Maddox and I shared a cab to the airport and went through security together, but it had taken him until now, until his plane is about to board, to actually ask the question: *What changed my mind?*

I take another sip of my drink, letting him think for a moment that I'm not going to answer. I swallow slowly, waiting until his eyes leave me. "Did you know that Jamie played the piano?"

He turns back to look at me. "Jamie did?"

"Yeah, he was really good. Like savant good."

"No . . ." Maddox says. "I didn't know that."

"Neither did Dad," I say.

Maddox nods as if that's answer enough. "What kind of songs did he like to play?"

Classics, I think, *like Chopin, Beethoven, Debussy, Mozart.* But I don't say that. Suddenly I don't want to talk about Jamie anymore. I feel like I've woken up and don't like the place I've found myself in.

"Dad owes me answers," I say instead of answering his question. "He doesn't get to hide from me anymore."

They call passengers from group two to begin boarding.

"I don't think he's hiding from you, Jeanie. I mean, he's wanted for murder."

I shake my head. "That's bullshit," I say.

"You don't think he killed her?" Maddox asks.

"I don't think that's why he's hiding. I don't think that's why he left. He left because he was a shit father, and he knew it. And he's hiding not to avoid going to prison, he's hiding because he's a coward. He's hiding from me. Well, he doesn't get to anymore."

Maddox takes another drink. "You sure you want to do this?" he asks.

I look over at him, meet his golden eyes; he has a concerned, stupid look on his face. "You came all this way to get me, and now what?" I ask. "You're trying to talk me out of it?"

"No," he says quickly. "I just want to make sure you want to do this. I don't want to see you get hurt." What does he care? He doesn't know me anymore. And I don't know him. We're strangers. He doesn't really care if I get hurt or not. It's just something people say. Even as I think it, though, I know it's not true. Maddox is the type to care; he's the type to care about you the moment he meets you. He can't help himself. That's just the way he is—and the worst part about it is, he thinks the rest of the world is exactly the same.

"You probably should've thought about that before hunting me down." I give him a small smile to lessen the blow of my words, but I can tell from his face that the smile doesn't quite come across.

They call for passengers in boarding group three and Maddox stands.

"Listen," he says, lifting his backpack around his shoulders. Who travels with a backpack? He looks like the fourteen-year-old boy I kissed all those years ago on the beach. "I have to go, but you don't. I came here to give you the information, to give you the option. I thought you deserved that. But honestly, if you don't get on that plane, I won't blame you, not even a little." He looks at the gate. The flight attendant is helping an elderly woman in a wheelchair get a tag looped around her luggage. An announcement from another flight calls for passengers Campbell, Levitz, and Greenburg to make their way to their boarding gate. "Either way, Jeanie, it really was good to see you." He smiles, then turns toward the gate. I'm angry all of a sudden. Mad that he's saying this. Things were easier when I'd felt his expectations. Now he's taking that away from me. I feel drained suddenly; I'm second-guessing my decision to come here. Before disappearing down the long hallway leading to the jet bridge, he looks over his shoulder and gives me one last wave. I return it with a perfunctory smile.

Once he's gone, I go to the large windows and watch until his plane takes off. They always seem to be moving way too slowly to actually lift off the tarmac. But it does; his plane laughs in the face of gravity and common sense and rises into the air. It looks unreal. Like an illusion. Maybe it is.

I make my slow way through the airport, browsing the book shops and stopping at a Glorious Britain for a bag of trail mix.

When I get to my gate, I sit by the window and watch the planes coming and going, wondering where all these people will end up tonight, or where they're coming back from. What vacations, adventures, funerals, or board meetings have they just sat through? A family passes, sporting horribly red tans on their otherwise milky English skin. The kids look dazed, and the parents look like they haven't quite shaken off their mai tais. I could go for a mai tai right now. I think maybe I have time to find the nearest airport pub and get a drink when they call the first group on my flight. It's my group, but I don't move. I still have time to get a drink. Or maybe three. Maybe I'll get drunk in the airport and find a cab back home. I still have some scotch in the cupboard.

They announce the next group as I pull out my ticket and stare at it. Seventeen D. Window seat. Another plane lands in the gate beside mine. More people get off. A young man is already on his phone, talking too loudly, trying to make sure the world knows how important his call is, how important he is.

They announce the last group. It's the smallest group. I watch as more passengers get up from the seats around me and make their way to queue behind the desk. Slowly it clears. More time passes.

"Paging passengers Kane Williams and Jeanie King . . ."

I can see the woman at the desk speaking into the mic. She looks at me for a brief moment as she continues the rest of her message: ". . . for service to New York." She looks like she knows who I am and is judging me for not moving.

A man rushes to the gate, ticket held aloft, luggage trailing behind him on wheels that squeak over the carpet. Kane Williams, I assume.

"This is the last boarding call for Jeanie King . . ." The woman is looking around as she speaks into the mic. She's got big round eyes, hair that may be either blonde or that dyed silver color that is so popular these days.

"Jeanie King, please make your way . . ."

Out the window, another plane is descending, I can practically feel the landing gear grunting out from beneath it.

I look down at my lap. My ticket is still in my hand.

". . . for service to New York. I repeat, this is the final boarding call for Jeanie King."

My name echoes through the terminal like a pebble skipping down a long dark tunnel.

Jeanie King.

Jeanie King.

Jeanie King.

PART II
California

CHAPTER 1

That night I dreamed I was lost in the woods, looking for Jamie. I couldn't find him anywhere. It was cold and all I had on was a T-shirt and shorts. I was calling out to him. I could hear Dad in the distance yelling my name, but I wouldn't respond. I was too focused on Jamie. I found him in a clearing, moonlight reflecting off his pale face. He looked at me, terrified.

"Jeanie?" he said.

And that was when I looked down at my hands. They were covered, dripping, in bright purple blood.

⊛

I was a desperate animal the first few days they didn't come back. Their absence was a tangible thing. I could feel it in my stomach; it was written in the walls of the cabin like petroglyphs. It wasn't abnormal for Dad to be gone for long periods of time, but Jamie never disappeared. Had he seen

Dad that night? Had he seen the blood on his hands? Had he known that I would never leave and so he made the decision to save himself? Jamie's absence gave the cabin an emptiness I'd never felt before. I could barely stand to be in there. So I left. I wandered the forests, the beaches, the pier. But then I'd get anxious that they'd return to the cabin while I was away, and I'd rush back. I willed them to come back. I imagined Jamie coming home saying he tried to run away but then got scared and turned around. And Dad, he'd have just gone on a bender; he'd slap me on the back and tell me not to worry so much.

"Sorry, Dad," I said out loud. I think I might have been in shock.

I thought about going to the police, I really did, but something stopped me. Some primal urge not to implicate my dad in whatever had happened. And perhaps this was the biggest betrayal. I didn't do what was best for Jamie. I did what was best for my relationship with my dad, a relationship that I didn't realize at the time was very, very dead.

The first night alone in the cabin, I stayed up all night, watching the wooden slats in the bunk above me, wishing to hear movement or the sound of breathing. When I finally did sleep, I woke to the sound of Jamie whispering my name: "Jeanie." I jumped out of bed and looked at his bunk, but it was empty. I searched the whole cabin, but it was empty, too. I should have been terrified, I know that, but I wasn't. I was heartbroken. I was empty to my core.

I fended for myself for food, but I was used to that. When the cupboards were running dry, I raided Dad's bedroom and found a jar of money that I used to buy bread and peanut butter and sugary cereal.

Maddox found me on the beach one day as I was searching for Jamie or Dad or the bodies of either. I almost wanted to laugh at the thought, that's how insane I'd become. The ridiculousness of Dad killing his own son.

"What's going on?" Maddox asked. He realized something was up, of course he did, he could see it on my face.

"Nothing," I said. Inwardly I pleaded with him not to ask about Jamie. I wouldn't have been able to form words.

"Is it your dad?" he asked.

"No," I said, thinking, *It's Jamie.*

"You've been really, I don't know, quiet."

I shrugged. "See you at school," I said and walked away. Not that I was going to school anymore. It was a long way to walk, and with Dad and Jamie suddenly ripped from my life, school felt like this trivial pastime that didn't have any meaning for me. I suppose that was why the first person to visit the cabin was Ms. Russo, the vice principal. She showed up in her Toyota Corolla, the small blue car juddering over the old ruts.

"Hi," she said with a smile as I answered the door. "Is your dad around?" She had black hair pulled back into a tight ponytail. She was pretty, with dark skin and red lips that even then I knew were plump and gorgeous. The boys in class all had crushes on her; I'd seen them in the hallway humping their lockers with flopping rubbery tongues hanging out of their mouths. They'd say her name while the others laughed.

"No, he went out with Jamie," I said.

"Okay," she said. "Know when he'll be back?"

I shrugged. I couldn't give her a specific time because then she'd come back.

"Haven't seen you at school for a while." She didn't phrase it as a question, but I knew it was.

"Sorry" was all I could think to say.

"Do you need a ride? I'm not that far from here, and if your dad doesn't mind . . ."

"I can ask him," I said.

"That'd be great." She smiled again, then half turned to leave, her gaze darting around the mess in the cabin. She looked into my eyes, lowering her shoulders toward me. "Listen," she said. "If you ever need help of any kind, you can tell me." She rested a palm on my shoulder, gave a small squeeze. "Okay? Even if it's something you don't want to tell your dad. You—"

"Okay, thanks," I said. I wanted her to leave. I didn't want to see that look of pity on her face, like she'd taken an assessment of our lives and understood it all. She didn't understand. She wasn't my mother. She couldn't help.

"Right," she said, straightening. "I'll be back to see about that ride, okay?"

I nodded, then shut the door quickly after her. She was on the phone for a while in her car before she started the engine and drove back down the dirt road, her Toyota nodding and dancing as it went.

◉

I got my period for the first time during those days alone in the cabin. I woke feeling sticky and looked down at myself. I was like a murder victim. I was so sick and horrified by it, I ran into the woods and buried my underwear beside a large maple tree. I stuffed toilet paper between my legs and walked bowlegged down to the corner store and found the bright pink boxes of tampons and pads. Not knowing which I was supposed to get, I grabbed a box of each. Mrs. Whitaker, who always worked at the corner store—we used to joke that she lived there, that she slept in the cereal aisle—watched me approach the counter, a strange look on her face.

"They're for a friend," I said as I placed the boxes in front of her. I felt like I was trying to buy drugs or guns or something.

"That's all right," Mrs. Whitaker said, her eyes big behind her large glasses. Her hair was gray and sat large on her head like thistledown.

As I turned to leave, she called after me, "Don't keep a tampon in overnight."

I stopped, half turned toward her. "I know," I said even though I obviously didn't.

"You know how to put one in?" she asked.

"Yes," I said.

She looked at me from over her large glasses, her eyes squinty and suspicious. "Come on," she said, stepping out from behind the counter.

"What?" I said.

"I'll give you a refresher."

I felt like crying then. A stupid time to burst into tears, but I couldn't explain how my body, let alone my emotions, worked. I was this mechanical thing, operating without a manual.

Mrs. Whitaker took me into the bathroom and showed me how to insert it properly, grasping the plastic body between thumb and middle finger, then using her pointer finger to push the applicator up. Even then I thought it looked, ironically, like an odd simulation of birth, the soft fabric forcing its way through the small opening. Mrs. Whitaker waited outside the stall as I took off my pants, removed the ball of sticky toilet paper I'd stuck to myself, and inserted the tampon. It felt weird. I didn't like it.

When I stepped out of the stall, Mrs. Whitaker had this sad, proud look on her face.

"How'd it go, hon?"

"It kinda hurts," I said.

"Being a woman always does."

Before I went to bed that night, I switched the tampon for a pad like Mrs. Whitaker had instructed. Felt like I was wearing a diaper. Lying down on my pillow, I heard the yipping baby-like cries of coyotes somewhere in the woods. Probably they'd just killed a deer, but I couldn't help picturing them digging up my soiled underwear, getting a taste of my blood and growing drunk on it, eyes dilating in animalistic pleasure. I felt akin to them with their wild cries.

I started to imitate them, screaming from my bed. I know, I know—I was certifiable, keening and wailing like some demon had come alive within me. Jamie would have told me to shut up. Not Dad, though. Dad would have howled right along with me.

⬤

The police arrived that Saturday afternoon. Two men in a squad car. An older one with a mustache and a younger one with blond hair like Jamie's—not as golden and beautiful, though.

"Shit," I said.

The knock was firm and official on the front door. "Hello in there," one of the men said.

I opened the door and faced them, defiant and confident. "Hi," I said.

"Looking for your dad," the older one with the mustache said. I could see his breath puffing in the cold air. "He around?"

"No. I think he went into town," I said.

"Really?" The mustache man was surveying the cabin, the same way Ms. Russo had. "When'd you last see him?"

I shrugged in a spastic, shoulder-twitching kind of movement. I felt like I was the one with blood on my hands. I felt like they were going to arrest me. I was the only one left, wasn't I?

"My brother is missing," I said.

They looked at me, their expressions unchanging. "How long has he been gone?"

"I haven't seen him and Dad for days," I said.

The mustached one looked at the blond one and then turned back to me. "Mind if we take a quick look around?" he asked. I did mind, but I let them in anyway. They did a quick search of the house, all the rooms, even the cupboards and the fridge.

"Listen"—the mustached man again—"why don't we go for a drive down to the station?" he said. "We've got a few more questions. Then we'll see about a place to stay."

"I'm staying here," I said, my voice starting to shake. "This is where I live." Even now, I don't understand why I clung on to that damn cabin. Why I didn't want to be pulled from it. Maybe I thought that Dad was coming back, that Jamie was coming back, and that if I wasn't right where they'd left me, somehow, I'd never see them again.

"I know," the officer said. "I know. We'll talk."

"You have to find my brother. His name is Jamie. He's got blond hair, blue eyes; he's a little taller than me."

"Okay," the mustached officer said. "Come with us. We'll have a nice long talk and figure out what we can do, okay?" Even then their tones sounded resigned. Like they knew they wouldn't find him. Like they'd already written him off as lost for good or dead.

I drove in the back of the police car like a convict. No one said a word. I watched the trees zip past the window, waiting for the shadow of Jamie and my father to materialize any second. Like spirits of the forest. Or ghosts.

CHAPTER 2

Years later, a continent away, my therapist would hear me tell that story, and he'd ask: "Is that the last time you saw the cabin?"

"The cabin? Yes, why?"

"Places can play a huge role in emotional memory. It seems to me that your cabin might hold an important place in your heart."

"Ha. No. Not in my heart."

"Well, at least it's significant, no?"

"Sure, I guess so."

"Why do you guess so?"

I never felt time passing in Dr. Gardner's office. It was the damn clock. No noise. Silent fingers falling then rising in a circular, never-ending pattern. I was outside of time. I was in Oxford. I was in Washington. In the woods. In the cabin. I was thirty-three. I was thirteen. I was seven.

"Because if I ever step foot in that cabin again," I said, "I'll probably burn it to the ground."

He nodded as if he expected as much. "That sounds quite significant to me."

☜

I told the police everything. Even the blood on my dad's hands. I'd turned into a regular old fountain of information. They asked a lot about Stacy—she had, obviously, disappeared as well. No body found, though. They promised to do everything they could for Jamie, but their tones made me feel like they knew something I didn't. Like they'd already resigned him to the book of lost-and-never-found children.

"You have to find Jamie," I told them.

"When was the last time you saw your brother?" the older, mustached one, who'd introduced himself as Officer Favre, asked. We were sitting in his office; I was in a chair by a window that looked out onto the red brick of the downtown shops. There was a poster on the wall with a picture of a golden police badge and the word LEADERSHIP in all-caps. On his desk was one of those little contraptions with balls on a string that you could set to tapping, one launching another into the air, then the two swinging back and forth like a pendulum. Absurdly, I wanted to reach out and set them into motion, to hear their little *clack-clack*ing like the seconds of a clock ticking.

"The day before they disappeared," I said. "We went to the pier together."

"And you didn't see him after that?" Officer Favre was looking at me while the blond one, who hadn't introduced himself, was taking notes.

"I dunno. I probably saw him in his bed. I don't remember."

Yes I did. But it wasn't anything important, was it? We walked to our bedroom together. I remembered watching him ascend the small ladder to the top bunk. I remembered the sound he made as he slid between his sheets. A sound as familiar and routine as breathing. I remembered listening for Dad. Listening for the return of his truck. I remembered Dad coming home with the blood on his hands, leading me back to bed. Jamie had still been there. I remembered his breathing. I remembered getting sleepy after Dad had left. Then I remembered the sound of my brother's voice.

"Jeanie," Jamie had said. Gentle, pleading. I was already half asleep. He'd told me something then. God help me, I couldn't remember what it was. What had he said? Was it about Dad? Was he telling me where he was going? Had I fallen asleep? Dreamed it? Shit.

"Jeanie." It was the officer now, but when he spoke, it was Jamie's voice. I stared at him in horror and he looked back with a confused look on his face.

"Yeah?" I managed, swallowing.

Officer Favre ran the skin between his index finger and thumb over his mustache. "Did your dad have any reason to harm Jamie?"

"No," I said. "I don't think so." Did he? He was angry at Jamie a lot, sure, but he didn't have any real reason to hurt Jamie. Not in a terminal sense, anyway. I felt tired all of a sudden. Like I didn't want to talk about this anymore. I'd said enough. I wanted to go back to the cabin and lie down. I wanted to close my eyes and watch my memories in rewind. To listen to what Jamie had said to me.

"Did they get along?"

I pictured Dad throwing Jamie across the room, the bruises on his arms. "Not really. But he wouldn't kill him." Was that even true? I rubbed my tired eyes.

"I see," Officer Favre said, pausing while my fists worked over my closed eyelids.

"So why didn't he take you?" the blond officer asked. I

looked up in time to see Officer Favre give the younger officer a hard look from beneath bushy eyebrows, but the blond man kept his eyes on me.

"You have to find him," I said, putting my forehead into my hands. I felt like I was going to fall asleep any second. *Jeanie* . . . Jamie's voice again.

After, they called Ms. Russo to come and pick me up at the station. They said I could stay with her for now. I wanted to go back to the cabin, but I was tired of arguing. I sat in the entryway on a chair by the doors. Officer Favre came by and handed me a candy bar. He stood over me, hands on his belt.

"I know it seems like there's nothing past this moment," he said, his eyes having gone all soft and kind. "But I promise, you'll get through this. Life will go on. It always does."

I think he'd meant to be comforting, but I barely heard him.

"We'll do everything we can," he said before leaving. I ate the chocolate bar in three huge bites, my mouth alight with sugar.

When Ms. Russo showed up, she had a determined look on her face. She gave me a hug, patting my back and nodding at me as if to say she'd known this was going to happen. She drove me to her house and, that night, she made pasta with thick noodles and ground beef. I didn't want to eat it as a sort of protest to the whole situation, but I was so hungry, I couldn't help myself—all I'd had that day was the chocolate bar, which wasn't sitting very well. I devoured the pasta. It was the best thing I can remember having in all the time in Washington.

"I've spoken to your aunt," she said, spinning her noodles around and around her fork without bringing them to her mouth. "And she and your uncle have agreed to take you back while the investigation is under way. We've gotten you on a flight tomorrow afternoon. I'll drive you to the airport."

"I can't leave," I said. And I wouldn't. I couldn't go without Jamie.

"There's nothing you can do here, honey. The police are searching. We have to leave it to them. The best thing you can do is be with your family right now."

I think I knew this was coming. Where else were they going to send me? But still, hearing the words, understanding that I was going back to California—back without Jamie—felt like a tearing of sorts. Like I was being ripped from the present and shipped back in time.

"What if Jamie comes back? What if he comes looking for me?"

Ms. Russo smiled a sad sort of smile as if she was trying to tell me what everyone else seemed to know for a fact: Jamie wasn't coming back. "I've talked to your aunt about this as well, and . . . listen, the police will be watching the cabin. I promise you, if Jamie comes back, he'll be on the first flight to Santa Clara."

"What if I refuse to go?" I asked.

Ms. Russo shook her head. "I know this isn't an easy time," she said. "I know there's probably nothing I can say that will make things better, but it does get easier. I can promise you that."

"How? Your dad ever kill someone? Did you lose your brother?" I was being snappy and she didn't deserve it. I knew that, but I couldn't help myself.

"We don't fully know what happened yet," Ms. Russo said. "In any case, you can't stay in that cabin by yourself. Your aunt is happy to have you back."

"No she's not." I didn't really know what I was saying. I had something like survivor's guilt. I felt like I should have been killed, too. I shouldn't have been left alive in that cabin. Some part of me thought that Aunt Eileen would think the same.

Ms. Russo looked like she was about to reach out a hand toward me. "None of this is your fault, Jeanie."

I didn't want to talk anymore, so I stuffed my mouth with pasta, despite the fact that I was already full; my stomach was churning like a windmill.

That night, after Ms. Russo had been asleep for maybe an hour, I snuck out the front door. It was easy. Her floors were covered with those thick seventies-style shag carpets, and her door didn't squeak as I opened it. The air outside was cold, and I regretted not wearing a coat over my hoodie, but I wasn't about to go back inside. I walked the streets with my hands stuffed in my pockets and my arms pressed against my sides.

From Ms. Russo's house, Maddox's place wasn't very far. I'd been there only once, however, so it took a bit of wandering to find it again along an old street with rain-cracked concrete. I crept over the half-ruined fence and made my way across the lawn as silently as I could. From there, I walked around the house, peeking in windows to try to find Maddox's room. The grass was tall along the side of the house. A pile of cement blocks leaned against the façade along with a rusty wheelbarrow and a garbage bag filled to bursting with something angular and sharp, parts of it puncturing the bag's black skin. The first window I looked in I could see a large bed with two bodies sleeping in it. I ducked quickly past and made my way around the back of the house. The next window was a bathroom. The next was blocked by a gray curtain. By the time I found Maddox's room, I was all the way on the other side of the house. Looking in, I saw clothes scattered on the floor, a bookshelf with novels and magazines spilling out of it, and some sort of game console or computer equipment either in the process of being taken apart or half assembled against the far wall. And there was Maddox, asleep in the bed. I felt a thrill at seeing him under the blankets, maybe half naked. I wondered what it would be like to crawl into that bed with him; I felt my skin go tingly at the thought.

I tapped on the window with my fingernail and watched him stir. I tapped harder, but he just settled back into his pillow.

"Maddox," I yell-whispered into the window, then closed my fist and gave a solid knock.

He jerked upright and looked around the room, unable to determine where the noise was coming from. I knocked again, and he turned to face me. His eyes were puffy with sleep, and he frowned at my face in the window. Then, as if my image had finally coalesced into existence, he sat bolt upright.

"Maddox," I said again. "It's me."

He said something that I was pretty sure started with a *J*: *Jeez, Jesus, Jeanie.*

I waved at him to come out. "Come on," I said, then turned and leaned against the wall of the house, waiting. I could hear shuffling inside, Maddox getting dressed. The cool air was biting at my cheeks and ears, so I pulled my hood up over my head. The window snapped open and Maddox started climbing out. He tripped and almost fell into me.

"What are you doing here?" he asked.

"I'm leaving tomorrow," I said.

"What do you mean? Where?"

"Let's get outta here first," I said.

"Here, come on," he said and led me around to the back of the house where he climbed up on the back-porch railing and used the gutters to haul himself onto the roof. I followed without question. I couldn't quite lift myself all the way up, so he gripped my arms and helped me. From there, we made our way across the flagstone shingles and onto a flat part of the roof. He lay down, pulling his hood over his head. I lay beside him, our shoulders touching. Above us, the clouds were glowing, lit by moonlight, and the moon itself was fat and gibbous. I tried not to think about Jamie and me, sitting together on our own roof, listening to Dad and Stacy.

"I heard what happened," he said. "Are you okay?"

"I'm fine," I said. I didn't want to talk about it. I'd been talking enough about it. That wasn't really why I'd come. I wasn't sure why I'd come, to be honest. Maybe to say goodbye.

"So you were in the cabin all by yourself?"

"Yes." I could feel him shifting beside me, his clothes dragging on the shingles.

"You should have told me," he said.

"I didn't even tell the police. What makes you so special?" I'd meant it as a kind of joke, but it came out too harshly. He went silent.

"So what happens now?" he asked.

"I'm going back to Santa Clara to stay with my aunt and uncle."

"Jeez." He ran his hands through his hair, which gleamed metallic black against the light of the moon. "I can't believe all this. I mean, your dad. He really—"

"Yes," I said. He really did kill someone. He really did take Jamie. *Please God, he couldn't have killed Jamie.*

"And what did the cops say?"

"That they'd do what they could. They've been searching everywhere as far as I know."

"I can't believe this," he said again.

"I know."

We sat in silence for a while. I didn't know what else to say.

He took in a big breath. "So how can I contact you?" he asked, and I loved him for the question. I loved that it was about something as simple as a phone number. I loved that he wasn't willing to let me go just yet. I gave him the number to my aunt's house, which Jamie and I had memorized long ago, and made him recite it back to me three times to prove that he'd memorized it as well.

"How far away is Santa Clara?" he asked.

"I dunno," I said. "It's like a two-hour flight, I think."

"I wonder how far it is by car," he said.

"You gonna drive to me?"

"Sure, why not? I could steal my dad's car. Maybe he'd disown me, and I could come live with you."

I smiled. "Or we could just run away right here right now."

He returned my smile, but I realized in that moment that if he'd said yes, if he'd turned the question into something serious, I would have gone. I would have left everything behind and gone wherever Maddox suggested. Maybe the two of us could find Jamie together. In that moment, I believed we could do it. I could envision limitless possibilities spreading out before us. Young love was stupid like that.

"Yes," Maddox said. But I could tell by his smile that he was continuing the joke and not seriously considering it. "Let's go to Vegas, make our millions gambling."

"Easy. Then what?" I said. I was happy to play along but was a little disappointed as well.

"Then we fly to Hawaii and spend our days eating coconuts, feeding seagulls, and throwing rocks at whales."

"That's cruel."

"Little ones, just pebbles. Just enough to let them know we're there, watching them."

I stared at the clouds overhead, their spines bulbous, curved like the backs of breaching whales. It was a good thought, a happy dream.

"Did you know that no one knows where blue whales go to mate?" I said, repeating Jamie's fact. The words carved out a hollow space inside me.

"That's crazy." Maddox shook his head. "Did you know

that we all come from the stars?" he said, like we were playing some sort of trivia game.

"No, what do you mean?" I asked.

"Like literally. We're made of stardust. The whole Earth,
all of life, is."

I looked up at the sky and the array of silver lights. "So
which one made you?" I asked.

"That one," he said, pointing at the sky like he'd already
considered this question.

"Which one?" I asked.

"See that really bright one?"

"Yeah."

"Then those three beside it?"

"Okay."

"I'm the middle one."

"I see," I said, smiling.

"How about you?" he asked.

"Duh. I'm the bright one."

He laughed.

We lay in silence for a while, watching the moon and the
stars appearing and disappearing between the passing clouds.
Then Maddox lifted a hand and placed it carefully on my
thigh. My heart played the veins of my throat like a harp. He
didn't move his fingers, didn't press against me, just placed
his palm high on my thigh, almost near my hip, and it was
the most intimate gesture of my young life. Even more than
the kiss. Slowly, I reached my hand down to his and placed it
on top of his knuckles. I didn't grip his fingers, didn't put my
hand into his palm for fear that he might let go of my leg, and
I didn't want that.

Had we been older, I might have taken his hand and placed
it farther, deeper. He might have rolled on top of me. We
might have fumbled at our clothing and figured out our bodies right then and there on his parents' rooftop. But we were

still young and had no idea how to get past a hand on a thigh. And so we sat like that, in that moment, for as long as we could—until the clouds cleared, our fingers froze, and I had to wrench myself from the moment or risk morning's light and Ms. Russo discovering my absence. We said goodbye—"This isn't goodbye," he said—at his window, hugging, holding each other like we'd never done before, both of us acknowledging that something had changed between us, something that had been absent when we'd kissed on the beach, and for the first time since Jamie disappeared and left a gaping chasm inside me, I felt a small taste of actual joy.

CHAPTER 3

Apparently Aunt Eileen and Uncle Derek had written to us while we'd been in Washington. Dad had just thrown away the letters. As kids, it had never occurred to us that we should be writing our aunt and uncle ourselves. In our minds, our life with them was over.

So when I arrived in Santa Clara and found my way back into the home I'd nearly forgotten during my time in Washington, I was surprised to see a brand-new baby girl nestled in Aunt Eileen's arms. My aunt and uncle were different, too: Uncle Derek's hair had gone gray, and Aunt Eileen had rounded out around the face and hips, though I supposed that was probably mostly due to the pregnancy, which they both repeatedly called "a miracle" or "God's blessing."

Aunt Eileen was already crying as I made my way to the door, my sad single bag of luggage over my shoulder.

"What's her name?" I asked. Aunt Eileen was basically sobbing at this point. Before answering, she wrapped an arm around me and pressed her cheek into mine. Uncle Derek approached slowly, placing a single hand on my shoulder as if unsure what his role in all this was supposed to be.

"You're gonna be fine, you know that, right?" Aunt Eileen said. "You're going to get through this."

I didn't say anything. I didn't know what I could say. When she released me and looked hard at my face, I felt guilty that I wasn't crying. I knew I should be, it was basically offensive not to, and yet, when I reached for the burning ball of emotion in my gut, I couldn't bring it to my eyes.

"What's her name?" I asked again.

"Grace," Aunt Eileen said, smiling, her nose full of snot. "You want to hold her?"

"No," I said.

She looked momentarily affronted by the vehemence of my *no*. But I couldn't hold baby Grace; it was a fact as true and pressing as gravity. "That's fine," Aunt Eileen said, looking from Uncle Derek back to me. "On your own time."

But I never held Grace while she was a baby. Not once.

"And why's that, do you think?" Dr. Gardner asked me.

"I don't like babies," I told him.

"It seems natural to me that someone in your position might feel replaced, might even feel jealous about a new child thrust so suddenly into their lives."

"I wasn't jealous of a baby."

"It doesn't matter that Grace was a baby. What matters is your feeling of belonging. And if that feeling was being challenged, you see?"

"I didn't care about belonging."

"And yet you never held baby Grace."

"She smelled like puke," I said.

"All the time?" Dr. Gardner had a suspicious look on his face.

"Yes," I said. "All the time."

That first night back home in Santa Clara, I went into my

old room and wrote a note to Jamie. It would be the first of many. Some of them longer than others. In one, I'd write four whole pages. But that first one was short and to the point.

Dear Jamie, I wrote. *Why'd you leave me?*

⬤

I was thirteen years old, at the end of eighth grade, when I was thrust back into my old life in Santa Clara without Jamie. Aunt Eileen didn't want to throw me into a new school with only a few months left, so I didn't start school until the following year. I was left in that house for the rest of that spring and all summer with a screaming baby and an aunt who seemed constantly near tears. She barely managed to maintain the house, the child, and her sympathy for me while Uncle Derek was at work. She kept asking why I didn't reach out to my friends, but I didn't want to. It had been so long since I'd lived there, I felt like I didn't really know my old friends anymore. I spent time reading, riding my aunt's bike around the neighborhood, and picking oranges from the tree out back. Any chance I got, I'd sneak onto Uncle Derek's computer and scan the internet for any reports on Dad and Jamie. So far, there was nothing other than the original missing persons reports. No sign of Jamie, Dad, or Stacy.

To help me deal with the "trauma of my situation," Aunt Eileen asked her pastor, Pastor Donnelly, to meet with me once every week. We didn't talk about Jamie or my dad, but he asked all kinds of questions about me and what I was interested in and how I was settling back into my life in California. I gave him clipped, glib answers. At the end of each session, he always prayed for me.

"Can I hold your hand?" Pastor Donnelly asked.

"No," I said.

When school started, it became increasingly clear that

things had changed. Some of my old friends had gone to other high schools, and the ones who didn't had scattered into cliques, none of which held any particular appeal for me, and so I found myself alone more often than not. No one wanted to hang out with the sad girl who'd lost her brother, whose dad was probably a murderer. And despite her earlier tenderness, I could tell Aunt Eileen didn't really want me back, either; she was too busy with the baby, too torn up with sadness for me, a sadness that I couldn't look at for too long or else I'd fall into something deep and black. Uncle Derek tried to treat me like he used to. He'd coax me outside to shoot baskets on the old hoop over the garage. I'd humor him, mostly because I didn't have anything else to do. I made him phone Officer Favre once a week to see if there was any news on Jamie. Sometimes he'd let me talk.

"Have you searched the bay?" I'd ask. "I mean like do a full sweep. He wasn't the best swimmer. Are there any islands nearby?" I was desperate, grasping at straws.

"Jeanie," Officer Favre'd say, "we're going to keep doing the best we can, and we'll be in touch with any updates. I think maybe you should talk with your aunt and uncle about all this. Don't shut them out. Family is important in times like these." But what help were Aunt Eileen and Uncle Derek going to be? They didn't know the area. They couldn't help me figure out what had happened. It wasn't until after I hung up the phone that I realized Officer Favre didn't want me to talk with them in order to come up with any ideas as to where Jamie might have gone; no, he was telling me I should talk to them in the same way I was forced to talk to Pastor Donnelly. He was trying to set up a counseling team to pacify crazy little Jeanie.

Jeanie. The last thing my brother had said. God, what had he been about to tell me?

My teachers were phoning home to tell Aunt Eileen that I

hadn't done my homework, I hadn't shown up for class, I'd thrown a ruler at a kid who'd said I had resting bitch face.

"At some point," Aunt Eileen told me, "you have to at least try to be happy."

It wasn't a time to be happy.

The only happy things in my life were the phone calls from Maddox, which had started that spring and summer and continued on into the school year. At least once a week, I'd get a call from him and we'd talk for as long as we could. Aunt Eileen had even bought me a new cell phone. And now that I had the phone, I wondered how I'd ever gone without.

"Any news?" I'd always ask Maddox. I wouldn't even have to mention Dad or Jamie or Stacy—he knew. And it was always the same: "Nothing, sorry."

"I miss you," he said one night, and something inside me switched on. A glow both warm and bright. I almost felt guilty for it. How could I be happy when Jamie was out there, God knew where?

"I miss you, too," I managed to say. The words felt alien on my tongue, but I liked the way they sounded. There was some sort of organic magic to the order of them, the shape of the vowels, the drawn-out hiss of the *s*'s and the clip of the *t*. We made vague promises about how we were going to visit each other, but we were confined because of our adolescence, our lack of transportation.

By the time my first year of high school was halfway over, Maddox and I were well and truly in the bloom of teenage love, there'd been no news about Dad or Jamie, and I was about to meet fucking Natalie Johannsen.

❦

"Everyone has that one friend, right?" I said to Dr. Gardner.

"What kind of friend do you mean?" Dr. Gardner asked.

"The one that is a total disaster. That you spend time with even though you hate everything about them."

"I'm not sure."

"Well, girls do. There's always that one. The one that fucks you up forever."

Natalie Johannsen was the type of freshman that acted like a senior, and the boys treated her like one. She wasn't in the popular group because the other girls hated her, but the boys loved her because she'd gotten her boobs early, she joked about how many blow jobs she'd given, and she was ruthlessly mean to almost everyone, which for some reason, was incredibly appealing to guys.

I met her while I was kicking Michael Nadler in the stomach. We were in the courtyard; he was standing over me while I sat on a bench beside a California laurel, whose late-winter flowers were small and golden like popcorn. He'd asked me if my dad was actually a murderer.

"No," I said, the book I'd been reading held open in my lap.

"I heard the police are looking for him," Michael said.

"I don't care what the police are doing. He didn't kill anyone." I looked back down at my book, unable to remember what paragraph I'd been on.

"That's not what I heard," Michael said.

"Well you heard wrong." My fingernails dug into the spine of my book.

"I guess that makes you the daughter of a killer, huh?"

I tried to ignore him.

"Everyone says you're crazy. Is it true?"

I tackled him to the ground, throwing my shoulder into his stomach as hard as I could. He wasn't a big kid, and I'd already grown to my full height. He fell on the ground with a "What the fuck!" I got up first and started kicking him in a blind rage.

"Stop!" he said as he curled up.

But I didn't stop. He tried to roll away from me, but I chased him down and kicked and kept kicking until Natalie Johannsen appeared out of nowhere and jumped on top of him. She was short but dense in the way some girls were. Her body had adopted a woman's shape but hadn't yet experienced the negative effects of gravity and time. She was tight and spry. Her hair was blonde and long and tied into a fishtail braid. She had a congregation of bracelets around her wrists that clacked together as she moved. She grabbed Michael's hair and raised his head to hers.

"You fuck with one of my bitches again, and I'll straight up kill you, got it?" she said.

He was basically crying at this point. "Yeah, fine."

She spat in his face and tossed his head back. She stood then, walked over to me, and looped her arm in mine as if we'd been best friends for years, as if I actually was one of her bitches. "Come on," she said, and I let myself be led away.

We found something in each other that day. A personification of our internal anger. Natalie didn't know why I was kicking Michael, nor did she have anything in particular against him. She just saw me and the rash way I could take out my anger on another human being—and in that, she saw a kindred spirit. Our two angers were different, though. Mine manifested in acts of physical violence while hers was much more subtle—degrading words, manipulative behavior. Turns out, anger is like love: it's got all kinds of languages. Ours complemented each other.

It was because of Natalie that I snuck out for the first time. Stole something for the first time. It was because of Natalie that I first had sex.

※

Natalie and I would cut class together. We'd go down to the drugstore and see if we could get anyone to buy cigarettes for us. And every once in a while, we found someone. We'd hide behind buildings and smoke them together, one after the other as if it were a race to see who could smoke the most. Often, her friend Tyler would be there. He was a sophomore with curly brown hair. He was tall and fairly good-looking but not good-looking enough to be accepted into the popular group. He was interesting to Natalie because he could play the guitar and he stole weed from his dad. We'd go over to his house and smoke on his back porch when his parents weren't home and sometimes even when they were. They didn't really care.

"My dad said these give you lung cancer," Natalie said, lifting the joint into the air and studying it like she'd seen something shimmering on its surface. The smell of skunk cabbage filled the air. My body was already feeling heavy. That's why I liked weed. It made me feel more compact, more solid. It was like a huge blanket was weighing me down.

"We're too young to get lung cancer," I said.

Natalie laughed. "That's exactly what I told him." She handed Tyler the joint. He was lying in the hammock, arms outstretched, eyes closed, not reaching for the joint. "Tyler," Natalie said. "Tyler, what are you doing?"

He lifted his chin to the sun. "I'm experiencing photosynthesis," he said. We all laughed.

"Hey, what're you guys doing on Saturday?" Natalie asked.

"Nothing," I said at the same time Tyler said, "Blossoming into a beautiful flower." I didn't think he was that high; he just liked to make people laugh, to be defined by how unseriously he took life.

"Think you guys could sneak out that night? Meet in the school parking lot? I stole some of my mom's pills I want to try."

"She didn't notice?" I asked, a nervous energy already turning my stomach. I knew I didn't really want to sneak out and try mystery pills, but I also knew that I was going to do anything that Natalie asked. She had that power over people, especially me. She'd taken me under her wing; without her, I'd have been friendless and alone in the world, which, in high school, was tantamount to death.

"No, I've had them for a few weeks now. She thinks she lost them. That woman is out of her damn mind."

"I'm in," Tyler said. "What are they?"

Natalie laughed. "I don't really know. But they fuck her up real good. I think one might be ecstasy."

Tyler passed the joint to me and I took a hit, the smoke warm in my lungs and eyes. "Jeanie?" Natalie asked.

"Yeah," I said. "Why not?"

☗

"Jeanie, can we talk?" Aunt Eileen asked one night.

"Sure," I said. I'd been on my phone, texting Maddox, who was telling me about a cheap flight to San Jose that he was going to buy tickets for. I couldn't let myself hope, but I was cautiously optimistic.

"Listen, I know things have been difficult. But . . ."

My eyes drifted back to my phone as she paused. Her worry had absolutely zero appeal to me.

"Jeanie, your teachers have been calling. They're worried about your future and, frankly, so am I, sweetheart. They say you don't turn in your homework, you miss class, and yet you ace the tests. Can you imagine how well you'd be doing if you just applied yourself?"

I shrugged.

"I know it doesn't seem important now, but getting your grades up in school will help set you up for college and for life. It's hard to have that perspective, especially given everything you've been through, but you're an incredibly talented young woman, Jeanie, we've always known that. Don't let your dad take that away from you, too." *Like he took everything else*, I thought.

I set my phone down beside me, anger suddenly flashing to life in my chest. I was often like that these days—mercurial. One moment I'd be completely calm and the next, a small thing would trigger some paroxysmal switch inside me, and I'd be instantly furious.

"You don't know shit about my dad," I said.

I'd never spoken to her like that before. Never sworn right to her face. Her mouth opened in shock, then closed in stern resolve. She looked like she wanted to scold me, to yell at me, to bend me over her knee and spank me like a child.

She stood up from the corner of the bed where she'd been sitting. "Just know we love you, Jeanie. We always have."

I watched her go, knowing that the look on her face before she closed my door hadn't been one of love or concern. It had been resignation. *At least she's not my real child.* That's what her eyes said, loud and clear.

❦

I snuck out the following night, Saturday. I met Tyler and Natalie in the school parking lot. We lay down in the empty spaces, took turns swallowing mystery pills, and laughed as the stars lit on fire.

I was sicker that night than I can ever remember being. I got home and somehow managed to make it to the bathroom to puke up what looked like rice I didn't remember eating. Amazingly, no one woke up. When I did finally emerge from the bathroom, the taste of puke was in my mouth and my nose, and my head was damp with cold sweat. My body wasn't ready for sleep. Pills, apparently, worked differently than weed—at least for my body. Instead of knocking me out, I was wide awake. My fingers felt weird when I rubbed them together, my mouth was dry, and while the room wasn't exactly spinning, it wasn't exactly still, either.

I decided to indulge in one of my nighttime rituals to take my mind off the weird things my body was doing. So I turned on Uncle Derek's computer in his office and started scrolling through Washington news reports. Inserting my dad's name, Jamie's name, our city into the Google search bar. Then things like *wanted for murder*, or *missing boy*, or *missing father and son*.

The computer had wavy lines dancing across the screen like water. I can't honestly remember if it looked like that because of the drugs or if Uncle Derek's computer was just a piece of shit.

When I saw the headline, my chest clenched: *Missing Boy Found Alive*.

I read quickly. A boy had been found in Boise, Idaho. No picture. No name listed. The family wanted to remain anonymous. The boy, it said, had run away from home and had been found trying to steal food at a Whole Foods. Just the kind of stupid thing that Jamie would do. The computer was a whirlpool now, agglomerate colors radiating from its edges. Was it adrenaline, or the next stage in whatever drugs I'd taken? I rubbed my fingers together but could only observe the contact visually. There was no sensation. I closed the computer. My legs carried me back out of the office toward the garage. The carpet was textureless beneath my bare feet.

I couldn't tell Aunt Eileen or Uncle Derek about this. They'd make me wait until the morning. They'd have to call Officer Favre and discuss what steps to take next. But Jamie was out there, in goddamn Idaho, and I had to get him; I had to do it now. I knew it. I knew I had to go to him right away or he was going to disappear again. This was a good idea. This was a *brilliant* idea. This was the fucking perfect idea.

I pressed the garage opener and winced at the noise it made. It had to be partly the drugs, but it sounded like an actual earthquake—fault lines rubbing together, shaking the very foundations of the planet. Once it was open, I found the spare keys Uncle Derek kept on a hook in the garage and started the car. I put the vehicle in reverse and hit the gas. The car felt like it was nosediving into the pavement. I stopped, realizing I hadn't hit the release brake. I looked down at the third little pedal to the left. Was I supposed to kick it, or was there a lever to lift? I couldn't remember. My brain wasn't forming the proper connections. The wheel was made out of rainbow taffy. It felt gummy and pliable beneath my fingers. I saw a little lever near the pedal and lifted it, then watched as the hood of the car popped up slightly.

"Shit," I said. I kicked the lever and it released. I could drive with the hood popped. It wasn't blocking my view. I pressed the gas again, knowing I needed to get out of there before Aunt Eileen or Uncle Derek woke up because of all the noise. But I didn't look behind me. I hadn't been to driver's ed; I'd never driven a car before; what the hell did I know about driving in reverse? The vehicle sped out of the garage. I twisted the wheel to correct myself. The car spun off the driveway and onto the lawn, bumping and jolting as it went. I had time enough to lift my right foot from the gas and slam my left foot onto the brake pedal just as the back of the car crashed into the birch tree in our front yard. For a terrible moment, as the car slammed to a stop, I was back on the highway with Mom and Jamie. The world was spinning around me, my limbs were lifting from my body, a herd of elk was dancing in and out of the windows.

I screamed, closed my eyes, and wrapped my arms around

myself, my hands gripping my elbows as if to keep my limbs in place.

When I looked up, my aunt and uncle were there, just outside the garage, racing toward me.

Uncle Derek was first to the driver's side, tearing the door open.

"Jeanie, are you okay?" His voice was low, grumbly from sleep, but he spoke hurriedly, slightly out of breath. Something in the car was beeping insistently.

"It's Jamie," I said, nearly choking on my words.

"What?" Uncle Derek said just as Aunt Eileen made it to his side.

"What happened?" she asked.

"Look, look," I said, exiting the car. My legs felt shaky, but I was determined.

"What's going on?" Aunt Eileen asked Uncle Derek, as if I were incapable of answering.

"Come on," I said, heading back toward the garage. Uncle Derek looked at the car is if unsure he wanted to leave it out there like that. Aunt Eileen held out a hand toward me, looking afraid I might fall over.

"Jeanie," Aunt Eileen said, but I kept walking. I led them to Uncle Derek's office and found the article I'd read on the computer.

"There," I said, pointing. "See." Now they'd understand. Now they'd know how serious this all was. They'd get baby Grace and jump in the car with me. "They found him," I said.

Uncle Derek was staring at the screen, a frown on his face. He read for a moment longer, Aunt Eileen looking over his shoulder. When he was done, he straightened slowly.

"It's not him, Jeanie," Uncle Derek said. "Come on, let's get you to bed."

"What do you mean? It *is* him."

"It's not. I promise."

"How can you know?" My voice was loud, echoing in my ears.

"Jeanie," Uncle Derek said, taking a deep breath. "That boy has only been missing for five days. And the article says he was nine years old." He looked at Aunt Eileen, concern in his eyes.

"What?" I said. That couldn't be. Where did it say that? I looked down at the computer, but the text was too small, the colors too bright.

"It's okay, Jeanie," Aunt Eileen said. "Come on, I'll make you some tea."

"No, it was him," I said. "This must be the wrong article." But it wasn't. I recognized the picture of the Whole Foods store the boy had been trying to rob.

"Come on, Jeanie," Uncle Derek said, putting a hand on my shoulder. "Jeanie?" They kept saying my name as if afraid I'd forgotten it. They should have been furious with me. Could they tell that I was high? Did they know how stupid their faces looked outlined in red-and-blue halos? They were treating me like a goddamned crazy person.

I wasn't crazy. It was Jamie. I wasn't fucking crazy.

I let Aunt Eileen lead me to the kitchen as Uncle Derek went back outside. Aunt Eileen placed her hands on my arm as if to keep me upright. She made me tea just like she promised, and I sipped it even though I didn't want any. She was crying silently, looking at me like I was a cancer patient with only a few days left to live. She kept saying stupid nonsense like, "Everything is going to be okay," and "Tomorrow is a new day," and "Do you want me to pray for you, Jeanie?"

The colors were gone by the time I went to bed. I could almost think clearly now. I lay beneath the covers, which Aunt Eileen had tucked around me as if I couldn't manage myself. I was furious. Furious with myself, with how I looked, with how Aunt Eileen and Uncle Derek looked at me. The pity in their eyes. I vowed then not to let them look at me like that again. I vowed not to be the crazy niece, the charity case they'd taken in out of the goodness of their hearts.

I had to move on with my life.

I had to let Dad go.

I had to let Jamie go.

Dear Jamie, I wrote in my journal that night, the pen feeling oddly tiny in my hands. *I can't keep looking for you. Please come find me.*

When I closed my eyes, I found the place where all the colors had been hiding: behind my eyelids, swirling fractal patterns of perfect, geometric beauty.

CHAPTER 4

Sophomore year, Maddox and I planned to go to homecoming together. He had saved enough for the flight and was planning on spending the whole weekend with me. Except his mom had a series of bad seizures and he had to stay home.

He cried on the phone when he told me everything that had happened with his mom. I'd underestimated his relationship with her. She was his connection to the Philippines. The way she'd make lumpia and pancit palabok for his birthday. How she called him Dodong. Both of them victims of his angry father. Maybe I hadn't wanted to see their connection. Because no matter how sick she was, how close she'd come to dying, she was still there. He still had her.

"Dad says he needs my money for the medical bills," he told me.

"That's bullshit," I said.

"I know," he said. But I hadn't been talking about his dad; I'd been talking about him. About the situation in general.

I'd been promised something, and I wasn't getting it. I felt abandoned, like he was choosing his mom over me. He was, of course, and it was fair, but still, I didn't like the feeling.

In the end, Tyler and I decided to go to homecoming together instead. Natalie was going with Cole, a lineman from the football team—"He's got a dick like a flagpole. My jaw is so sore"—so at the last minute, Tyler and I decided to go together out of convenience.

I liked Tyler; he always seemed to be in a good mood. Plus, the two of us shared a fear of Natalie.

"It's the voodoo magic she does on the weekends," Tyler said to me on one of the rare occasions that we were together without Natalie. "It's why she smells of toadstools and the blood of a fresh virgin."

"Does a virgin's blood smell different?" I asked.

"Oh yeah, it's like apples and oranges."

Despite being crushed by Maddox's absence, I was relatively placated by my decision to go to the dance with Tyler. And so, weirdly, was Natalie.

"That's perfect," Natalie said to me as we walked along the aisles at the grocery store, looking for weed snacks. "We'll carpool to my cousin's after."

Natalie's cousin was a thirtysomething businessman who worked in finance. We didn't really know the details, but he had a nice house in Green Acres with a pool and a hot tub and, apparently, lots of booze.

"So are you guys gonna do it?" Natalie asked as we scanned the different flavors of chips.

"Do what?" I asked.

"You and Tyler. You gonna jump his bones or what?"

"With Tyler?"

"Uh, yeah. It's homecoming and you're both still virgin as hell."

I laughed. "I don't know," I said. Even though I was sure the answer was definitely *no*, I didn't want to admit it. Natalie had this expectant look on her face.

"You'll need condoms then," Natalie said as if I'd told her yes.

"Oh, no, that's okay."

"You don't wanna get preggers. That'd be a bad look on your body." My hand went to my stomach as if to reassure myself of its flatness.

"Guys don't ever bring them," Natalie said. "Come on."

She led me to the pharmacy and the contraceptives. The brightly colored boxes made me anxious. The golds and purples flashed at me, promising a pleasure made of fire and ribbons.

"There's no way I'm standing in line with one of these boxes," I said.

"Fuck the line," Natalie said, grabbing a box. "Tuck it into your coat."

"What?"

"Just tuck it into your coat. People do it all the time with condoms. It's not a big deal."

I gave an exasperated laugh, my palms starting to sweat. "Natalie, I don't even—"

"Shh," Natalie said as she stuffed the box into my jacket and closed it around me. My arm went to the box so that it wouldn't fall to the shiny linoleum floor. An employee was shelving Advil farther down the aisle. A woman passed on the other side with a toddler swinging his legs over the back of the cart. "Let's go," Natalie said, smiling.

And we did. We walked out into the clear autumn air, the sun shining bright and golden. The package was pressed tight against my stomach, a small swell like the condoms had already failed to do their job.

Homecoming night, I wore a one-shouldered ruby dress. It had frilly lace in the front that unfurled like rhododendron petals. Aunt Eileen helped do my hair. She was eager for the task, chatting away like we'd been best friends this whole time.

Looking in the mirror, seeing my face plastered with makeup, my hair done up with curls and pins and enough hair spray to burn down a small village, I felt ridiculous. I thought of Jamie. Of the ocean. Of mollusk shells grainy between our fingers. Of our dirty faces, our salty skin, my hair tangled like the Gordian knot. I started smiling as if I were sharing a joke with my lost brother. The joke of how ridiculous I looked now. Through the eyes of those two kids, I looked hilarious. I started to laugh then, my shoulders shaking and my eyes beginning to water until Aunt Eileen's smile turned suspicious. "What are you laughing at?" she said, her last pin held between her lips.

"Nothing," I said, wiping my eyes.

"You're going to ruin your makeup," she said.

"Sorry."

At six o'clock, Aunt Eileen gave me a ride to the school, and despite the fact that Tyler and I had no romantic interest in each other, my heart was hammering in my chest at the sight of the other kids streaming through the doors. I got out as Aunt Eileen said, "Be safe, okay? No later than midnight."

"Gotcha," I said.

"And, Jeanie."

I paused with the car door open, the cool air rushing in.

"You don't get into a car with anyone who's been drinking, okay? Just call me, I'll come get you, anytime, all right?"

She was a good aunt, always had been. I was the one who was the disappointment, and I knew it.

"Thanks," I said, meeting her eyes. She looked like she was about to burst into tears. She took a deep breath as if she had more to say, but in the end, she just patted my shoulder as I made my way out of the car.

I met Tyler out front. He was wearing black dress pants and a tucked-in collared shirt. His curly hair was plastered to the sides of his head in a haphazard attempt at control. He had a small smile on his face, and it seemed like he was more excited to be playing dress-up than attending a dance with me.

"Shall we, my lady?" he said, holding out his elbow.

I laughed and took it.

The dance was everything you'd expect. Loud music. Walls decorated in sparkling streamers by the student body. I couldn't have told you what the theme was, probably something generic like "A Moment in Time." Tyler and I danced awkwardly, our bodies bumping into each other, both of us screaming to the music when we knew the song. We saw Natalie come and go, grinding her backside into Cole in a way that left me both fascinated and disgusted at once.

Tyler and I skipped the slow songs, stepping outside into the courtyard, where he shared some weed brownies with me.

"The high lasts longer when you eat it," he said.

I took a big bite.

When the dance was over, my feet were blistered and all the pins in my hair felt like they were trying to rip my scalp from my skull. Tyler and I joined Natalie and Cole along with two seniors, Nina and Gavin, to head to Natalie's cousin's place in Green Acres. Gavin drove us in his parents' car. Natalie's cousin's house was a fifteen-some-thousand-square-foot home on a quiet cul-de-sac. It was beautiful inside, with hardwood flooring and vaulted ceilings. A painting of a nude woman holding a cigarette hung over an unlit gas fireplace. The living room opened up to a sliding back door where there was a patio and a pool, lit from beneath in glowing blue light. Above the pool was the hot tub, which poured a fountain of water over layers of corrugated rocks.

Natalie's cousin was standing at a sunken bar filled with all kinds of bottles of varying shapes, sizes, and colors. He was attractive in a well-put-together way. Straight, combed black hair, an L-shaped jaw, and a collared shirt with the sleeves rolled up to reveal a tattoo on his left forearm. His nose was maybe a bit too big and his eyes a little too close together, but somehow it all suited him.

"I won't tell you not to drink," he said, smiling at us, playing the cool-older-cousin role to a T. "But I will say, if you *do* drink . . . I probably won't notice anything's gone, got it?" He laughed, and Natalie gave a "Woo!"

"I'll be upstairs if you need anything, okay?" he said to Natalie as he mixed a drink of his own from the bar. "Toodles." And he was gone. We were left to a house with a pool and a bar full of liquor.

Natalie made us drinks that tasted like peaches on fire. I sipped at mine and, despite the taste, was delighted at the warmth that started in my chest and spread out through the rest of my body. Because we didn't have swimsuits, we all stripped to our underwear and jumped into the heated pool. I was nervous at first, but I gave in to the joy of the moment, the intoxicating buzz of the alcohol, and my need to fit in. I joined with the rest, even taking the time to remove at least 70 percent of the pins from my hair. Because the air outside was cold and the pool was warm, tendrils of steam hovered above the surface of the water like twirling fingers. We swam and splashed as we drank. Overhead, the stars haloed a palm tree lit by golden spotlights. Beneath us, our skin glowed alien blue from the round fluorescent lights of the pool.

Cole was splashing Natalie, who kept flashing him her boobs to egg him on. Nina and Gavin had moved to the hot tub and were furiously making out. She was on his lap; for all I knew, they could have been having sex right there in front of us. It wouldn't have seemed out of place, either, given the energy of the moment. Nothing seemed like a bad idea, which is why when Tyler asked if I wanted to go inside and eat the rest of his weed brownie, I agreed.

We dried off and found the basement. It was a large open space with a pool table beside a group of brown leather couches and a giant TV.

"This place is nuts," Tyler said, laughing. He was still in his boxers, with the towel wrapped around his waist.

"I know," I said. My drink was still in hand and the alcohol flavor had given way to the peaches. It tasted bright and flowery on my tongue. We sat on the couches and Tyler unwrapped the brownie. He took a bite and then passed it to me. I took a smaller one, and we lay back on the couch, our skin tingling from the heat of the pool and probably the THC joining the alcohol in our bodies.

I don't remember what we talked about, only that we were down there for a while. We were laughing when Natalie finally came downstairs. She had on sweatpants and a white T-shirt but clearly wasn't wearing a bra.

"There you bitches are," she said. "I'm going upstairs with Cole." She began to swivel her hips back and forth. "I'm gonna give him a taste of my—"

"Jesus, Natalie," I said as Tyler laughed. "We get it."

"Good, 'cause I've got a present for you." She reached into her pocket and pulled out a roll of condoms, expertly bending one and snapping it off from the rest. "Here." She tossed it onto the couch. The plastic wrap made a cracking sound as it hit the brown leather. Something inside my stomach made the same sound. *Snap*. "You bunch of virgins need to man the fuck up," she said.

"Natalie," Tyler said, sitting up now.

"Come on, don't be pussies. You won't regret it." She stood up. "Now don't come upstairs until you both get good and laid, got it?"

"Come on, Natalie," Tyler said.

"I don't want to see that condom empty by the end of the night. I'm serious." She laughed and headed toward the stairs, her hips twirling again as she went. "Time to get mine," she said, grabbing her boobs and squeezing before disappearing around the corner.

Tyler and I sat rigid on the couch, staring down at the condom like it was about to burst into flames.

"She's fucking crazy," I said, and we both laughed, a tiny bit of the tension leaking out from our bodies. I didn't feel particularly drunk anymore. The pool water was beginning to freeze against my skin, and I was suddenly aware of how naked we both were.

Tyler picked up the condom. "I mean," he said, pausing. "I guess we could." The words sucked up any ambient noise in the room. I thought of Maddox. I wanted him to be there more than anything. But what did I owe him? What were we to each other, really? Phone calls? Vague promises? Maybe he was doing whatever he wanted with whoever he wanted in Washington. I wasn't beholden to anyone. Maybe that's just what the alcohol was telling me. Or the fact that I'd felt like he'd abandoned me. Like my dad. Like Jamie. Maybe I simply felt trapped in that basement—the stairwell behind us might as well have been filled with concrete. These aren't good reasons for what happened, and I know it. I wish I could explain how I felt that night. How it didn't even really seem like a decision I was making. It was just something that was happening. *Fuck it,* I thought. My new mantra. *Just fuck it.*

"Yeah," I said. "Okay."

He scooted hesitantly toward me, put a hand on my naked knee. My body responded by tightening, every muscle going rigid. But I pushed past it. I reached out and touched his thigh, grabbing a handful of the towel and sliding it to the floor. He put his hand on my towel, just above my chest, and pulled it down. My bra was heavy and waterlogged against my chest. Then Tyler leaned into me, and we were kissing, my head pressed against the cushion, his wiry body stabbing at mine in odd, uncomfortable angles. He smelled of alcohol and chocolate, and his lips were surprisingly warm against mine. His hand found the plane of my stomach and kept moving. I gasped when he touched me. I remembered Maddox's hand on my thigh that night on his rooftop; it had felt completely different from whatever was happening now.

I don't fully remember how our underwear came off, but soon there we were, naked bodies pressed into each other, thin and warm and fumbling. He found the condom and unwrapped it. His penis was pink, engorged, and fuzzy like a gerbil. I watched him roll the condom onto himself like I was watching someone open a can of beans: I was detached, unemotional. The alcohol and the weed were combining in my system to completely shut me down.

When he was above me once more, he looked at my face. He seemed scared. I wish I had stopped him there. I think he would have laughed, and everything would have gone back to normal, both of us relieved. But we were too young, too bound by the structure of our adolescent society, of Natalie's godlike command over us.

"You okay?" he asked.

All I could manage was a nod.

"You ready?"

I wasn't.

It didn't feel good. It hurt. He collapsed on top of me within minutes, maybe seconds. After, I lay there in silence, feeling empty. When I picked up the towel from beneath me, I saw the dark patch of blood and thought, that's it, that's the last thing I had left to break.

⬤

"Would you say that you were raped that night?" Dr. Gardner asked.

I was looking out the window at a magpie that had landed in a nearby alder. I liked magpies. I'd never seen ones quite so big as those in England. "No," I said.

"And why's that?"

"Why wasn't I raped?"

"Yes," he said, calm as a cucumber—though I'd never found cucumbers to be particularly calm vegetables; they're too phallic and warty. Potatoes, I should've said. Calm as a potato. "Why don't you consider it a rape?"

"Because it wasn't rape."

"What would have made it rape?" he asked.

"It would've been rape if I said no. I didn't. I said yes."

Dr. Gardner folded his hands in his lap like a poker player about to reveal his royal flush. "But did you feel like you *could* say no?"

The magpie in the branch ruffled his feathers and snapped his beak against the peeling skin of the alder.

"So who raped me?" I asked. "Tyler or Natalie?"

Dr. Gardner didn't respond.

"I guess I raped myself." The magpie gave a laughing chirrup as if he'd gotten the joke, then launched from the branch in a flash of glistening black and white and blue feathers.

CHAPTER 5

From that moment on, I decided that sex would never *not* be my idea again. I took control of it. The next weekend, I met Tyler at his house. We smoked a lot of weed. I took his pants off in the hammock and went down on him like I was Natalie. We weren't dating; really, we weren't anything. We were just two friends exploring our bodies. It felt both completely natural and terribly wrong at the same time.

By the end of sophomore year, Maddox had somehow managed to save enough to buy a car. It was an old Volvo that he bought from the neighbors down the street. He told me it was a piece of shit, but he didn't care. He was coming to me, whether his dad gave him permission or not. I was excited, but also wary. I was nervous that our seeing each other had become an obsession fueled by some misguided childhood connection. Did we really want to see each other at this point? Or were we going through the motions in order to fulfill a dream that the younger versions of ourselves had thought they wanted? I suppose it didn't matter either way. He had the car, and in a week, after finals, he was coming.

Tyler, Natalie, and I spent that week avoiding homework and school and smoking at Tyler's or in random parking lots. We even went back to Natalie's cousin's house where we skinny-dipped in his pool.

"You better not get pregnant," Natalie said while we soaked in the hot tub and Tyler went inside for a drink. The night was overcast, the clouds so hazy, purple, and low, they looked manufactured.

"We're using condoms," I said.

"That's good. You do not want that kid's baby."

I looked toward the house, into the golden glow of the windows, where Tyler was mixing alcohols in his glass.

"Tyler? Why?"

Natalie laughed. "Come on," she said. "I mean, he's fun and all, but he's not the brightest tool in the bunch."

"That's not how the saying goes," I said.

She laughed again. "Well fuck you."

Tyler returned with his drink and slipped on his way into the hot tub, spilling a healthy splash into the foaming water. Natalie nearly lost it. "See," she said to me.

"See what?" Tyler asked, smiling.

"I was just telling Jeanie how stupid you were." She winked at me.

"Screw you guys," he said, but he was still smiling. He didn't know that Natalie was being serious. And that was her absolute worst quality. Natalie was always serious. She always meant what she said. Her words were burrs; they dug into your skin and stuck there, and sometimes you didn't even know you had them until you twisted a certain way and felt their needles stabbing.

"So your long-distance lover is coming over this weekend, right?" Natalie said.

"What?" Tyler said, his face molding into a frown.

"He's not my lover," I said. I'd told Natalie about Maddox coming but had expressly asked her not to tell Tyler. She mouthed *Sorry* behind Tyler's back and touched two fingers to her forehead like she'd completely forgotten. She hadn't. "He's just a friend from Washington," I said.

"Oh," Tyler said. "Do we get to meet him?" He took a drink from his glass, doing his best to act casual, but Tyler's emotions were always written in bold font across his face.

"I dunno," I said. "He's not here for long."

"Oh, come on," Natalie said. "You can't talk about him for this long and not let us meet him." I could have punched Natalie in the face right then. And had she not been who she was, I might have.

"I'll think about it," I said.

"Bring him here," Natalie said. "My cousin won't mind. We'll all come over on Saturday. It'll be great. You can come, right?" She directed the last remark at Tyler.

"Yeah, sure." Tyler smiled at me and I did my best to return it.

"Yay," Natalie said, reaching out a hand for Tyler's glass. He passed it to her and she took a long drink.

When Friday finally came, Aunt Eileen dropped me off at Santa Clara Central Park, where I sat on a bench by the creek and watched a group of domesticated ducks waddle around by the water. I'd taken one of Tyler's edibles that morning, but it was backfiring. I was paranoid and anxious. My knee was bouncing, and my fingers picked at a loose bit of wood on the side of the bench. I pictured Jamie at the pier, picking at the wood and tossing the pieces in the water. I could see his fingers lifting the small slivers. I wondered where those fingers were now. If they were moving, or still and lifeless. And here I was, meeting Maddox without him again. And Maddox was definitely coming this time. He'd been texting me all along the way. *Seattle . . . Portland . . . Eugene. Man this car is a piece!* I'd told him where to meet and he'd texted when he was an hour away. That was forty-five minutes ago. I was deeply aware that Maddox was very close. Maybe he was parking the car in the lot. Maybe he'd be walking down that path any second. My heart was in my ears. I forced myself to stare at the creek as one duck chased another through the water, splashing. The sky was mostly clear; only a few clouds obscured the sun every once in a while as a high wind blew them across the expanse of blue.

I hadn't seen Maddox in person for years now and it was a daunting task: not just to see, but to be seen. I was much taller than I had been. I was nearly five-nine. My body had grown into my long legs and arms. My hair was better kept now that I wasn't in the woods all the time and had access to regular shampoo and Aunt Eileen's comb. It had grown thick and wavy and I often kept it tied up in a messy pony. My boobs had sprouted but couldn't compare to Natalie's. My face wasn't anything special; it was the type of face you might look at for an instant, wonder if it was appealing, and then look away and forget about completely. I had a nice nose, though—girls were jealous of my small, perfectly sloped nose.

I was biting the inside of my lip when I heard his voice. "Jeanie King." It came from far away. I looked up and saw Maddox coming toward me. I couldn't help but smile and scramble awkwardly to my feet—the back of one leg had gone numb from sitting on the uncomfortable bench for so long.

His hair was longer, brushed across his forehead and loose around his ears, but he wore it well. His lips were wide and open in a beautiful grin.

"Hey, stranger," I said, moving toward him.

"It's really you, right?" He was ten feet from me, taller than he had been, jawline stronger. His whole body had started to settle into the man he was becoming. I wondered what I looked like to him.

"I'm pretty sure," I said, looking down as if to make sure it was, in fact, me. By the time I looked up, he was reaching his arms around my waist and scooping me up. My feet lifted from the ground and he spun me like in a movie. I laughed.

"You're gonna hurt yourself," I said. He wasn't much taller than me, but he was broader around the shoulders, denser than the boy I'd played with on the beach all those years ago. It felt good to be so close to him, our bodies flush against each other—strange after being so distant for so long. He set me down slowly, and as soon as my feet hit the ground, he kissed me right on the mouth. A surprised noise escaped my throat, but Maddox wasn't deterred. His lips pushed against mine, and I found myself pushing back.

When we finally broke apart, the grin was back on his face. "I've been wanting to do that for a really long time," he said.

And if not for Tyler, if not for the memory of his mouth on mine, of his body in mine, it would have been an absolutely perfect moment.

❧

We spent a few hours walking around the park, the sun warm against our cheeks. His nearness was intoxicating. The taste of his mouth was still on my lips. At one point, he reached out and grabbed my hand, and I let him.

"This is so weird," I kept saying, and we'd laugh and talk about nothing in particular. We were in rare form, joking and laughing, giddy with the reality of each other's presence. When our legs grew tired, we found a bench by the man-made lake, the surface of which shone a metallic shade of dark blue. We sat at the bench, our conversation dwindling, the shared silence punctuated by small statements here and there. Eventually Maddox asked, "You been keeping track of the news?" I knew what he meant. He didn't mean the news in general. He meant Dad, Jamie.

"Not really," I said, and it was true. I'd stopped obsessing, stopped scouring the internet, stopped writing letters, and I hadn't called Officer Favre in months. I'd resigned myself to letting the story play out, to letting news find me when it came.

"We don't have to talk about it if you don't want to," Maddox said, obviously wanting to talk about it. "But people around town still talk, you know."

We were both silent a moment. I was hoping he'd shut up but was unwilling to tell him to. We still talked about what had happened on the phone every once in a while, but I didn't encourage it anymore. Though I'd never told him to leave it alone, either.

"Some people don't think Stacy is dead," he said. "They think they ran off together."

I laughed and the sound came out wilder than I'd intended. "So the blood on his hands? What was that?"

"Yeah," Maddox said. "But why, right? Why kill her? It's nuts."

I wanted to agree, but did I believe it? Maybe he could have killed Stacy in some kind of drunken rage, but not Jamie, right? Maybe it wasn't nuts. Maybe *Dad* was nuts. Maybe he'd always been nuts. Maybe the apple didn't fall far from the tree.

"I don't know," I said instead. "Sounds like nobody knows."

"Do you talk about it with your aunt and uncle?"

"No," I said. He must have heard the tone in my voice because he dropped the subject after that.

We listened to the soft sounds of the water, gentle against

the banks, nothing like the rush of the ocean unfolding upon the shoreline or fulminating against the rocks. When it became clear that the conversation wouldn't fully recover, we made our way back to the car and drove home.

Aunt Eileen and Uncle Derek were all nice manners and cautious excitement. I think they were hoping that Maddox was the missing piece to my fucked-up life. Grace was scared of him during dinner, but that night, when we watched a movie, she crawled into his lap without a word, like it was some sort of initiation. He looked at me, surprised, and I laughed. We held hands under the blanket.

Before heading to the guest bedroom downstairs, Maddox met me at my door in the hallway upstairs. The house was dark. Aunt Eileen and Uncle Derek had already gone to bed. Maddox kissed me again, softer, slower this time, resting his hand against my waist.

"Night, Jeanie," he said. Every time he used my name, I felt more myself, more grounded in my own skin. And no one else has ever had that effect on me, neither before nor since.

❦

The next day we went to the Rosicrucian Egyptian Museum because Maddox said he'd read about it online and wanted to see some mummies. The art and artifacts were interesting, but the mummy was gross. He was a pale greenish-brown color, and he had his mouth open as if he were snoring. His arms were crossed over his chest, which apparently meant he'd been some sort of royalty. After, we got burgers and fries like we used to do at the beach in Washington.

"These are way better," Maddox said, mouth half full of cheeseburger.

"The fries aren't as good, though," I said.

Afterward, Maddox and I drove to an empty church parking lot where he let me drive his car. I was anxious at first, picturing driving my uncle's car into the tree in our front lawn. But something about Maddox put me at ease. His instructions were slow and patient and encouraging.

"You're a natural," Maddox said as I backed into a parking space perfectly for a third time. "Now let's give it some gas."

"Okay," I said, smiling. I gunned it down the parking lot, which wrapped around the church and was almost completely empty. I took the corners hard, the dashboard shaking and the old tires screeching as I did.

"Yeah," Maddox said. "Keep going!"

I didn't care if anyone saw or if a cop came and arrested us; in that moment all that mattered was the feel of the car speeding over yellow paint and gray concrete, the smooth leather of the wheel between my fingers, the smell of pine coming from Maddox's dangling air freshener, and Maddox's laughter. He peeled back the sunroof and stood on his seat.

"What are you doing?" I said, stepping on the brake.

"Just keep going; don't slow down."

I pressed on the gas again and the car jolted forward, almost knocking Maddox into the back seat. "Whoa!" he said, laughing.

Then he stuck his whole upper body out of the sunroof. The wind caught his hair and flung it off his forehead. He lifted his arms wide as if a simulacrum of the holy cross, like the three outside the church building. I laughed and pressed harder on the gas, reaching sixty miles per hour across the back end of the church. Maddox yelled, a wild, young, animal scream.

Later, in college, I'd read a theory that time isn't a linear thing. Instead, everything is happening all at once, but the only way our minds can conceive of the events is in a progression. And while mostly I don't like that thought—I like time moving forward, clocks ticking, the past being emptied behind you like a sieve—I do like the theory in a selective fashion. I like to think that somehow, Maddox and I are still there, in that church parking lot, discovering our relationship, hands outstretched to the wind, laughing—a moment I can relive whenever I want to, like a firework that bursts and then disappears but is there again and again, an imprint of light every time you close your eyes to see.

That night, Maddox and I drove to Natalie's cousin's house in Green Acres.

"We really don't have to go," I told Maddox. "We can do our own thing."

"I don't mind," he said. "I'd like to meet your friends."

"They're okay," I said. "But we don't have to stay long if you don't want to."

"Okay, we'll play it by ear." He wasn't nervous to meet my friends like I would have been to meet his. Maddox was an anomaly: he'd always been so settled in who he was, he couldn't be bothered to worry about whether people liked him. To him, other people's opinions were their issues, not his. I often wondered what it would be like to live inside his head, even for a day.

Natalie, Cole, Tyler, and Samantha—one of Natalie's peripheral friends—were already in the pool, splashing and drinking. Natalie's cousin was away on business, so we had the house to ourselves, not that it made much of a difference when he was there, anyway.

I introduced Maddox, and Natalie made him a drink, mouthing *Oh my God* behind his back and biting her knuckles at me. I would have thought it was funny, if not for the fact that I knew Tyler was watching.

"Now get your clothes off, kids," Natalie said. She was in her bra and panties like she usually was, although I knew for a fact she had plenty of bikinis.

"We brought suits," I said.

Natalie made a pouty face as Cole called out "Lame!" from the pool. Tyler was drinking by the hot tub, pointedly looking away from me.

We went inside to change, and already I felt like this was a colossal mistake, bringing Maddox. So why did I do it? Did I like two boys fighting over me? Did I want to hurt Tyler for taking my first sexual experience away from me? Or was it simpler: Could I really not refuse Natalie?

"They seem nice," Maddox said.

"They're probably all drunk already, so don't judge too harshly."

He laughed. "Got it."

We put our suits on and joined the others in the lukewarm pool. It felt colder, or maybe I wasn't as drunk as I normally was. I was pacing myself, more concerned about Maddox's presence than I was about managing my buzz. But my lack of drinking was having a physical effect on me. My skin broke out in goose bumps. I was practically shivering.

Maddox, however, had jumped into the water and started doing the crawl from one end of the pool to the other. We all watched him swim like none of us knew a pool could actually be used like that. It was a pool party; who actually swims at a pool party? Answer: Maddox. He liked to swim. I remembered that from our time in the ocean. I could picture the calm green inlet we went to during the summer when the water wasn't as freeze-your-bones-off cold. As we all watched him, I felt weirdly protective toward him. I didn't like the others' judgmental stares. I wanted to pull him from the pool and leave immediately.

"So what was our girl like when she was just a sprite?"

Natalie asked once he'd stopped, water dripping from his hair and eyelashes.

Maddox shrugged. "Pretty similar," he said. "Maybe a little wilder."

"Ooh," Natalie said. "Do tell."

"I don't know," Tyler said, a malicious smile on his face. "She's pretty wild now."

Natalie laughed. "You would," she said.

I couldn't bring myself to meet anyone's eyes, so I watched my fingers dance above the surface of the pool as if I were playing piano like Jamie.

"Her hair was crazier, and she always had a streak of dirt on her face," Maddox said. The others laughed. "Though we all did back then."

"I don't think I bathed much," I said.

"Gross," Natalie said, taking another drink. She was already growing bored of the conversation.

"I don't think you bathe much now," Tyler said. "Smells like fish up in here."

Natalie snorted her alcohol and then screamed, waving an arm in front of her face, "It burns, oh God!" Everyone was laughing but Maddox and me. Tyler was trying to get to me, trying to humiliate me in front of Maddox. I was furious at the time, but now, looking back, how can I blame him? What I was doing was far worse.

"I'm gonna show Maddox the rest of the house," I said.

"Oh, come on," Tyler said at the same time Natalie yelled, "Go get it, girl!"

I led Maddox back inside, and we dried off and put our clothes back on. When we both emerged into the kitchen, dressed and moderately dry, I said, "Let's get out of here."

"We just got here," Maddox said, oblivious to the tension.

"I know," I said. "But I'd rather be with you."

Maddox nodded. "Me too. Should we tell them we're leaving?"

"No," I said. "They'll probably drink enough tonight to forget we even showed up."

We drove back to the church parking lot, and as soon as he parked the car, he leaned over and kissed me. We made out for a minute or two, our body temperatures rising, fogging up the windows.

"Let's move to the back seat," I said.

We could almost lie down back there. We bent our bodies, trying to find the perfect angle where we could press as close to each other as possible. Maddox cracked a window and cool air spilled into the car through the small slit. Things were getting heavy. I paused to take off my bra underneath my shirt and he stared at me like he couldn't quite believe what he was watching. I smiled at the look. When I had it off, I took his hands and placed them beneath my shirt. They were surprisingly cool—or my chest was surprisingly warm. His grip was soft but urgent. When I reached down and grabbed between his legs, he groaned. The sound sent a jolt through my body. It emboldened me. I reached for his jeans and pulled at the button. I felt his hand on my wrist and thought it was an encouragement, I was so blinded by the moment. This was right, I thought. This was what it's supposed to be like. Things with Tyler were all wrong. This would make things right. This would be my real first time. But when I pinched his zipper between my fingers and pulled, he said, "Wait."

That single word drained something out of me, and I lifted my gaze to meet his face.

"What?" I said, a hint of anger sharpening the edges of the word. "You don't want to?"

"I do," he said. "I mean, just maybe not here."

"Somewhere else?" I asked. "We could go back to Natalie's

cousin's, sneak into one of the rooms upstairs. They wouldn't even notice."

"That's okay," Maddox said, sitting up. "Can we just, I don't know."

He didn't want to do it. He wasn't ready. I was practically shaking. It was fine that he wasn't ready. It was natural. Normal. Good. Right? It didn't mean he didn't want me. It didn't mean that he was bothered by the fact that my dad was probably a murderer. That everyone in my life had abandoned me. He wouldn't be the same. And yet, in the end, why would he be any different? I had a fundamental flaw, and everyone else could sense it, could see the indelible stain on my soul.

Something was happening to me. Something was breaking and falling and shattering all at once. Our limbs were still close, but I felt an ocean away from him. Maddox couldn't want me. Maybe he didn't even know why exactly. But he wasn't living the same life I was. He wasn't making the same mistakes. We'd become irreparably different people. Born from two different stars. He'd already left me behind. He just didn't know it yet.

"Yeah," I said, "sure."

We were silent a moment. Maddox rolled up the window.

"Actually," I said, "let's just go home."

"Jeanie—"

"No, it's okay. You're right. We should probably get back."

"I don't want to go back," Maddox said.

"But I do," I said, my voice shaking slightly. "Please just drive."

He drove me home in silence. Both of us were affected by what had happened, but I was the only one who understood it for what it was. I wasn't good enough. I was fucked up. If he stayed with me, I'd fuck him up, too. Only now do I realize what I was doing: rejecting him before he could reject me.

Leaving him before I could be left. I was never going to be that little girl alone in the cabin again.

When he said good night at my door, I let him kiss me one more time, but I saw the look on his face and could do nothing about it. He understood. He was losing me and he didn't know why.

CHAPTER 6

"Tell me what you like about sex," Dr. Gardner said. Commanded, really.

I waited for him to smirk or smile like he should've, like any man should've, asking a single woman that question. He didn't. But I knew the excitement some part of him felt. The joy at being given permission to ask a woman about sex with a straight face. I could practically feel him struggling to maintain the flaccidity of his penis.

"You mean, like, other than the obvious?" I asked.

"The obvious being what?"

Oh God, he wanted me to spell it out for him. Talk slow. Touch my lips.

"Well, women have these things called clitorises . . . clitorisi . . . clitori?" Clitoratti? I could've gone on. "Anyway, and when—"

"Yes." He held up a hand, palm facing me. "Other than the obvious," he said, and I almost felt put out. It'd been nice watching his subtle discomfort as I ruined his psychological boner. But the truth was that it really wasn't about physical pleasure. I mean, it felt good at times, but I never came. Never never never. Not even with this Irish guy a few years back that looked, I swear to God, just like Colin Farrell. I didn't know why it didn't work for me. I supposed it didn't matter. Maybe some girls just couldn't. But that wasn't why I did it, anyway.

"There's just this feeling during sex," I said. "Like nothing else matters except that exact second, that single moment. You're never more in your body than when you're having sex. You can block out everything around you. Your mind kind of shuts down, you know?"

"Interesting," he said.

"Why's that interesting?" I asked.

"What I'm hearing is that you like to have sex because it helps you push out other emotions."

"I didn't say that," I said.

"Do you think there's some validity to it?"

"I don't know," I said. I was getting testy, though I didn't know why. "You're the expert, you tell me."

"It's not wrong for a woman to like sex." He lifted a leg, crossed it again.

"I didn't say it was."

He was silent, staring at me, undressing me with his eyes. "Let's talk about something else for now," he said, leaning his head against his headrest—satisfied, satiated, sated.

"Yes," I said, dragging a single fingernail over the arm of my chair.

Maddox went home the next day because I asked him to.

"Jeanie, come on," he begged. "Let's at least talk about it."

"I can't," I said, and I was insistent.

Eventually he left, reluctantly. "I'll call you," he said.

It was a beautiful sunny day.

☙

"What happened with your Washington boy?" Tyler asked me that weekend as we lay partially naked in his bedroom, the sheets draped over our bodies.

"We're too different," I said.

"Natalie was sure you were in love."

"I wasn't," I said.

☙

Maddox and I spoke on and off for the rest of that year. He grew desperate and insistent, and I holed up in my shell.

"I'm going to come back down," he said.

"Please don't," I said. "I just need to figure some stuff out." *Like what the fuck is wrong with me.*

"Please, Jeanie," he said. "Don't do this."

Eventually the phone calls slowed, then stopped. Our contact devolved into an irregular text here and there until the end of junior year, when those stopped as well. Maddox had faded from my life, or rather, I'd phased him out.

I distanced myself from Natalie and Tyler, too. Natalie, bless her black heart, spread rumors about me being a horrible slut and said that I tried to get her to have sex with me and Tyler.

Junior prom I slept with my date, Anton Baskin, a good-looking guy who I was pretty sure asked me to go with him because he wanted exactly what he got out of the night. I didn't feel anything.

"You have to start thinking about your future," Aunt Eileen told me.

But the future was a black void for me. And school was utterly uninteresting. For most high school students, school was life, the epicenter of their little universes. For me, school was an extracurricular activity. Optional at best. My grades weren't terrible. I had a 3.4 GPA, which was impressive given that I often skipped class, rarely did homework, and wrote dark poetry in my notebook more often than I took notes.

Aunt Eileen attempted to pour herself into me, to heal the wounds inside my soul, exorcise the demons. But she was too busy with Grace to give me what I needed. Not that anything she could have done would have helped anyway.

At the beginning of my senior year, I had the dream about Dad and Jamie in the woods again. Only this time, when I found Jamie, he was playing the piano. His fingers were covered in blood as they danced across the keys, smearing the white notes with bloody slashes and round, red finger-prints. "Jeanie," he said. The last words he'd spoken to me. "You're . . ." I woke in the middle of the night, shaking. I felt my body start to convulse, like I needed to sob my guts out but couldn't. Something wasn't right. Maybe I was having a seizure. The silence of the house at midnight was disturbed by, I swear to God, the sound of the piano. The music was soft and light like rising fog, like moonlight through trees in an endless forest.

"Shut up!" I yelled. The music played on. No one stirred from their beds. "Shut the fuck up!" I called again, my arms still shaking as I sat up. I thought I heard movement from Aunt Eileen and Uncle Derek's room, but I wasn't sure. I jumped out of bed, my mind a red haze of anger. I was having horrible racking convulsions. I almost didn't make it down the stairs. My limbs didn't feel like they were working right. It was like they were elongated, nightmarish, like they belonged to someone else; I was trapped inside my brain, watching them move. I went to the garage, grabbed the biggest hammer

I could find and raced back inside, the leather grip cold and solid as a blade.

I wasn't thinking. I wasn't myself. I was outside myself as I approached the old piano in the living room. As far as I knew, it hadn't been used since Jamie had practiced on it as a kid. I lifted the fallboard and raised the hammer and slammed it down hard on the keys. "I said, shut . . . the . . . fuck . . . up!" I screamed, smashing the hammer down on the piano with every word. I was still lifting and striking, lifting and striking when the lights came on. Aunt Eileen and Uncle Derek were standing there, staring at me like I was some murderer who had just broken into their house. I tossed the hammer on the floor, looked at the cracked keys, the splintered wood. A single white key lay on the floor, perfectly intact, as if it had realized what was happening and jumped out of the way just in time.

"Jeanie!" Aunt Eileen said. "What's going on?"

I looked down at the ruined piano, the broken keys, the splintered wood resting on the carpet. I looked at my hands, half expecting to see them covered in blood.

"Nothing," I said.

"This is not nothing, Jeanie King," Aunt Eileen said. "You'll—"

"I'm going to bed," I interrupted. Uncle Derek stood silent, his hands on his hips, looking at the ground as if he was embarrassed.

"No, we need to talk about this," Aunt Eileen said, but I was already moving. My body floated past her like a shapeless spirit, my legs lifting me up the stairs toward my bedroom as my skin grew translucent, my arms wisplike at my side. In her bedroom, Grace began to call out for her mama, and the sound was so sharp and piercing, it almost scattered my nebulous pieces into complete oblivion.

CHAPTER 7

Aunt Eileen made me see Pastor Donnelly twice a week for the rest of that year. His office smelled like old leather and there was a big picture of a blond Jesus in the corner, looking down on me with pitying eyes, like he had this secret he was sad he couldn't tell me.

I gave Pastor Donnelly the answers he was looking for. I told him how sad and angry I'd felt. How horrible what I'd done to the piano was. How I would try harder in school. Make new friends, blah blah blah.

"I think we're making some great progress," he told Aunt Eileen. She nodded, tears in her eyes, and shook the pastor's hand like he'd pulled my soul from the pit of despair.

***

That winter, I was sneaking out a lot to drink with a casual friend named Indie. He was younger but somehow had all kinds of alcohol hookups. I'd give him the occasional hand job but couldn't be bothered to do more than that. I got into a fight with Natalie in school and slammed her head into the locker. Turned out, Natalie, for all her talk about being a badass and even the way she'd handled herself with Michael when I first met her, was pretty timid when it came to any real kind of violence. She cried like a baby when she saw the blood pouring from her eyebrow. I was sent home and threatened with juvenile detention. Instead, I agreed to go to the church youth group, where kids tried to bring me to Christ in what I'm sure they thought was the coolest most casual way possible.

During my senior year, I began to realize that I needed to leave California. And I felt the best way to do that was get accepted to college. Then I realized that I didn't just want to leave California, I wanted to leave the country. Mom had been from the UK, and the thought of relocating to the place where she'd grown up was this bright and golden thing, hovering in front of me. The US was tainted now, anyway, by the ghost of my father, the ghost of Jamie, and the promise of the girl I was turning into.

I focused on my grades the rest of that year and ended up with a 3.8 GPA, which gave me a 3.5 overall. I applied to several UK colleges: University of Edinburgh, Cambridge, University of London, and Oxford, which is where Mom had gone to school. I knew my grades might not have been Oxford-good, but apparently my essay was. I wrote about my life: the life of a girl who lost her whole family. I wrote about my semifamous father, my lost brother, our time in the woods, the toll it had taken on me, how I'd overcome it with focus and dedication, and how I wanted to go to Oxford to be close to the memory of my mother—which wasn't complete bullshit, at least—and how I wanted to study psychology because I wanted to get inside the head of my father. I had an interview over the phone with one of the tutors at Magdalen College, pronounced *Maudlin* for some inexplicable reason, which was a part of Oxford.

And that's when I heard his voice for the first time. A mellifluous tenor. *William.* I hadn't been nervous before that moment. Before I heard his voice. I didn't really care about my education or my psychology degree, to be honest, so much as I cared about getting out of the country.

"Jeanie" was the first word I heard from him, the phone pressed against my ear. "Lovely to meet you."

"You too," I said. I hated how childish my voice sounded. I resolved to smoke more, to rake at my voice box until I had that sexy, rusty edge.

"I have to say I was very impressed by your essay. Very impressed."

"That's great."

"I must confess that I did some research on your story and found it absolutely fascinating."

Fascinating. Like my life was some sort of docuseries he'd binge-watched in the evening with a glass of wine.

"Thanks" was all I could manage.

"Tell me, where do you think your father is?"

"Excuse me?"

"I'm just curious if you have some idea. Family members often have an inkling, a suspicion that they can't prove. Sometimes the police have their hands tied—too much red tape. That sort of thing. Do you?"

"Do I what?"

"Have any idea where he went."

"No," I said honestly. Was this how things were supposed to go? Was this part of the interview, or hadn't we started that yet?

"And Jamie . . ." He paused as if expecting me to fill in the rest of the sentence. Maybe this was part of it. A test. I opened my mouth to respond, but he continued: "What about Jamie? Do you have any idea what could have happened to him?"

"I don't," I said. For some reason, my heart was pounding. I was weirdly thrilled and scandalized at once. "Do you?" I asked him. I don't know why I said it. Maybe I didn't like the way he was handling things. Maybe I wanted to make him feel guilty. Turn the tables. I heard a sound on the other end of the line, something that could have been papers shuffling or an intake of breath.

Instead of answering the question, he told me about the psychology department at Magdalen College. About the faculty, about tutors, about the final exam, which he called "writing papers."

He asked a few more generic questions and at the end of the conversation, he told me abruptly that he was happy to invite me to attend the school.

"We'll send an acceptance letter to make it official and all that, but really it's just formalities from here on out."

"Thank you," I said. "I really appreciate it."

"I'm excited to work with you, Jeanie King." The way he said my name in full, it was like he was casting a spell.

I got the acceptance letter in the mail a week after that. Aunt Eileen couldn't have been more delighted. Or perhaps she was relieved to be rid of me. Sometimes the two emotions looked the same.

It had been years at this point, but for some reason, I called Officer Favre again. I did it while Aunt Eileen and Uncle Derek were at a playdate with Grace.

"Officer Favre." He said his own name into the phone as if I didn't know who I'd been calling.

"Hi, Officer Favre. It's Jeanie King."

"Jeanie," he said, drawing out the vowels like he was sitting back in his chair, like he'd just won a bet with his colleagues about whether I'd call. "How are you? Haven't heard from you in a while."

"Yeah, well, I haven't heard from you, either." This didn't make sense. He'd never been the one to call me.

"True. What can I do for you, Jeanie?"

"I just . . . I'm moving."

"Oh, off to college I imagine, huh? Time flies."

"Yeah. I mean. I'm moving out of the country. I'm going to study at Oxford."

"Oxford?" He sounded genuinely surprised. "Well good for you. I mean that, Jeanie. I'm glad to hear it. A lot of kids that go through something as, you know, traumatizing as what you've been through end up spiraling. It's very common and, well, I'm just glad to hear it."

"Thanks." We were both silent on the phone for a minute. He was waiting for me to continue, but I was scared to bring up my brother after all this time. It was like I was worried that he was expecting me to be over it. As if I knew that he was sitting there, willing me not to say the name.

"Hey, so if you hear anything about Jamie or my dad, you know, I'm gonna have a new number. I don't have it yet, but can I call and give it to you? I'd like you to call me, not my aunt, if you find anything. Is that okay?"

Another long pause. *Say something,* I thought. *Dammit, just speak!*

"Jeanie—"

"I know. I'm not asking for answers now. I'm not hassling you anymore, I swear. I just want you to call my number in the UK. I don't think that's too much to ask, you know?"

He cleared his throat. "Of course. Of course."

"Thanks," I said. "I'll get you the number when I have it."

"Okay. That's fine."

He was waiting for me to end the conversation. I wasn't sure I wanted to yet. I was expecting more from him. Some little detail. Some promise. Some indication that they were on to something but weren't supposed to tell me.

"Are you still looking for him?" The words sounded childish. Like I was asking, once and for all, if Santa was real. *Is Jamie alive? Have you given up?*

"Jeanie." I could hear it in his tone, the resignation. I couldn't stand it. I couldn't bear his pity. It was nails in my skin.

I hung up the phone before he could say anything else.

❦

I hugged Aunt Eileen at the airport before I left. She squeezed tight. I also hugged Uncle Derek and little Grace, who clung to my waist and cried despite the fact that I hadn't put much effort into our relationship. Kids were like that, I supposed.

As I stepped between the mechanical glass doors of the airport, I turned around and saw Uncle Derek opening the car door while Aunt Eileen watched me, Grace holding her hand, tears in both their eyes. I realized then that the distance separating this little family and me would only grow. Not just physically but emotionally. They weren't my parents, they'd only tried to be, and I'd never let them succeed, not even a little. And now that I was leaving, they were becoming something else entirely, like the rest of my life in California. A memory.

A firework.

Fading.

Close your eyes. Do you see all the colors?

❦

The first time I was ever on a train was that trip into Oxford from Heathrow. I stowed my luggage in the compartment, hoping no one would steal it, and found a seat by the window. Across from me was a grandma-aged woman next to a young girl wearing a pink tutu; she was eating a bag of cheesy puffs, her fingers orange from the artificial flavoring, the bag crackling every time she put her little hand inside. For some reason, I wanted to cry then, at seeing that little girl, more than I had in years and years. I felt tears begin to sting my eyes, but I forced them down, took a deep breath, and that's when the train started down the tracks.

I was facing the opposite direction the train was going, so it was discomforting at first, watching the towns and greenery slip past the wrong way. But slowly I relaxed, sank into my seat, and grew to love it. I was distancing myself from the life I'd fallen into, the past I wanted to forget, the self I wanted to be torn from. That's what that train ride felt like, and that's what they've always been to me: movement, change, a seam pulled from fabric, splitting past from future with the violence of its tearing.

⊙

Oxford was a beautiful place. The small pubs, the colleges like castles rising over narrow, cobbled streets filled with locals, tourists, bikers. Cars hummed along the roads; red double-decker buses moved and stopped, brakes squealing and doors hissing open. History was settled into the bones of the place. I remember looking up at the Saxon Tower on Cornmarket Street, seeing the small stone slit windows and thinking those are the type of windows fair maidens scream out of or arrows are shot from—even though the tower was technically part of a church and for all I knew had seen neither fair maiden nor arrow fire. But the thought that it *could* have was something altogether new and thrilling to me.

The people were pleasant without being too forward. There was a sense that if you were completely happy, well that was just fine for you, but you had better keep that to yourself in public, thank you very much. You could smile and wish someone a good day if you passed them on the street, but you were in no way obliged to do so. I liked that. It made me feel more connected to the people than the phony *Hi, how are you? Great how are you?* Back home, everyone was great, everyone was having a good morning, every day was absolutely fine. Not here. Here, you could keep your head down and know that the rest of the world was doing the same, surviving our shared tragedies together.

I was put in a dorm room in the Waynflete Building, which had carpeted floors that were a vague grayish-purple color. The room had a desk, a bed, a small closet, and a window overlooking the Cherwell, which rushed across ancient, green, leaning trees and housed all kinds of migratory birds. I didn't have much luggage, so when I unpacked, the room still felt empty. My meeting with my tutor was that afternoon, but instead of going, I went for a walk and ended up at The King's Arms and ordered a pint like a proper Englishwoman. No one ID'd me or looked at me funny, having a drink by myself at the corner of the bar. The bartender was a young guy with dark hair and earrings. Something about his look said *pirate* to me.

"So where you from?" he asked as he slid me my beer across the old wooden counter.

"California," I said.

"Here for school?" He was probably seven years older than me. Maybe a little less. It was hard to tell.

"Yup," I said, taking a sip of my beer. It was flat and lukewarm but creamy and delicious all the same.

"And how is it so far?" he asked.

"Just moved in today. Haven't seen much. But the room is nice, I guess."

"That's good. Well, enjoy, yeah?" He started to turn away, toward an older man who'd just sidled up to the bar.

"You wanna see it?" I asked him.

He looked at me from over his shoulder. "Your room?" he asked.

And it turns out, he did.

Can you feel him? Waiting in the wings. Not knowing he's about to enter. Not knowing he'll be the pièce de résistance of my debauchery. He was the perfect storm, exactly what I was looking for: He was unlike Maddox in every way. Unlike my dad. Completely unavailable.

See him with his bright smile. His brown and silver hair. The way he looks at you over his glasses. The way he calls your name in class. The way the sound of it on his lips makes you feel, somehow, like a complete impostor. You like that feeling. It makes your skin tingle.

Lectures started after the weekend. Saturday was rainy, but Sunday was only overcast, so I ended up going for a run around University Park. This would be my new thing, I thought. Running. Exercise. I would stop drinking and get fit as shit. Count calories. Make lists. Keep a calendar. Become someone different.

After my run, I used my student pass to tour the colleges, marveling at their structures. Magdalen College's sprawling campus and green cloisters, Christ Church's iconic Tom

Tower, and the pointed steeples of All Souls rising like jagged battlements. The way some roofs seemed to overlap one on top of the other from the inside, extending upward to infinity; and the cracked stone pillars lining intricately manicured greens no one walked on, as if to disturb the grass was the worst offense. And yet, many of the classrooms were modern. Lighting, projectors, large lecture halls. I didn't know why this surprised me. I suppose I'd expected dungeons, turrets, old men in beards scratching numbers on ancient chalkboards.

My first lecture was in a large hall with wooden stairs, a wooden podium, white walls hung with pictures of Magdalen College as if to remind students how lucky we were to be in such a brilliant place with so much wonderful history. The chairs had green cushions and were impressively uncomfortable.

I heard his voice before I saw him. I recognized it from our phone call immediately, but it was deeper in person, more commanding. "Seats please, if you will." The students went silent and sat down. I'd already been sitting in the back next to a girl with large hoop earrings.

He walked to his little podium and began fiddling around on the computer in order to get the projector working.

"Jesus," the hoop earrings girl said, staring at him like a fox in heat. That's when I really looked at him. Blue blazer and jeans with brown dress shoes. Brown hair slightly tousled, graying around the ears. Skin that seemed somehow tanned despite the perpetual English clouds. He had this intense look on his face as he stared at the computer. It was like he was calculating astronomical sums that were so important the future outcome of the world depended on them. I wanted him to look at me like that. I wanted to be that important, that fascinating.

"All right," he said, looking up from his computer as the projector displayed the PowerPoint onto the screen. *Experi-*

mental Psychology, it read. He proceeded to lecture on the history and practice of psychology, including some of the major players, important breakthroughs, and groundbreaking treatments. He didn't, however, click past the *Experimental Psychology* title page, which made him look like an absentminded professor or an eccentric genius.

By the end of the lecture, most of the girls and even half the boys in class were in love with him. I was the only student in class that day, however, who would ever see the inside of his bedroom.

He found me that next week in a pub down the street, on my second pint. I'd stopped going to the pirate bartender—whose name turned out to be Eugene, which was infinitely *un*piratey—because I'd already *hosted* him in my bedroom and didn't really plan on doing so again. He wasn't disappointing; he was just, well, efficient. Okay, disappointing.

My professor went up to the bar and ordered his pint while pushing up his wide-rimmed glasses—a beautiful nerd that didn't know he was beautiful. When he saw me, he stared like he was trying to place me, which I knew couldn't be true, the lecture hall was too big for him to have noticed me. Either way, my heartbeat was in my throat, knocking around my tonsils.

Amazingly, he approached my table, his footsteps matching the sound of my pounding heart.

"You were at my lecture, weren't you?"

I opened my mouth and, no joke, a tiny squeak came out. I prayed to God the bar was too loud for him to hear. "Oh yeah," I managed. "Hi, Professor."

He waved his hand as if the formality hung like a scent in the air between us. "Professor is for the classroom. You can call me William in a pub." He smiled like he'd made some sort of joke. "Mind if I sit?" he asked.

I shook my head, and he sat beside me.

"And you're Jeanie King," he said, his accent making my name sound royal.

I opened my mouth again, but thankfully the motion was squeak-free this time.

"You missed your tutorial. I'm your tutor, you know. There's you and two other students. We meet at my office on Wednesdays at one o'clock. You need to be there, you understand? It's an integral part of your education."

Maybe I should have felt chastised. He was reprimanding me like a disobedient student; instead, I had to stifle a smile. He'd remembered me. Maybe even sought me out. God, maybe he'd followed me here.

"Did you follow me here?" I asked, shocking the both of us.

"No, of course not," he said, but a small flash of fear burst in his eyes like an aneurysm.

Holy shit, he did *follow me here.*

"Would you like me to leave?" he asked, the fear evaporating from his expression.

"No," I said.

"Listen, I think it might behoove you"—*behoove*, he actually said *behoove*; I pictured bison wearing wellies for some reason—"to join us next time."

"Is that your professional opinion?" I felt oddly empowered now. That look of discomfort on his face had emboldened me. I took a sip of my pint; it was almost gone.

He looked taken aback, a feeling I doubted he had very often. I was putting him on edge, knocking him off his otherwise perfect balance. I wondered if I was annoying him. But I didn't think so. In fact, I thought the opposite: as flustered as he seemed, I was pretty sure I was fascinating him. Like a broken watch he wanted to take apart and put back together.

"It's a requirement," he said, commanding me. "Every student must meet with their tutor." He gave me a wan smile that he must have learned in a how-to-smile-professionally class, in which he earned himself a B-. "Wednesday," he said. "One o'clock."

I lifted my pint to my lips and drained the rest of my glass. I didn't feel like myself. I was role-playing. I wasn't the Jeanie King I'd left behind in California. I was powerful. In control.

I liked the feeling very much.

"I appreciate it, William." His name on my lips, me holding it out to him like a wallet he'd dropped on the sidewalk. I stood up to leave.

"Cheers, Jeanie," he said.

I left that bar so buzzing with energy that I went to The King's Arms on my way back to my room and picked up Eugene, the non-pirate bartender, and took him back with me. He couldn't believe his luck.

CHAPTER 8

Being in Oxford, knowing that my mom went to school here, was having a strange effect on me. I'd find myself wandering the streets and looking into shops, wondering if Mom used to shop here. Did she get her groceries at this Sainsbury's? Was this the pub where she used to hang out? It was disorienting and comforting, walking with the ghost of my mother. What was she like then? Did she dream of having a family in the States? Raising twins? Dying in a car crash, face pale and eyes empty?

I could still picture the green-and-gray tennis shoes she used to wear when she went jogging with her friends. I can hear the sound of her keyboard clacking as she wrote the short stories that she managed to sell to a few obscure literary magazines. It was strange how grief manifested. I could watch a movie where a mother dies in a car accident and feel nothing at all, but I see a small ironed crease in a little girl's pants and I'd remember her ironing my blue dress before family pictures, making me wear it even though I didn't like the color or the fit and thought the lines from the iron made it look ridiculous. I'd think of those vague creases in the fabric and a hole would open inside me, deep, endless. Not an equivocal emotion, floating in the ether. It was physical. I could point to the exact location in my chest where I felt it. *Where does it hurt? Right here, Doc.*

◼

The next lecture, William set two chairs down in the front and asked for volunteers. The room was still at first, everyone staring at those empty chairs, so full of potential and import. Eventually the boldest began to raise their hands and William chose a tall guy in the front row and beckoned him with an open-palmed gesture. He stood, shoulders stooped, and moved toward the chair.

"Have a seat," William said.

The guy sat, giving the class a *what have I gotten into?* look, lips stretched and turned downward. A few students chuckled.

"What's your name?" William asked him.

"Devin," he said.

"Devin, we're going to run an exercise often used in talk therapy sessions. It's called the empty chair technique, in which you imagine that an individual from your life is sitting in this chair, here." He placed both hands on the top of the chair across from Devin. "Now, Devin, I'd like you to imagine that your mother is sitting in this chair right now."

Nervous laughter from Devin and the rest of the lecture hall.

"All you have to do is talk to her. Tell her exactly what you would if she was sitting here today."

Devin rubbed his hands along his thighs as if he was nervous, though he seemed to be the type of guy who embraced
the spotlight.

"We're all going to be quiet now and let you have the floor.
Whatever you're comfortable with, feel free to say to your
mother."

William smiled at Devin and moved aside, leaving the tall
student alone with the empty chair in front of the class.

"Uh, hey, Mum," Devin said. Murmuring of amusement
from the rapt audience. "What are you doing here, anyway?"
A few real chuckles. Devin looked over his shoulder at William, who nodded and waved a hand encouragingly.

Devin turned back to the chair. "Thanks for the crisps you
sent. I still can't find them here." Devin scratched the back of
his head, growing, perhaps, actually uncomfortable.

"Tell Sarah I say hi. Miss her. Tell her she can come visit on
her birthday. I'll take her for a pint."

More silence. More rubbing the back of his head. He
laughed. "I don't know what else to say."

William didn't come to his rescue. He let the silence stretch.
Devin said a few more innocuous statements. Told his mom
to tell his older brother to piss off. Devin laughed, but no one
else did. Eventually he looked back at William, who stood
and thanked Devin.

"Let's hear it for our first guinea pig. Not an easy task, well
done." The students applauded.

"Now," William said. "Another volunteer."

Amazingly, there were more. They said all kinds of things
from the very personal to the vague to the sort of vulgar. This
one girl actually started to cry. William gave her an awkward
one-armed hug, and the collective female population decided
immediately that she was a complete skank.

Before William ended the exercise, he looked around the
class and asked if there were any more volunteers. His eyes

roved around the dark rows of students, and then paused, very dramatically, on me.

I forced myself to return the gaze, even lifting my chin in defiance as my palms grew sweaty. When his eyes moved on, I felt something snap, like a rope connecting us had been cut in two. I thought of Maddox. I'd been trying not to think of him as often lately, but something about that feeling, that snapping, brought him back to mind.

"All right, we'll call that experiment finished for today," William said. He walked back across the front of the class to his podium, which sat like a dais from which he administered his judgment.

⊜

I knew he was married. Of course I did. We all did, every one of those girls who was in love with him, or at the very least, in love with the idea of him. Let's say in the lecture hall of maybe fifty students, there were at least twelve girls who had a crush on him. Let's say of those twelve, only five had actual real, womanly stirrings for him. The rest liked him in a hang-his-poster-on-the-wall kind of way. Then, of those girls, only three would actually do something physical with him given the opportunity. Then, finally, of those three, two would be willing to do something only if he was the very clear and direct instigator. Only one of them—guess which—would be fucking crazy enough to do the instigating herself.

⊜

"How are your lectures?" Eugene asked me while he plugged in the electric kettle in the narrow kitchen of his houseboat on the Oxford Canal. It was a ninety-five-foot boat with living space, a small kitchen with a gas burner, one bedroom, and a bathroom equipped with toilet, sink, and shower. Not exactly spacious, but there was something quaint and full of character about it—I liked the rough green and red chipped paint along the walls and tables. I liked the gentle way it would list with the current or with our bodies, shifting back and forth like ballasts. Outside, a kingfisher watched the water from an overhanging branch of a willow, whose leaves reached toward the bank like outstretched fingers.

"Fine," I said.

"Learning anything interesting?" he asked, watching the water in the kettle begin to boil.

"Is that what school is for?" I asked.

"Wouldn't know, to be honest. Never went to university. I'm more of a free-thinking artist, myself. That's one of mine right there." He pointed to a painting hanging awkwardly beside the window. It was a landscape of the exact view outside, one image mocking the other in its inaccuracy. I couldn't decide if his braggadocio was endearing or a turnoff.

"Wow, that's great," I said in the manner of unimpressed audiences from time immemorial. But he wasn't the type to pick up on something like that.

"Thanks," he said as if he'd expected as much.

He produced two mugs from a green cabinet. One was black with a red rose in the center, the other had a picture of a cat giving the middle finger.

When the kettle finally came to a boil, he set the tea bags carefully into the mugs and poured the water. It steamed and spat slightly as it gushed into the mugs. He blew on each before handing me the one with the pissed-off cat.

We took the first few, cautious sips of tea. It scalded my tongue slightly, but I didn't mind.

"So what are we doing here, exactly?" Eugene asked. It was a vague question, but I knew what he meant. Knew it had been coming. Despite his carefree lifestyle, his confident exterior, Eugene was a sensitive soul.

"We're having tea on your houseboat," I said.

He smiled. He knew the game I was playing. "I mean what's going on with the two of us? We just fuck buddies or what?"

I set down my cup of tea, which was a little disappointing because I was enjoying it, but the angry cat was flipping me off with extra vehemence now. "Do you want to talk, or would you rather go back to your bedroom and have a shag before I leave?" I liked using British idioms like *shag* to the British; it set them on edge, like they were hearing adult words coming from a child's mouth.

He laughed, setting down his own mug. "Come on then." He led me to the bedroom, and I went willingly, all the while knowing that this—the fact that he didn't say, "No, I'd rather not have a shag just yet"—was the very reason our relationship would never last outside the bedroom.

When I left the houseboat, I walked along the canal as the day sank steadily into twilight. I lit a cigarette as I passed the rows of houseboats lined along the banks. I liked to smoke while walking. I'd convinced myself that the damage I was doing to my lungs was mitigated by the exercise. Someone was having a party on one of the boats. I saw a fire burning inside, people laughing, music thumping. It smelled like smoke and wet moss.

Once I cleared the row of houseboats, I saw a bird, wings outstretched, gliding over the water. At first, I thought it was heading directly toward me. I even stopped walking, grabbed for the pepper spray I kept in my purse. But the bird veered left over the canal, landing on the shore, just above the edge of the water. It was a heron. Instinctively I touched my neck where the necklace Dad had given me used to sit—the one that once belonged to Mom. I'd stopped wearing it because instead of reminding me of her, it just made me think of Dad, of what he'd done to me that night before he'd given it. I couldn't bring myself to get rid of it, though, not when it had been Mom's. Sometimes I pulled it out and looked at it, touched the slender golden neck of the bird without ever putting it around my own.

In front of me, the heron lifted its wings wide before settling them back against its body. Long and majestic, it looked like a thing out of mythology, elegant in the monochrome gray of the evening. I realized then that, because of the necklace, herons would always make me think of her. In a strange way, I'd forever see them as actually *being* her. I wasn't necessarily religious, but I was maybe what people would call spiritual. I would even admit as much if it didn't make me sound like I rubbed crystals for fertility and believed cancer could be cured by things like expensive bath salts. When I looked at that heron, I saw her, craning her neck in the car toward us, hand outstretched, feathers protruding from skeletal limbs like fingers. "Everything is going to be fine," the heron said. Then it took a single careful step into the water, watching me through beady eyes behind its long pointed beak.

I put out my cigarette as if I felt guilty to have been caught smoking it, then continued down the path, breathing in the cool night air through lungs free of smoke. I heard a splash a moment later and looked back over my shoulder. The heron was gone.

CHAPTER 9

There was a knock at my dorm room the next day. I'd been reading poetry. I found I really enjoyed it. Kay Ryan, Simon Armitage, Jill Alexander Essbaum, and classics like Blake, Whitman, Dickinson, and Sylvia Plath. I'd been reading a lot of Sylvia Plath.

> *If the moon smiled, she would resemble you.*
> *You leave the same impression*
> *Of something beautiful, but annihilating.*

I answered the door to find a dark-haired girl with a long, but pretty, face, wearing a red sweater that was attempting but failing to hide the outline of the most beautiful breasts I'd ever seen. She was smiling at me.

"Hi," I said.

"Hi, sorry to bug you. I'm Manda, I live down the hall on plain side." Her accent was posh English.

"Manda?" I asked. "Or Amanda?"

"Just Manda. Not my choice."

"I like it," I lied. "Jeanie," I said.

"Nice to meet you." She smiled. "I wanted to stop by and invite you to study group. We're both in Experimental Psychology, yeah?"

"Oh yeah," I said. I hadn't noticed her before.

"Anyway, just being friendly. It's a small group. We meet down the street at Paul's flat."

She said the name Paul as if I should recognize him.

"Oh, thanks. When is it?"

"Now actually. Sorry for the late notice. Kinda thought of it as I was passing."

"That's very nice of you." My first instinct was to reject her invitation. Studying with a group of strangers sounded terrible, but some primal urge within me pushed back. A hunt-in-groups Neanderthal impulse opened my mouth and I found myself agreeing to go.

"Brilliant," she said.

We walked out of the building and down the street as she told me about the group.

"Paul is super smart. He basically runs the show, but honestly, sometimes we don't even study, just have a drink and chat, you know? It's pretty fun, super low-key."

"Sounds good," I said. If Manda noticed my lack of enthusiasm, she didn't say anything.

"Trevor is kind of an asshole, but he's the kind of asshole who mostly does it for show, you know. He's actually not so bad once you get to know him. And do you know Kerry? She's on Longwall Street."

I didn't know Kerry. Or Trevor, or Paul. I was immediately regretting this outing. I almost made up an excuse and pissed off to the pub or the canal to see if Eugene was around. But before I worked up the courage to ditch her, Manda said,

"Here we are," and stopped in front of an old Georgian building. She rang the buzzer to number 42.

A scratchy voice sounded from the honeycomb metal box. "Hello?"

"Hey, it's Manda."

"Hey, Manda, it's Trevor. How've ya been?" the voice said.

Manda rolled her eyes, but there was a smile on her face. "Let us in, Trevor."

"Us?"

"Brought a friend."

"Is she pretty?" Trevor asked. Voices sounded from behind him.

Manda looked at me, embarrassed. "Come on, Trevor."

"She can't come unless she's pretty."

There was a fumbling sound from the speaker before the door clicked and Manda opened it to let us into the building. We stepped into a long hallway that ended in stairs covered in old carpet. We made our way up the winding, cramped stairway.

"I should have said yes, sorry," Manda said on the second flight of stairs.

"Yes to what?" I asked.

"To Trevor. I should have told him you were pretty," she said.

I shook my head. "You should have told him to fuck off."

Manda laughed—a giddy-sounding thing, a mix of shock and relief.

When we reached the flat, a tall guy with a long face and glasses opened the door for us. He wasn't attractive, but he had a sort of Oxford sophisticated look to him that was appealing. Large glasses, maroon sweater, unkempt hair. "Sorry about Trevor," he said. "I dunno why we keep letting him come."

"'Cause you'd be bored to tears without me, sure," came a voice from the kitchen.

"Paul," the tall guy said, holding out a hand. I shook it.

"Jeanie," I said.

"Welcome. Tea?" he asked.

"Sure," I said. I was still getting used to being immediately offered tea at any social gathering.

Trevor, unfortunately, was very attractive—the assholes often were. He had brownish-reddish hair and green eyes that looked otherworldly and mysterious. He smiled often, but it was a mischievous smile, like he knew something about you but wasn't going to tell.

Kerry was a Black girl with beautiful eyes and thick dark hair.

"You should have said yes," Trevor said in an Irish accent I hadn't detected over the intercom. He was speaking to Manda while smiling at me. "She's only gorgeous."

"Are we gonna actually study today?" Kerry asked.

"We probably should so Jeanie doesn't think we're a bunch of eejits," Trevor said.

"We already think you're an *eejit*," Kerry said, emphasizing his pronunciation.

"And you're right about that, aren't ya?" Trevor said, smiling. He was the type of guy who was incapable of being insulted. Whether he defended himself or adopted your criticism as his own, his confidence was infallible.

When the tea was poured and we were all sitting down, Paul made a joke about one of the psychology professors and his combover.

"It's the most impressive thing I've ever seen," Paul said.

"I want to take it home," Trevor said. "Put it in a terrarium and raise it as my own."

Everyone laughed; Kerry rolled her eyes. And it went on like this for a while. Small jokes, laughter, banter—a familiar social protocol firmly established within the comfort of this small group. They asked me a few questions and I gave them short answers.

"Where you from originally, Jeanie?" Paul asked.

"Washington."

"Is it nice there?"

"It's by the ocean."

"Love the accent," Trevor added.

"You sound like a leprechaun," I said, and they all laughed, especially Trevor.

Eventually we got down to the studying. Everyone talked about their different assignments. Given that I hadn't been meeting with my tutor, I didn't have much to add.

They spent a few minutes debating which psychologist was the most influential to experimental psychology. I sat in silence, listening to the conversation like it had nothing to do with me.

"Wilhelm Wundt is considered the founder," Kerry was saying.

"Yes, but Titchener's work dramatically expounded Wundt's original ideas," Paul said calmly.

"I like B. F. Skinner," Trevor said.

"You just like to say his name," Kerry said.

"I bet the *B. F.* stands for bullfrog. Or bumfuck."

Manda stifled a laugh as Kerry rolled her eyes again. "My God," she said.

This went back and forth for some time before Manda turned to me and asked, "What do you think, Jeanie?"

They all went quiet at that, polite to the new girl.

I shook my head. I didn't want to choose a side. "I don't really care either way," I said without realizing how my lack of interest might come across. I was the new girl. I was supposed to show some sort of enthusiasm in order to garner acceptance into the group. My comment didn't just reject the discussion, it inadvertently rejected them, rejected this get-together. I looked away from their stares toward the door, wondering if I could just walk out. No one would stop me. They'd probably be relieved.

"I'm with her," Trevor said. "Doesn't really matter, does it? Who's the most important. What matters is the work itself."

"Of course," Paul said, looking at me.

The conversation was amenable after that and, by the end of the meeting, we were all laughing at Trevor's impression of one of their shared tutors.

I was taking my mug to the sink when Paul approached me. "Hey, thanks for coming," he said.

"Yeah, thanks for having me."

"It's a weird group, but it can be pretty fun. We don't study every time. Sometimes we just hang out, have a chat."

"Manda told me," I said.

"Ah, good." He lifted a hand to the back of his head and rubbed. *Oh shit,* I thought. *He's hitting on me.*

"If you want, I could—"

"So same time next week, or what?"

"Yeah," he said. "Yeah."

"Well, I'll see ya then." I made my way around him, met Manda at the door, and we walked back together. The air felt fresh outside; there was a sweetness to it that had been lacking in the old building, in that small room filled with people.

"Kerry's in love with Trevor," Manda said.

"Really?" I said. "Looked like she wanted to rip his head off."

Manda laughed. "That's love. He wants her, too, but until he grows up a little, it'll never work out. Sometimes people are too different, you know?"

And I did. I knew exactly. Knew that I wasn't meant for people like Paul in the same way Maddox had deserved someone better. It was why, in the end, when Manda came to my door the following week, I told her I was busy, had too much work to do. She nodded, wished me good luck, and left by herself—happy to be rid of me, I'm sure. The truth was, I was like a cancer. My attitude toward my studies, my relationships, toward anything serious, was a black hole, sucking everyone down with me. I would have ruined all of them, and I think they knew it, too, deep down.

While Manda and I continued to be periphery friends, I never went back to the group again. I did, however, sometimes picture myself, a different version of me, who *would* have gone back, who would have studied, who would have laughed at their jokes and contributed to the conversation. I thought about a different version of Jeanie King who dated guys like Paul, discussed Titchener's contributions to psychology, and thrived in the world of the living.

❧

I was smoking at the edge of Eugene's bed. It was the last night I'd let myself sleep with him before moving on. I was set on becoming a passing figure in other people's lives. I wasn't a long-term friend, girlfriend, sister, daughter—I was transient. The window was open to siphon out the smoke. Something was stirring in the bushes across the waters of the dark canal. Eugene had told me he saw an otter once—maybe that's what it was. Beside me, Eugene was snoring softly, blankets pulled over his shoulders to protect him from the cold air.

"Do you believe in God?" Eugene had asked before falling asleep. If he didn't pass out immediately after sex, he tended to get existential.

"I don't think so," I told him. "Do you?"

"Yeah, of course," he said. "What do you think happens when you die?"

"I don't know," I said. "Nothing, I guess." A vast and

endless nothingness. I wasn't entirely sure I really believed that. I didn't think I'd sprout wings and a harp and float into the clouds, either, but everything I felt, all that emotion, the good and the bad, couldn't just cease to exist. I felt too much—my feelings were too tangible to not be eternal. But where did they go? I had no idea. *Dear Mom, where are you?*

"Maybe everything just keeps on happening," I said.

"What do you mean?" His voice had gone sleepy.

"Well, we're all just a collection of atoms, stardust, really," I said, thinking of Maddox. "A random pattern formed into bodies. So, given the space of infinity, it stands to reason that this pattern will form again. You and I will be here together, again and again."

"That doesn't sound so bad." He stretched out a warm palm over my cold thigh. "But where's God in this equation?"

"God is the vastness of infinity," I said, proud of my own cleverness.

"The Bible says God is love," he said.

"What could be more loving than all the time in the world?"

There was a pause in the conversation, his breathing slowing. "Do you really believe all that?" he asked, eyes closed.

"I'd like to," I said, surprising myself because I meant it.

"So do it" was all he said. And to him it was as simple as that. You want to think something, you do it. The mechanism of the mind was a push button. Believe in an eternal soul? Sure, why not?

Years later, a couple Jehovah's Witnesses would come by my house, and I'd invite them in for tea. They seemed surprised by this, but I couldn't help myself. They were just so interesting in their little suits with their Bibles and their pamphlets held in front of them like Girl Scout cookies. I let them tell me all about God and his gift of salvation, and, in the end, I held their hands and accepted the Lord Jesus Christ into my heart. As they left, their elysian faces were bright and hopeful. I'd given them each jewels in their heavenly crowns. It was almost as good as sex. In fact, I liked it so much, I day-dreamed about traveling around the country, going from one Kingdom Hall to the next, asking if there were any Witnesses who'd like to lead my everlasting soul to eternity. I'd let them save me again, again, and again.

After Eugene fell asleep that night, I finished my ciga-rette and dressed quietly. The old wood of the boat groaned beneath my shifting weight, every step sent it teetering one way, then the next. I made my way outside. The air felt cool in my smoke-heated lungs. Something stirred in the bushes—maybe the animal I'd heard earlier—as I walked down the small path past the line of other boats. I looked, hoping to see an otter, or, even better, the heron. But there was only stillness, moonlight splitting across the water like strands of tinsel. The sound of the water in the canal was soft, nothing like the ocean, and yet, walking along those banks, I couldn't help but think of the Pacific, the sand beneath my feet, the seagulls overhead, and all the people in my life walking beside me like ghosts.

I thought of Jamie, of seeing him again by the ocean, when our exact collection of atoms formed once more, a trillion years from now.

CHAPTER 10

On the next Tuesday evening at seven o'clock, I found myself standing outside William's office. I hadn't been going to the Wednesday meetings, and I wasn't entirely sure why. The idea of sitting with him and two other students discussing our papers, our degree, our plans for the future made me want to jump off a cliff. And yet, something drew me here, something about the look he'd given me at the pub. The way I'd clearly intrigued him. How vulnerable and powerful I'd felt at the same time. I wanted to feel that again.

I was about to knock on his door, or maybe I was about to chicken out. I was like Schrödinger's living-dead cat. My fist raised in the air: my living-dead knock. I never got to find out, either, because the door snapped open and there he was, blazer and glasses and tousled graying hair with a computer bag slung over his shoulder. He nearly bumped into my upraised hand, stopping just in time.

"Jeanie, hi. Are you all right?"

I moved my raised hand to my hair. In my stomach, I

felt something scurrying, something with millions of tiny feet. "I . . . you said I was supposed to meet with my tutor."

"Right," he said. "That's tomorrow."

"Yeah, but since I missed the other meetings, I thought you could catch me up. Sorry, though, you're just leaving, aren't you."

"No," he said, staring at me, unsure, off-balance. "Come on in then." He stood to one side and I slipped past him into his office.

"You sure?" I asked.

"Of course."

The office was small and smelled of old wood and books. There was a window overlooking the quadrangle and a fireplace, unlit, in the corner of the room. A mahogany desk stood on one side of the room and a large bookshelf was on the other, full of thick texts with a stack of magazines perched on top. Beside the window were two matching leather chairs. Other than that, the room was relatively plain. No decorative adornments, no clacking stack of metal balls on his desk, no swinging pendulums, no fancy mouse pad. A framed photograph of a castle by the ocean sat above the bookshelf, and that was it.

"It's Bamburgh," he said, following my gaze to the castle. "Beautiful place."

"Did you take the picture?"

"Uh, no. My wife did." The word *wife* shaved off the edges of the room, making the place feel oblong, obscure.

"It's a great photo," I said.

"Thank you, Jeanie. Why don't you have a seat over there." He motioned toward the leather chairs by the window. I stepped slowly and sat cautiously, afraid the leather would groan beneath me, and the sound would be enough to send me bolting from the office. Thankfully, it was silent.

He sat down in the adjacent chair, staring at me like I was supposed to make the next move.

"So is this where you tell me what I'm supposed to be doing with my life?"

He smiled. "Not at all."

"Are you going to give me a lecture?"

"I can, if you'd like." He was joking. It sounded strange coming from him. "But before we get into anything academic, why don't we talk?" he said. "As a sort of primer."

"Okay," I said, a strange bubble of excitement popping in my chest. This felt oddly inappropriate.

"Would you like some tea? Sherry maybe?"

"Sherry?" I asked.

"Yes, it's not abnormal, if that's what you're worried about. It's quite appropriate to share a glass if you'd like."

"I'm fine," I said. I'd just come from the pub, in fact. I'd had a few pints and was worried that my head was already too unclear.

He shifted in his chair. "Why don't you tell me about yourself."

"What would you like to know?" I asked.

"Anything. What your interests are, your favorite novels, your hobbies, what have you."

"I don't have any hobbies."

"I'm sure that's not true. Anything can be a hobby."

"What are your hobbies?" I asked.

He ran a single finger across a small crease in his forehead. I leaned back against the chair, sinking into the leather. "I play tennis," he said, sitting up straight as if proud of the fact. I couldn't, for the life of me, imagine him playing tennis.

"I doubt that," I said.

"Excuse me?"

"I bet you've never held a racket in your life."

He actually laughed at that, shaking his head as he did. He looked at me then, a salivating sort of expression. I could tell he wanted to bottle me up and collect me, to own me, to possess me. I liked that look. I liked the feeling it gave me. I wanted to be collected.

"Maybe," he said after a while, "you'd like to tell me your whole story, like you did in your application. From the beginning."

"But you already know it," I said.

"I'd still like to hear you tell it."

"It's a long story," I said.

He leaned back in his chair, folding his arms over his stomach. "Tell me," he commanded.

⊛

I continued to meet with William in his office on Tuesday evenings. He never mentioned anything about my studies. I just told him about my life and he listened, a rapt and attentive audience, asking questions off and on.

"You're doing really well," he told me one evening. I wasn't sure what he'd meant, what I was *doing well* at, or what, exactly, he was expecting of me. He put a hand on my shoulder as I stood by the open doorway. It rested there, heavy and warm, his pointer finger nearly touching my neck. I looked into his eyes, saw uncertainty there. He removed his hand and I left.

⊛

"What do you want out of your life?" he asked me once.

What do I want? Everything, I thought. I am full of want. Brimming with it, from the bottoms of my toes to the top of my skull. My want is intransitive, voracious. It'll eat the world. Human beings shouldn't be capable of such terrible want. But I am. I pine. I lust. I desire. I hope. I want! *Perhaps when we find ourselves wanting everything,* Sylvia Plath said, *it is because we are dangerously near to wanting nothing.*

"I just want a drink," I told him, and he smiled.

❦

"What makes you happy?" he asked me.

All the things they tell you not to do. Drinking, smoking, sex. I wasn't ready to say any of that.

"I like riding trains," I said.

"You mean you like to travel?"

"No. Just the ride. Just being on trains."

"And why is that, do you think?"

I looked out the window, imagined the world zipping by in an array of color. "I really don't know."

❦

"Let's do something different today," he said. He stood from his chair and stepped toward the door as if to prevent anyone from entering.

"Do you remember the exercise we did in class a few weeks ago?" he asked.

"Which one?" I knew which one.

"The empty chair exercise."

"Oh. Yeah."

"I want you to imagine your father is in that chair."

"Do I have to?" I asked.

"You don't have to do anything you don't want to. But I'd like you to."

I couldn't say no to him. The gray around his ears was slightly windblown today; his hair looked like silver wings outstretched on either side of his head. "Okay," I said.

"Whenever you're ready." He leaned back against the doorway. He wasn't wearing a blazer today. He was more casual in a blue sweater that had a gray collar protruding from it, framing his well-tanned neck. He had a great Adam's apple, something I didn't know could be appealing, but it was, in its size—not too large nor too tiny—and in its perfect V shape.

I turned to the chair. It was the emptiest thing I'd ever seen in my entire life. I stared at it for a long time, picturing Dad sitting on his Adirondack chair, sharpening his knife. Dad sitting on a stone behind me while I took aim at a milk jug. Dad sitting by the fire drinking whisky.

I couldn't for the life of me picture him in that room, in Oxford, with William watching from the sidelines.

"I don't know what to say," I said, looking at William. He nodded at me encouragingly but remained frustratingly silent. The room was empty of sound. No clock ticking on the wall. No cars rolling along the street. Time had stopped. I felt disoriented. I felt my limbs elongating, my body pulling apart. I was beginning to panic. My arms gripped my chair and my stomach sank to the floor. I was breathing too fast. Or maybe not. Maybe I wasn't breathing enough. Maybe I wasn't breathing at all. My head felt light. It was lifting toward the ceiling. I was being pulled apart at the seams.

"Just say the first thing that comes to mind," William said. "It can be anything."

His words pulled my limbs back into themselves. The room still felt disjointed, as if something had changed, as if some small vital thing was different, like I'd been transported through the multiverse and landed in a world that was exactly the same except for one indecipherable thing about his office.

"Where the hell are you?" I said to the empty chair.

Another bout of silence. I kept my limbs where they were this time.

"Don't imagine he's somewhere else," William said. "He's right there. In front of you. What would you say?"

I broke eye contact with the chair. Stared hard at William. Something had come over me. Electric fingers danced along my veins.

"Can you sit in the chair?" I asked. "I don't like it being empty."

He gave me a look like he normally would have said no, like he knew he shouldn't. I like to think that he knew what was happening even then. That was the moment he should have stopped it. He should have backed away. Told me to continue with the exercise. But he didn't. He walked silently across the room and sank slowly into his chair, facing me.

I looked at him, saw the rare uncertainty in his eyes.

Then I rose from my chair and stepped toward him. He should have said something then as well, but he didn't.

"Are you my therapist now?" I asked him bluntly.

"I'm not a therapist," he said. He sounded almost breathless.

I felt my legs, as if moving on their own, lift and straddle the chair, felt him beneath me. He took in a quick breath, caught himself.

"So what do I call you in here?" I asked as I grabbed his wrists and placed his palms around the base of my back.

"What do you mean?" He was staring at my eyes intently, as if scared to look away. I liked the thought. I liked the idea that I was making him scared.

"In class you're Professor, in the pub you're William. What are you now?"

He smiled. "Perhaps it's best you call me Dr. Gardner in here."

"Dr. Gardner," I repeated. There was something comically pornographic about it.

I lifted my hands and put them on either side of his face,

framing it. We sat like that, breathing for a long time, his eyes drilling into mine like two burrowing screws. The room around us departed for other universes, and it was just him and me, approaching a black hole, the event horizon. I felt dizzy, my hands still on his face, his on my back, our chests rising and falling in unison. Bodies intertwined.

Then, as if an alarm had gone off, both of us began to move.

PART III
New York

CHAPTER 1

NOW

Planes are not the same as trains. There's something less romantic about them. Something hospital-like that sets me on edge. When you're on a train, there's a sense of movement, of places and time passing. But a plane feels outside of time, as if the distance from the ground somehow renders you timeless. You're floating above the world like God herself looking down. It's all discomforting to me. I like the idea of time passing. Perhaps it's why I have so many clocks in my house. Their ticking comforts me.

I do, however, like looking out the window, watching the hills flash with sunlight, the vast plains stretch open and empty. The clouds are so solid seeming, hovering as if held aloft by some magic. It's this one thing, the view, that makes flying a conundrum for me. Otherwise, it would be an easy, blanket hatred.

The flight attendant, a red-headed woman with bright lipstick and a square face, asks if I'd care for a snack or something to drink.

Whisky, I want to say. But it's not even ten in the morning.

"I'll have a Coke," I say. I don't normally drink sugary drinks, but for some reason I make an exception when flying. Like somehow, this high up, it doesn't really count. The effervescent liquid, its intoxicating sugar rush, fits right into the experience for me. I both enjoy it and completely dislike it at once.

Especially this time. Especially considering where I'm heading.

"Let me guess, big business trip?" the older man sitting next to me asks. He's got a grandfatherly smile. I can't decide whether it's a little bit creepy or kind.

"Uh, no," I say. "Why?" I don't really want to talk, but I have to admit to being a little curious. What assessment has this man made of me?

"Your knee hasn't stopped tapping since you sat down. Figured you didn't like flying, or were on a business trip, perhaps a stressful one." He leans back in his seat.

I press my hands against my knee as if my leg has a mind of its own and I can control it only by force.

"You don't seem like you're scared of flying," he says.

"I'm not," I say. "Just connecting with someone I haven't seen in a while."

"I see. Sounds important."

"Not really." I like to downplay things. Dr. Gardner tells me this all the time.

"You know," the man says, "I was a doctor for thirty years."

"Wow," I say trying to give him genuine enthusiasm without encouraging him to tell me his life story. I don't want to be mean, but I also don't want to talk. My knee starts bouncing again and I pinch myself.

"Yup, I'm the guy that if someone has a heart attack on

the plane and the flight attendant says, 'Is there a doctor on board?' well then I gotta raise my hand and do my duty." He half raises his hand to help me picture the scene.

"I see."

"I know you're not having a heart attack, mind you, but they do have medications to help you deal with that." He points to my knee; we both see my hand gripping it and I let go.

"To help me with a bouncing leg?" I ask.

"Anxiety," he says. "It's the most common mental illness in the world."

"I don't have a mental illness," I say.

"I'm not saying you do. Just saying if you needed help with it, medication can be your friend." He winks at me and I decide he is the kindly grandpa type. "Didn't mean to pry," he says.

I look out the window and thankfully he takes the hint and lays his head back onto the headrest. He's asleep in seconds. I've always marveled at how people can sleep on planes. With the noise and the motion and the uncomfortable seats. We're being jettisoned over the world in a metal box, and this old man is snoring like a newborn. Beneath us, waves spike and shimmer.

▣

Maddox is waiting for me at JFK.

"You didn't have to wait," I tell him, though I can't deny I'm happy to see him. I've got my small carry-on bag slung around my shoulder. It's a half-empty blue duffel; I packed light.

"I didn't mind," he says, smiling an annoyingly sneaky smile, like he knew I was going to come all along, like he never doubted it for a second.

"What if I didn't come? It was a near thing."

"I had my book," he says, holding up a paperback with a vague black cover and large white lettering.

"Anything good?"

"Space opera, you wouldn't like it." He laughs at himself.

"How do you know that?" I ask.

"You always made fun of me for this stuff."

"Maybe I've changed."

"Yeah, and maybe I haven't."

We share a cab to Midtown and both of us are fairly quiet. It's the presence of the cab driver, and the being together again under the strangest circumstances possible. I stare at his hand, resting lightly over his right knee. All of it is too much. I look away. Slowly, the monolithic skyscrapers fill the windows. Towers are looming, leaning over our cab as if any second they might tumble down on top of us. Cars crowd the streets, honking like angry geese. On the sidewalk, groups of people move by in shoals. A woman pushing a grocery cart flips me off for some reason. I'm so horribly uncomfortable my knee starts tapping again and I let it.

We get out on Seventh Avenue and I take in the miasma of smells: concrete, drying piss, roasted peanuts, burning hot dogs, and sweet garbage. Somehow, the overall effect isn't entirely unpleasant. A light rain is falling on the cars, which are still honking and braking and jutting along as if dancing to some mechanical street rhythm.

Maddox's apartment is in a large art-deco building just a couple blocks from Central Park. It overlooks a street lined with parked cars, restaurants, metal scaffolding. Inside, there's a small kitchen with cream-colored cupboards and laminate countertops. Under the counter are three barstools. Beyond that is the living area, with a large brown couch and a TV that sits on top of a wide dresser beside a sliding screen door that leads to a modest balcony. The bedroom is to the left. The door is half open.

"It's nice," I say.

"It's small," Maddox says. "But you'd be surprised; everything costs so much in this city."

"Oxford isn't exactly cheap, either," I say. The only reason I can afford my terraced house is because of my inheritance from Mom. I wonder if Maddox knows about all that. I wonder how much he's dug into my life.

"So when do we leave for Stumpsville or whatever it was?" I ask, sitting down on his couch. The cushion sinks beneath me, the fabric soft and worn.

"Downsville. And we can leave in the morning. A friend of mine is coming to town and letting us borrow her car while she stays at my place."

"That's kind of her," I say.

He shrugs. "She likes coming into the city."

I'm full of questions. *What's her name? How did you meet her? Did you date? Are you dating now?* I don't ask any of them. They're stupid. "Is it a long drive?" I ask instead.

"Couple hours."

Maddox is standing in the kitchen like he's waiting for something. "How're you feeling about it?" he asks.

"About the trip?" I don't know why I make him spell it out. I know what he's asking.

"About seeing your dad again," he says.

"I don't know. I kind of doubt he's actually there."

He nods. "Right. So why did you get on that plane then?"

I ignore the question. "So am I . . ." I start. "I mean, should I get a hotel or—"

"Oh no, you can stay here," he says. "I mean, if you want. Saves you money."

"Sure," I say like it's the most casual thing in the world.

"You can have my bedroom. I'll sleep on the couch," he says.

"No," I say. "It's fine. I'm not gonna kick you out of your own room."

"No, really," he says. "I've slept on the couch before. I don't mind. Besides, it's really uncomfortable. You wouldn't be able to sleep."

"Then neither would you," I say, putting an elbow on the armrest as if to claim it.

"I'm used to it. Trust me."

I shake my head. "I can't. It feels wrong."

"Let's just leave this decision for later then, huh?" Maddox says. "Can I get you anything? Coffee? Tea?"

"Tea," I say quickly.

"You know, I'm not even sure I have tea." He checks his cupboards and comes out with a ginger-pear white tea. Americans don't know how to drink tea. "This okay?" he asks.

"Yeah, it's great, thanks."

He asks me if I want to take a shower, but I don't; I'm not comfortable enough with his place, with this situation to take one yet. Strange, how I can be naked in front of a stranger after a single drink, but with someone like Maddox, a wall, a locked door, and a closed shower curtain are still not enough.

"Do you mind if I do?" he asks. "I always feel sticky after flying. I think I might be a germaphobe."

"No, go ahead," I say.

"I'll be quick, just make yourself at home."

I sit on the couch by the window, sipping my tea and looking out at the street. A man jogs by, a young Asian family pushes their baby in a pram—stroller, here—and an older woman with white hair walks an equally white and fluffy dog. I sip my tea, my nerves just now beginning to settle. The tea is hot but not scalding and surprisingly delicious. I close my eyes. Take another sip.

That evening, Maddox takes me to a rooftop bar that over-looks the city. It's cold outside, but hovering over the wooden tables and chairs are large metal propane heaters, standing sentinel like robots out of one of Maddox's science fiction novels. Lights are strung around the eaves of the building and over the railings, beneath which sit plastic potted plants, exuberantly green. Beyond the railing, the city glitters like rising, sparkling stalagmites in an endless and immense cave. We've got a seat by the railing, and I'm looking out across the impossible assortment of concrete and glass and light.

"You never really get used to it," Maddox says.

"The view?"

"Yeah. It sort of becomes less beautiful over time, but you don't really get used to it. It's always impressive."

"I could never live here," I say. I don't mean it to sound so negative. Maddox just smiles.

"I thought the same when I got here. Too many people. But there are places to find solitude, and the ocean is basically next door."

It's my turn to smile. "I miss the ocean."

"Me too," Maddox says. "I mean Washington. You know. The beach." Walking with Jamie and me, he means. Or maybe just me. Seagulls. Starfish. Sand dollars. Geoducks.

We order our drinks. Maddox gets a beer, but I need something stronger. I order a whisky. Lagavulin 16, one of my favorites. It's not cheap, but I plan to pay my own way.

"But you like Oxford?" Maddox asks.

"Yeah, I do. For a city, it's strangely quiet. It suits me."

"It does suit you," he says as if just realizing.

I don't push him on what he means by that. I don't really want to be analyzed. "To be honest," I say, "New York doesn't really suit you."

He laughs. I forgot how easy he laughed.

"I mean, I guess I always pictured you someplace with forests, climbing trees with your kids," I say.

"Oh, I've got kids now?"

"Yup. You're the type of guy to settle down."

"And you aren't?"

I shake my head. Our drinks arrive. "No," I say after taking my first delicious, smoky sip. "I'm not."

"And how many kids do I have?"

"Oh, at least half a dozen," I say.

He laughs again, a full-belly sound.

"I must be Mormon."

"You aren't," I say, smiling now. "She is."

"Wow. You seem to know a lot about my life." He picks up his beer.

"I've always been able to read you like a book," I say. Suddenly I have the urge to reach my leg over and touch him under the table. Or maybe my hand. I could do it, too. That's the weirdest thing about it. Maddox has been so distant for so long and now here he is. Just there. An arm's reach away.

"I always pictured you as a hired killer," he says.

I laugh out loud, nearly spilling my precious Lagavulin as I do.

"Oh yeah?" I ask.

"Yeah, but you'd only take on specific contracts, like the really bad dudes."

"Really?"

"Yeah," he says. His smile is wide and perfect. "You could totally cut a bitch."

"Oh, totally."

"Funny the lives we've chosen for ourselves. Me with my army of kids and you out there keeping the streets clean with your poison darts."

"I wouldn't use poison darts," I say.

"No?"

"No. Too easy to miss with a poison dart."

"What would you use?"

"I'd use a Nighthawk pistol with a silencer. Two shots to the head. Double tap."

"Jeez," he says. He's impressed and maybe a little shocked. "You've clearly thought this through."

"Who says I didn't actually come here because I've been hired to kill you?"

"It all makes sense now," he says, taking his first sip of the beer he's been holding.

Eventually we order another round of drinks and food. This time Maddox gets a Lagavulin like me.

"Whoooo!" he says after his first sip. "So smooth." His voice is rough, and I laugh.

"You get used to it," I say.

"How?"

"Drink paint thinner on the weekends."

After, we make our way back to his apartment, and I begin to feel my insides churning with something. It's not the alcohol. My stomach and liver are tried-and-true warriors at this point. No, it's the night closing in on me. Maddox's apartment looming in the distance. The small space. His presence is like the past coming back to haunt me. And there's the thought of my dad in the morning. I feel that feeling again. Like my body doesn't belong to me. I haven't felt this way in a long time. I've kept it at bay by running or smoking or drinking or fucking. I haven't had enough to drink, that's the problem. By the time we reach Maddox's apartment, my limbs feel like they're elongating, my head floating. I'm walking through fluid. It's like being in a nightmare.

"So," Maddox says, throwing his keys on the counter, "do you want to—"

"Actually, I'd like to go for a run if that's okay." I'm holding on to his counter like a maniac. My palms are sweaty.

"You okay, Jeanie?"

"Yeah, I'm fine. No problem. Just need to blow off some steam."

"Okay, sure, I'll go with you, let me just—"

"No," I say, straightening. Already the idea of going for a run is bringing my body back into itself. "I'm fine. I just, you know, tomorrow is kind of messing with me."

"Totally, I get it."

"Central Park is close, right?"

"Jeanie, I don't think you want to run in Central Park alone at night."

"I'll be fine." Anything out there feels less dangerous than everything in here. "Mind if I use your bathroom to change?" I ask.

"Of course."

When I'm dressed in my trainers and yoga pants, Maddox gives me directions to the park, practically begging me to let him come. "It's huge, you could get lost so easily."

"Please," I say firmly. "I won't be long." Reluctantly he agrees, and I make my way to the base of the building and out into the cool night air. I start running immediately.

⊞

I know I'm not in a good state of mind. I know I drink too much. My therapy is probably more damaging than it is healing. I don't feel normal; I feel askew, like everyone else is walking straight and I'm walking just slightly sideways.

There's a species of ant in the Amazon that is vexed by a particular form of fungus that infects their minds. Once infected, the ants don't do their jobs right, they wander aimlessly up branches until the fungus bursts through their heads and releases its spores into the canopy of the forest. When the colony sees an ant with these symptoms, the other ants will carry their infected comrade outside the colony and deposit it to die. That's how I feel. Like any minute, someone— Maddox—is going to take a good look at me and see the multicolored spores swirling in my eyes like fireflies.

The park is quiet at night. Quieter at least. There are a few couples walking under the streetlamps. I can hear ducks slicing the bladed tips of their wings against a body of water aptly named the Lake. I gain confidence when I see the wide walkways, the pewter glow of the streetlamps and the familiar foliage. I run a little faster. I pass a wide-open stretch of grass with a baseball field. I keep running, my lungs working hard, my head slowly clearing. My heart beats faster, but the run has a calming effect on my body. I start to feel like myself again.

I take a few turns, confident I can find my way back. After about twenty minutes, I find myself on a narrower path with denser trees and no streetlamps. I look around, wondering how far I've come, if I should turn back. I decide I better. I'm not worried yet, though. I turn around and start running back the way I came. I run for another ten minutes or so before I realize there's a man about thirty yards behind me, out for a run himself. He's tall and has a hood over his head, obscuring his face. I tell myself it's perfectly natural, just another man out for a jog. I keep running, keep my pace. When I turn around again, he's still thirty yards away. We're running at the same speed. It's not odd. It's happened to me before. You randomly run into someone who's doing the same route, the same speed as you. Only, all those other times were during the day, down paths I knew by heart. I pick up speed. I'm in pretty good shape, but I'm pushing myself now. I count to sixty twice then turn around and look again. Same man. Same distance. I go even faster, almost sprinting. When I look over my shoulder, I see that he's sprinting as well. Not gaining or losing ground. Now I *am* beginning to panic. At what point do I scream for help? Call the police? Would anyone hear me? How soon could the cops even get there? Where would I tell them to go? I'm running as fast as I can now, my feet slapping the ground the only sound I can hear against the stillness of the park. I scan the path ahead for any sign of people. There's no one. I feel like crying. After everything, I'm going to get raped and murdered in Central Park. How long until Maddox comes looking for me? When will he call the police? Where will they find my body?

I stop suddenly and turn around. The man stops, too, keeping his distance. What the fuck is happening?

"Leave me alone!" I scream at him. Someone must've heard that. I turn and run again. When I look over my shoulder, he's running once more. It's a nightmare, I think. I have to wake up. My legs feel numb as I push them against the ground, faster and faster. I can see the streetlights again. There's pavement beneath my feet instead of loose rocks and dirt. I'm running faster. He's still behind me. I can hear him now. His footsteps are echoing mine in perfect rhythm—now he's speeding up. Is he catching me? I can practically feel his hands reaching out for my neck. I want to scream, but I can't.

I see a traffic light ahead and race for it. A man in a long jacket and gloves is standing by the light and I don't care that he's another stranger, I race toward him, anything to be away from the runner.

"Help!" I yell at the man. He's Black with a silver beard and wide eyes.

"Hey now," he says.

I practically tumble into him.

"You all right, honey?"

I could cry at the sound of his kind voice. I place my hands on my knees and turn around, see the stretch of streetlights along the path. There's no one there.

"Yeah," I say. "I'm okay. Jesus."

"You sure?" he asks. "Need me to call someone?"

"No, I thought . . ." My breath is quick, my heart trying to fling itself from my body. "I thought someone was chasing me. I'm sorry. It's okay."

I ask him for directions to Maddox's street and he gives them, even offering to walk me there. Who says New Yorkers aren't kind. I tell him no, and he graciously leaves me alone.

I've recovered my breath by the time I reach Maddox's door, though my limbs are still shaking. I look at my phone and see I've gotten two texts from Maddox, just checking in. It's twelve thirty. I use the key he gave me and slip inside. The lights are out. I make my way around the kitchen before I realize that Maddox is lying on the couch, which he's pulled out to make it into a bed. He's under a large blanket. He has a Kindle in his hands and glasses on his face. Since when does he wear glasses? Even after everything, seeing him in those glasses does something to my insides, something that doesn't quite make sense, given what just happened. Already I'm wondering if the whole thing was a hallucination. Did I really see the man? Should I tell Maddox? No. No need to alarm him. No need to prove him right.

"You're in my bed," I say.

He gives a tired laugh and sits up. "How was the run?"

"Exhilarating," I say. "I need to shower."

"Be my guest," he says, pointing to the bathroom beside the kitchen.

I take a long shower, washing the sweat and fear from my body. The bathroom is small and fills with steam; I breathe it in as if it might get me high.

When I emerge, my skin is soft and pink, my hair still mostly wet. I'm wearing a T-shirt and sweatpants. I've kept my bra on because I'm assuming Maddox is still awake. And I'm right. He's looking at me over his glasses, Kindle still in his hands.

"You off to bed?" he asks. "Big day tomorrow." He winces as he says the last part. He knows that I'm stressed, but he doesn't know the half of it.

"You're in my bed." I don't know why I'm pushing it again. Maddox is just being nice. He's giving up his bed for me. And why not? He dragged me all the way here, didn't he? No, he didn't. He found my dad for me; he's doing what he thinks I want. He's doing too much. That's what it is. I need to win this.

"I'm sleeping there," I say.

"Come on, Jeanie, my bed is comfortable. Besides, I'm already settled in. Go take it and enjoy."

"I'm sleeping there," I repeat.

His eyes narrow. "I'm not moving," he says.

"Fine," I say. I lift the blanket and slide into the bed. "Scoot over."

"What are you doing?" he asks.

"Going to bed," I say. I pull the blanket over my legs, still sitting up. I reach around my back and unsnap my bra. I can feel him watching me as I pull the unsexy cream-colored undergarment out the sleeve of my T-shirt and toss it at the foot of the bed.

"Good night," I say, then lay back on my side of the bed, no pillow or anything. I can feel Maddox's weight beside me, his breathing, the slight rustle of his legs against the blanket. I wonder, for a brief moment, if he might put his arm around me. I wonder what I'd do if he does.

Instead, he laughs. I don't move when I feel his weight lift from the bed. I see his outline standing in front of his bedroom door.

"Good night, Jeanie King," he says. The pillow smacks me in the face. I sit up sharply to throw it back at him, but his door has already closed.

I smile and set the pillow behind my head. I lay back. It seems impossible that just half an hour ago I was running for my life through Central Park. I'm losing my mind, I think. I settle deeper into the pillow and close my eyes. *At least I won this battle*.

In the middle of the night, when I wake and see the empty spot where Maddox had been, see the solid door, closed between us, I realize that I haven't actually won anything at all.

CHAPTER 2

"Sometimes I think it would be easier if there was a pill that could make you forget everything, you know?" I told Dr. Gardner during one of our Tuesday sessions.

"But we are our memories," he said. "If you erase your past, you wouldn't be you. You'd be a hollow shell, empty of everything that made you who you are today."

"But I'd have my same personality, right?"

"Well, yes, probably."

"I just wouldn't know why I was the way I was."

"Correct. But you'd still have the same emotional and psychological hang-ups. You just wouldn't know why they were there, rendering them impossible to work through."

I wondered at his use of the word *rendering*, wondered if I'd ever heard another human being use the word in a sentence before. For some reason, it sounded violent to me. "But how can my hang-ups still affect me if they're no longer a part of my story?" I asked. "If I've erased them from my mind, I wouldn't need to work through them."

"That's not what I'm saying."

"What are you saying?"

"Let's say you have trouble with commitment, for example."

"Yes," I said. "Let's say that." I smiled, but the joke was lost on him.

"Let's say you can't hold a steady relationship. This could be due to a past experience that you've yet to work through. It would be nearly impossible to process such an experience if you have no memory of it happening. But emotional memory and brain memory are two different things, you see? You'd still feel the effects without actually remembering them. If the memories were gone, the tools that would help you move forward would be gone as well."

"Yeah, well, I think I'd be okay with that," I said.

"No, you wouldn't, you'd—I don't know why this matters. It's not possible either way." He flattened his tie against his dress shirt, smoothing out the nonexistent wrinkles over and over again. I should have let the matter drop, but it was like an open wound. I couldn't help but poke it to see how much it hurt.

"What about hypnosis? Don't people use that to forget?"

"The opposite," he said, his hand settling into his lap. "People use it to remember."

"Oh, right," I said. "Maybe I'm thinking of alcohol." I laughed. Dr. Gardner didn't. He stared at me, straightened his tie again. Maybe he was waiting for me to say something else. It was a trick therapists used, letting the silence stretch until the patient decided to spill the beans.

"You know," I said, "your tie is a bit wrinkled. Just there." I pointed in the general direction of his chest. He didn't look. His eyes were fixed on mine, unblinking and robotic.

"I think maybe that's all for today," he said.

The rain looks almost like snow the way it falls over the city. Soft and drifting. If you look up, you can see individual dots hovering around the tops of the buildings as if hung on strings. The drizzle doesn't seem to deter foot traffic as we make our way down the street toward where Maddox's "friend" has found parking.

"How'd you sleep?" Maddox had asked me that morning over more of his ginger-pear tea.

"Terrible," I said.

"Told you it was uncomfortable. I slept like a babe." He smiled, sipping his coffee. "Toast?" he asked.

I agreed and he made toast with jam that was so full of sugar my lips felt coated with a thick film. Now, walking down the street with Maddox, I can still taste it. I look up at the sky and let the rain sprinkle my face, wash the sugar away.

"I don't mind the rain, either," he says. "Growing up in Washington, I suppose you either develop an appreciation for it or you sink into depression."

"Oxford isn't as rainy, but if the clouds bug you, you'll never manage."

"Hope you don't have seasonal affective disorder," he says.

"No," I say. "I have all the other ones."

He laughs. I smile.

Maddox's "friend" is a gorgeous Latina named Luciana. Of course she is. She's the exact opposite of me. Shorter. Wide hips. Tiny waist. I'd hate her if I weren't so awed by her. She's friendly, too. Outgoing in a way I've tried to emulate in certain periods of my life but have always failed at.

"Hi, you must be Jeanie." She shakes my hand, smiling. Her skin is warm.

"Thanks for letting us borrow your car," I say, trying to imitate her wide-lipped smile.

"No problem at all," she says. "I take the chance to use Maddox's pied-à-terre anytime I can." She laughs like it's a joke. I wonder if she speaks French. I think to ask her. If she speaks French, I'm leaving. I can't ride with Maddox in a car owned by a woman as beautiful as she is if she also speaks French. It's too much.

Maddox thanks her again and they embrace. She gives him a quick kiss on the cheek.

"Let me know if you have any trouble with the dishwasher," he says. "It's supposed to be fixed, but that thing's a piece."

"Will do, thanks." She waves one last time, smiling a perfect, white-toothed smile.

We get in the car, which is a 2016 Mercedes—of course—and Maddox starts the engine.

"Ready?" he asks, looking over at me. "What?" I'm giving him a look.

"Oh, nothing," I say. "She seems nice."

"Stop it."

"No, really. Like super nice. Like Miss America levels of nice."

He laughs. "Okay, we dated for a while. It didn't work out."

"How'd you let that fish get away?" I've never liked that phrase.

"She's definitely not a fish," he says, and I'm both proud of and annoyed at him at the same time. "And I don't really know. Some things just don't work for reasons that don't make sense, you know? She and I just made better friends."

"How long did you date for?"

"About two years, I think."

"Jesus," I say.

"It sounds like a bigger deal than it was. It was sort of a distance thing for a while and never got too serious."

We sit in silence while Maddox navigates the traffic out of Manhattan. I'm a little impressed by his driving. I haven't held a license for years. You don't really need one in Oxford—everyone just walks or takes the bus. And if I ever needed to go farther than the city center, I'd much rather take the train.

"What about you?" Maddox asks, both hands on the wheel, eyes darting from one mirror to the next.

"What about me?" I ask.

"Anyone significant in your life?"

I laugh, though it wasn't meant to be funny.

"What?" he asks.

"No," I say. "I'm not really the dating type."

"And what's the dating type?"

"I dunno. Someone who wears slippers."

Maddox's laugh is a barking thing. "Slippers?"

"Yeah, do you have slippers?" I ask.

"No. And I'm assuming you don't, either."

"No," I say.

"Well maybe someday we'll have to buy some slippers." A taxi cuts him off, but Maddox just applies the brakes and lets him in.

"Not me," I say. "I'm a closed-toed shoes, itchy sweater kind of girl."

We grow silent after that as Maddox makes his way over the George Washington Bridge. From there, we drive along the Hudson for a while, on a highway next to a line of deciduous trees, their boughs mostly naked and spindly in preparation for the coming winter. We take the 17, a small two-lane highway, passing evergreen-covered hills and towns that look abandoned.

"Where are you taking me?" I ask, looking out the window.

"Downsville. I know. It's kind of a nowhere town."

"Things are looking pretty *Deliverance* around here."

"I swear I have nothing but good intentions," he says, and we grow quiet again.

Eventually I ask him about how he got into investigative journalism, and he tells me about his start writing short stories and failing to get them published anywhere. How he witnessed a murder on the street and wrote about the experience. The article was eventually published in the *Washington Post*. From there, someone at the *New York Times* got a hold of him and he slowly worked his way up. I ask all the appropriate questions and am amazed and appalled in equal measure when necessary. After, he asks about my job at the dinner shop. I shrug the question off with a pithy answer and he leaves it be. He puts on the radio and we zone out to terrible pop songs.

A little over two hours later, we pull into Downsville. Everything looks old and run-down, as if one great wind might blow the whole place over. A gas station, a church, a bank, old houses.

"Downsville," I say.

"I know," Maddox says.

"The name kind of fits, doesn't it?"

He laughs and pulls up to a building with red and white trimmings, a white picket fence, and a bell tower sitting on top of the roof. In front of the building is a sign that reads THE OLD SCHOOLHOUSE INN & RESTAURANT.

"Cute," I say. In truth, it *would* be kind of cute if not for the location. This dead town.

A woman with a chipped tooth checks us in and tells us about an old covered bridge that is quite the tourist attraction. Maddox is kind to her, even making sure he understands how to get to the bridge before taking the room keys—which are actual keys—and heading up the stairs.

My room has a single bed and overlooks the green front yard. The bed is puke-green, the walls are lined with a vaguely floral pattern, and a blue lamp sits on an old wooden desk. Beneath my feet, the swirling patterns of a Venetian rug repeat, folding themselves again and again into infinity. It's disorienting to look at. When Maddox finishes dropping his stuff off in his room, which is right next to mine, he knocks on my door and I let him in.

"Not bad, huh?" he says, smiling.

"So what now?" I ask, throwing my bag onto one of the beds.

"Now it's up to you," Maddox says. "We have the rooms for two nights. It's"—he checks his watch—"almost noon. We can go grab something to eat, explore the town, or we can go find your dad." He says it so casually. It's that simple to him. *Go find your dad*. Words strung together in a haphazard fashion. They sink into my gut and sit there, boiling like battery acid.

"Wait, *we*?" I ask.

"Well yeah, I'm not letting you go alone."

"Is that supposed to be some sort of macho gesture?"

He opens his palms as if to show me there's nothing in them. "Sure."

"Bullshit," I say. "You want your story."

His lips do something between a smile and a shrug. "Can't it be both?"

"Yeah, fine, but you're not going."

"Jeanie, I don't know this guy I'm sending you to. I don't know—"

"If you're going, I'm not going." I cross my arms over my chest.

"You're kidding," he says.

I sit down on the bed. "You can drive me to the airport whenever you're ready." And I'm serious. Maybe I'm just looking for a way out, or maybe it's that if this becomes about his story, I don't want any part of it.

He pulls the car keys out of his pocket and swings them around his finger.

I reach out my hand. Maddox doesn't say a word as he sets the keys into my palm. It's as close to angry as I've ever seen from him. But it's not quite that. Flustered at best. It's almost cute.

"I'll text you directions," he says. "It's a little weird to get to."

"Okay," I say, heading toward the door. I haven't told Maddox that I don't have my license anymore. I don't want to give him another reason to come with me.

"Hey," he says before I've left the room. "Good luck, Jeanie." He's not smiling now. He's concerned. I don't like the look on his face.

"Thanks," I say. I wish I could sound more sincere, but I can't. I'm barely keeping my limbs from floating away as I step out the door. *He's not actually there,* I tell myself. *Neither of them are. This is all a waste of time.* Behind me, the door closes with a snap.

⬤

I take the 206 north out of town toward Bear Spring Mountain. Alders and evergreens zip by me as the gentle slope of the mountain rises to my left. Run-down houses dot the roadway; they look depressing. I wonder how people can live out here. I wonder how my dad might. I miss my house in Oxford, my clocks, my small patio out back. I miss Josephine, my fat cat. I very seriously contemplate turning around, telling Maddox to take me home. I could be on a flight tonight and home by the morning.

I don't turn around. I've come too far.

Following Maddox's directions, I take a turn that has no signage. It's a gravel road that follows the base of the mountain into a wooded area. The car bumps and rattles along. I think of Dad's truck dipping on the rutted road to our cabin in Washington, the smell of old apples from the rotting cores he'd always leave in the cup holder.

The road curves and opens to a large field, where the grass is as tall as a small child. The road forks and I stay to the left. One more curve over a cattle guard that shakes the vehicle like an earthquake, and I see the house. It's a small blue ranch with a wide front porch and a wooden shed just to the left of it. In front of the house is an unkempt yard with a riding lawnmower bleeding rust onto the front lawn.

The gravel sounds like tiny bombs detonating beneath the car's wheels as I pull up to the house. When I kill the engine, the silence feels like two bricks pressing on either side of my head. Small sounds make it through: birds chirping somewhere nearby, a dying fly droning near the windshield. I wait to see if anyone will step out the front door. Surely the man that lives here—Tony Carmichael, Maddox had said—would have heard my approach. Nothing stirs.

I pop open the car door, the sound loud in the afternoon air. The sky is bipolar: half is covered in dark rain clouds while the other half is brilliant sunshine—something about it unsettles me. I make my way across the lawn and up the step onto the wooden porch. The blue paint is peeling along the banisters, and the screen door is hanging off its hinges. Maybe I've gotten the address wrong. This house looks abandoned. I try the doorbell, but when I don't hear a sound, I knock. There are no footsteps for at least a full minute, so I knock again, louder this time.

"Hello?" I call. "Anyone home?"

Another few seconds go by before I finally hear footsteps, a voice calling out something I can't understand. The door swings open violently, and a man stands before me, buttoned shirt open to reveal a gray-haired chest and the swell of an equally hairy belly hanging over blue jeans. He's got a mustache that belongs on a magazine, but it's ruined by the gray stubble dotting his cheeks in uneven patches. He's got a full head of gray hair and eyes that are strangely kind, light blue, with crow's feet etched into his skin, dark lines that look like they've been tattooed on his face.

"Tony Carmichael?"

"Who're you?" he asks. His mouth keeps moving after the words are gone as if he's chewing something.

"I'm Jeanie King," I say. "I'm here because I think you know where my father, Johnathan King, is."

His mouth opens. I half expect to see tobacco or some partially chewed lunch in his mouth, but there's nothing. "Bullshit," he says, though the way he's looking at me, examining my face, I can tell he knows it's not bullshit. "You some kind of reporter?" he asks. His mouth has closed. He's on the verge of slamming the door in my face.

"Do I look like a reporter?" I say, not really knowing what I'm implying, but he eyes me up and down and seems to be satisfied.

"What's your mom's name?" he asks. And in the question, I realize something: Dad is here. He's close. Holy shit, Maddox was right. Tony wouldn't be asking me these questions if he wasn't actually hiding him. Sickness pulls at the base of my spine.

"Samantha King. Originally Samantha Bradford," I say. "She went by Sam."

Tony starts chewing again.

"I'm not here to get anyone in trouble," I say. "I don't want to turn him in. I don't want you in trouble for hiding him. I don't give a shit."

"So what do you want?" he asks, eyes still small and

unsure. Maybe he wants me to start crying, to tell him I've missed my dad, that I just want the chance to see him one more time. Instead, I say something approaching the truth.

"Mostly, I want to look him in the eye and tell him he's a fucking asshole."

Tony's lip twitches and it's either shock or a small smile.

"Let me get my coat," he says, turning back inside.

⊚

He takes me up the hill on a quad that rattles and sputters, jerking its way over uneven ground. I hold on tight to the little handlebars on either side of me, but I still feel like I'm about to fall off constantly. I feel suddenly lonely, on this machine with this man, who I know next to nothing about, heading toward my dad.

For the moment, the sun has won out against the heavy iron clouds, but I don't feel its warmth because of the cold wind blowing against my face. Tony takes a couple turns along the road, climbing a steeper slope. Beside us, a fence appears, behind which a small structure that looks like an outhouse sits half open. It's overgrown with moss like it's being eaten alive by the woods. Eventually we enter a small clearing with a gentle slope. And there's the cabin. Dad's new cabin. A ramshackle place, much woodsier and more makeshift than our old home on the coast. It has a single window, no porch, and is made of slats of wood with no paint. This is it? It's perfect, really. It looks exactly like the place where a soul goes to die.

Tony pulls up close and turns off the engine while I scan the windows of the cabin to look for any sign of life within. There's nothing.

A squirrel is chattering in a nearby tree. Overhead, a plane flies across the blue section of sky, spewing white contrails behind it. I picture the passengers in their seats. A flight attendant navigating the aisle with her overlarge cart of snacks and drinks—all of it a world away from me and this cabin.

"Looks like he's out," Tony says.

"Where?"

"Hunting. Checking his traps. I don't know. Honestly, I don't see him very often."

I look at the old man. He's wearing a flannel jacket and gloves with his blue jeans and brown boots. "You knew him from the army?" I ask, though I already know the answer from Maddox.

He nods. "I owe him my life. Literally."

I want to ask him more, find out what happened, but something more pressing makes its way to the surface. "Is he alone up here?"

"Alone?" he says.

"Yeah, does anyone else live with him? My, my brother Jamie went missing the same time as Dad, I just thought . . ." I can't finish the sentence.

"I'm sorry, I didn't know that."

Of course he didn't; of course Dad wouldn't admit to whatever he'd done to Jamie.

"He's here by himself." He has the decency to look away, even though I'm not crying. As far as I can tell, my face is stone. Jamie isn't here. Jamie is dead or gone. I knew it, and yet I'd let myself hope. A part of me wants to jump back on the quad and head back to the hotel. But I can't. Even if Jamie's not here, at least Dad knows what happened. He has to.

"So he should be back soon?" I ask, trying to sound casual.

"Hard to tell. He's got one of my old quads, so he's not on foot. But I can't tell you where he's gone to. I don't keep tabs on the man."

I look toward the cabin door. "Do you mind if . . . I think I want to do this part alone."

"You want me to leave you?"

"Yes," I say.

"I don't know how long he'll be gone," he says. "Could be a while."

"I can take care of myself," I say more confidently than I feel.

He nods. "Fair enough. He can give you a ride back down when you're ready."

"Thank you," I say.

He gets on his quad and starts the engine, looking at me like he knows he's supposed to tell me something else but can't quite bring it to mind. In the end, he rattles back down the path the way we'd come.

When I go to open the door to the cabin, it catches on something, but with a sharp tug, it snaps loose, and I step inside. It's a small space. A cot in one corner, a chair and a table in the other. A sink with a hose dangling above it. Shelves covered with tools, pots and pans, and bags of what might be spices or seeds. Two kerosene lamps are sitting on the floor waiting to be knocked over and broken. Beside the kitchen sink is a gun rack with three guns mounted on it. A Browning double-barrel 12-gauge, a bolt-action Remington 700 model, and Dad's old .308. I pick up the .308, hefting its weight in my palms. It's been a long time since I held a gun. All kinds of memories rush back to me. The sound of cans splitting, the rip of gunfire, the pungent smell of nitroglycerin. Beside the guns are boxes of ammo. I pick up a box of the .308 rifle cartridges and slide one into the chamber. The action is smooth and well oiled, the bolt sliding easily into place. It feels strangely good.

I hear the growl of an engine and for a second, I think maybe Tony is returning. But when I look out the window, I see a different quad coming toward the cabin from a trail to the north. I feel like I'm going to be sick. I feel like my body is going to float away from me. I feel a rope tugging at my insides. He's getting closer. I can make out his long hair and beard from here. He's older, grayer, bigger. Hair wild. He looks very little like the man in my memories. And yet it's him. I'd know the shape of him anywhere.

And suddenly I'm angry. My limbs are nearly shaking with it. All the other emotions congeal into this one solid feeling. I'm mad that he's here, riding this damn quad. That he's been hiding from the world, from me. That Jamie isn't with him.

I'm pushing the window open. It jams, but it's cracked enough for me to stick the barrel of the gun out. I look through the scope, see him on the quad, still coming like nothing is different. He has no idea I'm here. The crosshairs are hovering over his heart. I've already switched the safety.

What am I doing?

Had I planned this all along?

Dear Dr. Gardner, I've lost my mind.

Dear Jamie, this is for you.

My finger hovers over the trigger.

I take a deep breath.

My body grows still. Muscle memory.

I lower my aim. Lead the quad. Can't do it. Yes, I can.

The trigger feels liquid beneath my finger as I squeeze it tight. I don't even notice the recoil, but the report is loud, a flash-bang. The barrel strikes the base of the window and there's another crack: wood splitting. I see Dad stop suddenly, the tire I shot already sagging. He jumps from the quad, dropping to the ground.

I'm shaking now. I look through the scope, just to find him. I see his shoulder from behind the vehicle. There's no ammunition in the rifle now. I'm just watching, curious as to what he'll do. I see him rise slowly from behind the quad. He's got something in his hands. He's resting it on the seat. He's looking at it intently.

I lower my gun too late. The crash of his return fire. The shimmering flash of the window breaking into pieces. The sharp tug of the bullet entering my chest, exiting through my back. I don't remember hitting the floor, but I find myself sitting on the ground. Something warm blossoming inside me. I notice a pile of shards of glass on the wooden floorboard beneath the window. They look like diamonds. They sparkle a multitude of colors. It becomes all I can see. Such bright colors.

I don't remember passing out. Though no one ever does.

CHAPTER 3

The room is swimming. Something is burning inside me. This isn't right. Everything is wrong. A man's head hovers above me. His mouth moves and words spill out of it, black like tar. "Don't move," he says. His eyes are red coals. He's grabbing my chest now, his hands hot on my skin. I can hear a ripping sound and see bits of my flesh in his hands as he tears them to pieces. He's gutting me like a fish. Shredding my skin. But it's not my skin. It's my shirt. He's tearing it. Why? What is he doing? I need to get out of here, but I feel leaden.

"This is going to hurt," he says. He's got something in his hand. A cup of clear liquid. He pours it on me, and the sound of screaming fills my ears. I don't pass out as much as I dive headfirst into darkness.

When I wake again, the pain is still there, my head is thundering, but the room isn't as liquid. The man, my dad, is still above me, my naked chest exposed. I reach to cover myself and feel a cloth over my chest. At least there's that. I look at Dad and see that he's tying something into my skin. Holy shit.

"What the hell are you doing?" I ask. My voice is softer than I meant it to be.

"Stitching you, girl," he says.

"You have to take me to the hospital." I lay back, my eyes half-lidded. I can't feel the stitches going in. Why is that? I should be able to feel them.

"Can't," he says. "You shot the tire out of my ride and I can't carry you the whole way. Better you rest here. I know what I'm doing." The sound of his voice brings old memories to mind. I don't like it. Don't like what it does to me. Don't like any of this.

"Call someone," I say.

"Can't," he says. "No radio, no phones, no contact."

I shift to reach for my phone. "I'm calling for help," I say.

"You can do that, I suppose. But if you do, I'll be arrested."

This shouldn't stop me, but somehow it does.

"You shot me," I say.

"Didn't know it was you. You shot at me."

"Just your tire. Believe me, if I'd wanted to hit you, I would have." What am I trying to do, impress him? Still?

He doesn't say anything. He just pulls the wire or whatever it is he's using to stitch me. I can feel the tugging now.

"Already did your back. It was a nice clean wound, just under the collarbone," he says. "And you're lucky I only had the twenty-two. Otherwise your shoulder would be pulp. Ruined my window, though."

"You've got to be kidding me," I say. The pain is starting to build, but it feels like it's coming from deeper inside me—the base of the iceberg as opposed to the sharpened tip. He ties off the wire and presses a wet rag to my naked shoulder.

Then he stands and returns with a canister of water and a pill in his hand.

"Take this," he says. I pop the pill into my mouth and take the water. It nearly scalds my throat it's so cold. "Now you should rest."

"I'm fine," I say, starting to sit up. I look outside and see that the day has turned to evening. Crickets are singing in the brush. A chill wind is blowing through the open window.

"You've been shot, girl. Now rest."

I laid my head back, realizing that I'm on his cot. I have no memory of getting there. I reach into my pocket for my phone but find it's missing.

"Where's my phone?" I try to sit up again.

"Relax," Dad says, "I've got it."

"I need to text someone."

"It's Maddox, isn't it?" Dad asks. "Tony told me he's been asking around about me. I suppose that's how you found me."

"He's probably going to call the police if he doesn't hear from me."

Dad goes to the far end of the room and retrieves my phone from some hidden compartment I can't see. "How do I unlock this thing?" he asks.

"I'm not telling you," I say.

He looks at me, the phone small in his big, old hands. There's real worry on his face. A look I haven't seen from him before. How much of his life has he spent being worried? Looking over his shoulder? I don't feel bad for him.

Dad hands me the phone and sits down on the floor, cross-legged like some yoga guru. In front of him is the hearth, now blazing orange from the fire he must've built while I slept.

I look at my phone and see that Maddox has texted four times and called three. I text him back.

Everything is fine. I'm staying the night.

Then, on second thought, I text again. *Sorry if I'm MIA for a while. Bad reception out here.* I put the phone down on the cot beside me and laid my head back on the pillow. I can feel Dad watching me.

"What are you doing here, Jeanie?" he asks.

My shoulder and chest are burning, but I feel more clear-headed. "What do you think?" I say.

"Why?" he asks. "Why come and find me?"

"I didn't. Remember? Maddox did."

"You're not answering my question," he says, stabbing the fire with a black metal poker.

"I don't need to answer shit," I say, trying to reclaim my anger. And why shouldn't I be angry? He abandoned me, and now he fucking shoots me—okay, I did try to shoot him first, but still. "You're the one who has to answer me," I say.

He looks at me. His eyes are red, or maybe that's just the reflection of the fire, I can't tell. His beard is gray wires sprouting from his face like the inside of machinery. His hair reaches to his shoulders, but I can see the parts on top where it's grown thin. His face is rounder than I remembered, his cheeks are beginning to hang from his jaw. Time has found him.

He twists around and grabs a jug of something clear. Takes a drink. "Ask me anything," he says.

I open my mouth and instead of asking about Jamie or one of the other millions of questions I have, I say, "Fuck you." I'm enjoying my anger. I'm not sure I want to hear his answers yet. I just want to be mad at him like I wasn't ever allowed to be back in Washington. I realize something then: I'm not afraid of him. Fear had always been mingled in with any emotion I'd felt for my dad, but not anymore. There is just an emptiness now where the fear had been.

He takes another drink, looks back at the fire. We sit in silence for a long time. I drift off for what feels like only seconds. When I open my eyes, he's still awake, staring at the fireplace.

"Have you been here ever since you left?" I ask.

"I moved around a bit before contacting Tony. We were friends from Iraq."

"And he's been helping you?"

"He gets things for me when I need them. But mostly, I'm on my own. There's okay hunting around here. Lake's nearby with trout. Tony brings me fruit and vegetables and whatever else."

I wonder what it's been like for him out here. Alone in the woods for so many years. How has he not gone insane? Maybe he has.

"So . . ." He pauses, deciding how to say whatever it is he wants to say. His voice sounds slightly hoarse. "What are you—"

"No," I say. "I told you, you don't get to ask."

He nods as if he understands. "Fine."

Another silence. Wind whistling into the cabin through the broken window. I take a deep breath. It hurts.

"What happened to Jamie?" I ask, my heart smacking against the hole in my chest, pain in every beat.

"To Jamie?" he asks, the wrinkles of his face contracting.

"You killed him, didn't you?" The words shake as they leave my mouth.

"Kill him?" His eyes are on me, confused, intense. "My God, Jeanie. Do you hear yourself?" He lifts a hand to his forehead.

"He's gone, Dad. What else could have happened to him? He wouldn't have left me!" I'm almost shouting.

The silence that follows is menacing. The fire snaps. It feels like the whole world is holding its breath, time is standing still. Dad is staring at the fire. Good Lord, he didn't kill him. I can tell; he wouldn't have been able to hide that from me. He doesn't know about Jamie. He doesn't know what happened. If Dad didn't kill him, it means he actually left. He left me. But it also means he's out there, somewhere, doesn't it? And suddenly I don't want to talk to Dad about him anymore. He doesn't get to share in my pain about Jamie. He wouldn't care anyway. He never loved Jamie. Maybe he never loved me, either.

"Jeanie," he says, "what do you—"

"I told you, no damn questions."

He shuts his mouth, sucking his teeth. His eyes reflect the orange glow of the flames.

"Did you kill Stacy?" I ask—the next big question.

He takes a deep breath, rubbing his hand on his forehead again. "Yes," he says.

I know it shouldn't surprise me, but it does, laid bare like that. A wound ripped open, the pink insides revealed.

"Why?" I ask.

"I didn't mean to," he says, turning his gaze back to the fire. "I think she was high that night. Normally she wouldn't have hit you. She wasn't the best, I know, but she wasn't all bad. She wasn't the type to hurt a kid."

But you were, weren't you? I want to say. *Maybe you didn't kill Jamie, but you drove him away.* I keep my mouth shut.

"I forced her into the truck that night. I was drunk, shouldn't have been driving. She was so mad. God, she was fucking manic. She wouldn't stop hitting me. I told her to stop or I was gonna crash the car. She didn't stop. I was rough with her, I know that, but I had to get her to stop hitting me or I really was gonna crash. I gave her a good smack, just to stop her, but it made things worse. She got crazy, like real crazy. Screaming and spitting and clawing. She opened the passenger door and told me she was gonna jump if I didn't stop and let her out. I didn't stop." He pauses and takes a drink from his jug. "Then she fucking jumped. I didn't think she would.

I really didn't. When I found her, she'd hit her head on a rock or something. And she was gone. Just like that." He looks through the clear jug of alcohol as if it's a crystal ball and he's seeing the scene in it.

The silence that follows is a penetrating thing. It burrows its way into my skin.

"You didn't kill her," I say, more to myself than to him. "Not really."

"Yes, I did, Jeanie. Don't kid yourself. I killed her."

I don't want to fight over this. I don't really care. "Why did you leave without me?" I ask.

Dad grunts a laugh. "What did you want me to do? Lug you around the country, avoiding police and living off fucking garbage? You don't know what I had to do to survive, Jeanie. And if I'd taken you, what, then suddenly I've got kidnapping on top of everything."

"You could have stayed," I said.

"If I'd stayed, I'd have been arrested. Gone to jail. Is that the life you wanted for me? Is that how you wanted things to end? No. It was—"

"Yes," I say. The word is sharp on my tongue. I use it like a whip.

"Yes what?"

"You should have stayed. You should have let yourself get arrested."

"You're kidding." His smile is wan, lifeless.

"No. At least then you wouldn't have left. You'd have been taken—"

"I—" He tries to interrupt me, but I barrel through. Something long buried is bubbling to the surface.

"Like Mom." The two words sound like coins dropped in an empty bucket. They reverberate between us.

His lip twitches. He stabs the fire with the poker again.

"She didn't have a choice. You did," I say. "And you made

the wrong one. She wouldn't have done that." The words are molten liquid on my tongue, pouring out of me. But with each one, I can feel an opening in my chest, as if space is clearing for my lungs to stretch. I realize that my coming here wasn't just about Dad and Jamie. It was about Mom, too. Deep down, maybe I'm just a girl who misses her mom. It feels good to admit it. Feels right. Like I can finally breathe. "She was a great mom. When you left, she did her best. I know she was sad sometimes, but she tried not to show it. She was kind. She played games. She tucked me in at night. You used to be like that. You probably don't remember, but you did. I remember putting tiaras on your head and you'd laugh. But something happened to you. I don't care what it was, all I care about is that it changed you, and you came back all wrong. And instead of finding help, or fixing yourself, you fucked everything up. God, you fucked me up. I've been so fucked up." I place my right hand over my face, though I'm not crying. I still can't.

Dad's eyes are fixed on the fire. His face is placid like he hasn't heard a word I said.

"You want me to apologize," he says. It's more a statement than a question. I know in that moment that he won't. He won't admit to wrongdoing. He's too far gone in his own delusions. Or perhaps his own trauma.

"I don't want anything from you," I say with resignation.

"Should I apologize for serving my country? The sacrifices I made? Should I apologize for wanting to be with my family again? Is that it?"

"You never wanted to be with your family again. You wanted to drink and shoot."

"And didn't I teach you to shoot?" he asks. He doesn't say Jamie. Jamie never properly learned. Jamie got smacked in the head when he missed.

"I never wanted you to teach me to shoot," I say.

"What did you want?" he asks, turning to me, his face growing red, his voice louder. "Huh? What did you want from me?"

"I don't know," I say, raising my voice to match his. "I wanted you to be my dad! That's it."

He grows quiet, his body relaxing. He sets the poker down beside him. "I've always been your dad."

I don't respond. I don't feel like I need to. Whatever he says next doesn't really matter. The last of the molten anger has spilled out of me. I'm empty and it feels good. I close my eyes, lean back against the pillow behind me. I'm so tired.

"I won't apologize," he says. "No matter what happened, I've always been your dad and you can't take that away from me. I left because I had no other choice." He sounds more emotional than I've ever heard him. Maybe he's gotten soft in his old age. I picture him standing in the rain that day of the storm. He and Jamie and I screaming into the thunder. How solid he'd seemed. How large. At the time, I would have bet everything I'd owned that if lightning had struck us, he'd have lifted his mighty fists and punched it back into the sky. The tragedy of growing up is realizing your parents were just as vulnerable as you've always felt. That you were never as safe as you thought. That the rotten, festering thing inside you is something they put there, and you have to deal with it alone.

"I wish it had been me," he says, his voice soft. "It should've been me who died on tour. I've wished for that a million times a day, every day since coming home without her." *Her*, he says. Like Beetlejuice, he can't say her name, can't conjure her into this room. Then he laughs, a sad little chuckle. "You know the first thing I thought when you shot out my tire? I thought, thank God, this is it. Thank fucking God. And yet I couldn't help myself, could I? Even now, the damn instinct to survive kicks in. I'm too weak, really. You think it's a strength. Survival. That's what they teach you in the service. But it's not. It's a weakness. Mankind's biggest and most pathetic flaw." He takes another drink.

I realize I feel sorry for him. I've wanted to blame him all this time, but now I find I can't. We are made up of the choices we make, that's what William would say, but we're also, each of us, affected by a million different traumas a million times a day. I remember reading Flannery O'Connor at Oxford, memorizing the line: *Anybody who has survived his childhood has enough information about life to last him the rest of his days.* We're all survivors of something, aren't we? So who's to blame? Dad? The war that made him the way he is? The parents who gave him his genes? His natural proclivities that caused him to make the choices he has? Or is it something that goes further? Deeper? Is it society? Wars? Economic depression? The fall of Adam and Eve? The stars that birthed us? Or maybe God himself? I have no answer. But empathy has swallowed my anger.

In the ensuing silence, I close my eyes again. I sleep like I'm dead.

CHAPTER 4

The morning is bright; the grass shines with beads of dew. Two ravens are fighting in a nearby pine, making odd human-like grumbling noises. The glass from the broken window has been cleaned up, and Dad is nowhere to be seen. I sit up slowly. There's a tight pain in my chest and shoulder. It's not as terrible as I'd have imagined. Maybe it'll get worse. I find it both odd and exhilarating that a bullet has punctured my body and made its way out the other side. I feel different. Lighter. Like the bullet was my baptism and I've been cleansed by the saving power of hot metal through soft flesh. I've been pierced like Jesus. I lower my feet to the floor and stand slowly. I'm okay, and that realization startles me. I shouldn't be okay. But Dad bandaged me well. I can feel the gauze he's wrapped around my chest and shoulder. It's tight and a little uncomfortable, but I can live with it. God, I've been shot. I hear voices from outside, and when I look through the window, I can see Dad with Tony. They're replacing the tire I shot. I put on my jacket carefully and leave my ruined, bloody shirt in the middle of the floor.

I'm done with this place. I've had enough. Getting shot will do that to you, I guess. I step outside onto the wet grass and inhale the cool morning air. It reminds me of the coast. I have an intense and sudden desire to see the ocean. *My vision of the sea is the clearest thing I own*, Sylvia Plath wrote.

I walk down to the quads just as Tony is tightening up the last lug nut.

"You almost done?" I ask.

"Yup, just finished," Tony says.

"Good," I say, "I'm ready to go."

Dad looks at me as if he'd expected me to stay.

"Listen, Jeanie," he says. "Why don't you . . ." He can't finish the thought. *Stay awhile. Talk it out. Don't leave like this.* Maybe he wants to ask about my life, wants to know what kind of woman I've become. Maybe he wants to try to ask about Jamie again.

"I'd like to go," I say.

"You're still hurt."

"I'll be fine."

"We're not done talking," he says.

I nod. "I live in Oxford." The name of the city brings up the ghost of Mom; we can both feel her presence between us. "Come and find me if you want."

"You know I can't do that," he says.

"Bye, Dad," I say and step onto Tony's quad. Tony looks between us, then straddles the quad on the space in front of me.

Dad places his hands on the handlebars, looking at me as if Tony isn't even there. "Your mother always saw the best in me," he says. "When she died, she took it with her."

I nod again. "I understand," I say.

I look at him for half a second, waiting for the words to

form on his lips. *I'm sorry.* He looks like he wants to say them, but they're clogged in his throat. They can't claw their way out. He's as fucked up as we all are.

"Please go," I tell Tony. He gives Dad one more look before he starts the engine.

Dad lets go of the handlebars and steps away from the vehicle. There's more to say, but I'm done saying it. I'm done with this whole damn adventure. I'm ready to go back to my life and start living it without the plague of my father hovering over my shoulder. I'm ready, for the first time ever, to move on. I almost feel bad that I've come and left so quickly, that I've gotten what I came for and left him in turmoil. But I leave that feeling behind, too. The wind lifts my hair behind my head, and the quad rattles down the dirt road. Every bump sends a sliver of pain into my wound, and with each flash of hurt, I feel more alive.

⬛

There are some things in life you just never get to know. I think about that sometimes. How I'll probably die before we figure out for sure if aliens exist. I probably won't ever know what wiped the dinosaurs out, how the universe first came into being, or where the whales go to mate. Is that where you are, Jamie? Swimming among giant, otherworldly creatures in a kingdom of suffocating pressure.

People go missing all the time, their names written forever in the great book of lost souls. You never get to know where they've gone. You can only imagine.

I imagine Jamie escaping the cabin. I imagine him wanting to take me with him but knowing I'd try to talk him out of it. And he'd have done what I asked. Maybe he found a new family to live with. A new school. Maybe he found someone to love. Maybe he's even now teaching piano lessons to his kids or performing for thousands under a different name. I like that thought. I like picturing him like that.

Maybe, if there is a God, in the end, we get to ask him all the questions we never got answered. That'll be my first and, probably, my only.

Dear God, what happened to Jamie?

⬛

I knock on the door to Maddox's room at the Old Schoolhouse. There's footsteps from inside and the door snaps open. Maddox is standing in front of me, his eyes wide. It feels like I haven't seen him in months. Like I've been out of the country and am just now returning. I can't help but smile at his long sigh.

"Jesus, Jeanie." He closes the distance between us and wraps his arms around me. I wince from the pain in my shoulder, but it feels good to be so close to him. "I was so worried about you. I almost called the cops."

"Really?" I ask.

"Yeah. What happened? Everything all right?"

"Yeah, it's fine. I mean, I did get shot."

He frowns, not sure if I'm joking. "You got shot?"

"Yeah, it was a mistake. Dad shot me. He thought I was trying to kill him." It all sounds really bad coming out like that.

"What?" His frown has dissipated and his face is widening into all-out shock.

"Can we just get a drink?" I ask.

"A drink? You need to go to the hospital."

"No," I say. "I'm fine. Dad patched me. He's got field training. What I need most right now is a drink."

It takes a little while to convince him. He nearly drags me

to the car to get me to go to the hospital. But when I open up my jacket and show him the wrapping, he seems both scandalized at the amount of skin I'm showing him and temporarily appeased by the professional-looking bandaging.

Maddox forces an inordinate amount of Advil into me and we head down to the bar, Maddox still looking at me like I'm about to collapse at any second. The room is all wood and old lighting. The heads of animals protrude from above the bar, their marble eyes staring lifelessly. There's even a stuffed baboon in the corner, its mouth open, large ivory incisors sharp. This is a strange town.

The bar is closed, given that it's not quite ten in the morning, so we order breakfast. Maddox gets eggs and toast, and I get the eggs benedict with hash browns and a side of sausage. I'm starving. During breakfast, I tell Maddox everything that happened, everything Dad and I said. He listens as we eat. He has all the right reactions, asks concerned questions. Then he tells me we're going to the hospital, he doesn't care what I say.

The Advil has taken a tiny bit of the pain away, but my shoulder still throbs. I feel a little bit clammy. "Okay," I tell Maddox. "Let's go find a hospital."

The nearest hospital is in Walton, so we have to drive farther north to get there. Once admitted, they ask surprisingly few questions, as if a bullet wound isn't all that uncommon out here. I tell them it was an accident and they seem to understand. They redo the stitches in the wound on my back but leave the ones in my chest rather than reopen the wound. They bandage me up—not much better than Dad had done, to be honest—and then give me some powerful painkillers and antibiotics. After that, they send me on my way. All in all, a relatively easy process, considering.

☙

"So how do you feel?" Maddox asks. The day is bright, the sun meandering across the blank map of blue sky. It looks lost up there in all that open space. I trace the multitudinous paths it could take from one horizon to the next. Lucky, I think, that it doesn't have to choose. I'm envious of that. If only life were as simple as following the trajectory of the sun. But maybe that's the great joke of it all: maybe it really is that simple. The path of our lives as easy as the pull of gravity.

"Fine, I think." I do feel lighter, like I've unburdened myself of something. But I can't say that I feel good, or happy in this moment. I still don't know what happened to Jamie.

"I'm so sorry this happened. I feel like it's my fault."

"It's not your fault," I say.

"I'm the one who practically dragged you here."

"I'm glad you did."

"You got shot," he says, looking over at me briefly before turning his gaze back to the road.

"It happens," I say. To be honest, getting shot has contributed the least to all the emotions roiling inside me. But Maddox laughs, shaking his head. I'm smiling, too.

"I guess you've got your story now," I say.

He shakes his head. "No. I don't."

"What do you mean?"

"I'm not going to write the story."

"Why?"

"Because you don't want me to," he says.

I almost reach out a hand and touch him. "Are you going to tell the police?"

He shakes his head again.

This shouldn't feel like such a relief. I'm so grateful to him, I can feel it like a dull glow in my body. Although that could be the painkillers. I lean my head back against the headrest. I haven't felt this good without a drink in a very long time. I drift into that wonderful, honey-warm place between waking and sleeping. Maybe twenty minutes go by and then Maddox whispers, "You sleeping?"

I open my eyes. "Sorta, not really."

"Look, cows." He nods to his left, where in a wide green field, behind a wire fence, a herd of cows are chewing on the grass, their sloppy jaws circling, tawny hides almost golden in the sunshine.

"Ever play 'hey cow'?" Maddox asks.

"Hey cow?"

"Yeah. Like this." He rolls down the window. The wind rushes in, and Maddox sticks his head out. "Hey cow!" he yells. And for half a second, I see him as the high school boy all those years ago in the church parking lot, body lifted out of the sunroof, hair tossed in the wind, youthful and eternal. Four or five cows look up from their chewing. He rolls up the window.

"What the hell?" I say.

"How many looked up? Four?"

"I don't know, sure."

"Great. Four points for me."

"That's it?" I ask.

"That's it."

I start laughing, and he joins in. I laugh until it hurts, until we're both giddy with it. Soon we're laughing at each other for laughing so much. But it's more than that. We're laughing at the dumbass cows, laughing at my dad, laughing at the new hole in my body. I laugh so hard, there are tears in my eyes. I wonder if that counts as crying.

⊡

It's evening by the time we make it to Manhattan and trade Maddox's apartment for Luciana's car. Maddox doesn't tell her what happened, for which I'm grateful. He orders sushi, and we eat it with a bottle of white wine.

"You supposed to mix alcohol with your painkillers?" he asks.

"A few glasses won't kill me." And that's really all I have. We share the bottle and leave a little behind. I don't even really want it. Between the painkillers and the sushi—probably the best Alaskan roll I've ever had—and being here with Maddox, I don't need to get drunk. I decide for the millionth time that I'm going to quit drinking, even though in the back of my mind I know I won't. Or, rather, I will for a little while, feel good about myself, and then binge drink myself blind. But I don't want to think about that. I don't want it to ruin the good mood I'm in.

We don't talk about anything important that night. Instead, we run through times in Washington and the quirks of New York: Maddox tells me he once saw John Malkovich in Times Square eating a bagel.

"What kind of bagel?" I ask.

"Uh, I think it was an everything bagel."

"I knew it," I say.

"Knew what?"

"I knew he was an everything bagel kind of guy."

That night, I let him talk me into sleeping in his bed. He was right, the couch wasn't that comfortable, and I don't want to put my shoulder through the pain.

"You seem different," he tells me after we've turned off the lights and I'm climbing into bed in sweatpants and a T-shirt. My bandage is still wrapped around my chest.

"What do you mean?"

"You seem, I don't know, lighter since talking to your dad. Or maybe I'm just relieved you're okay."

"Well, other than getting shot"—bringing this fact up will be my new thing, I've decided: *Remember that one time I got shot?*—"I think I do feel lighter. I said what I wanted to say to him."

"But he didn't apologize."

"I suppose that would have been better. But I don't think I needed him to."

Maddox nods. He's sitting at the edge of the bed like he's about to tuck me in. I weirdly like it.

"You know, you're the best friend I ever had," he says, looking at the floor.

"I know," I say. He's silent for a moment, as unmoving as an effigy. He wants to say more. I let him think it through in silence.

"What happened between us—"

"I know," I say again. "I'm sorry. It wasn't the best time in my life."

"We were just kids," Maddox says. He smiles. "Good night, Jeanie." He stands, then leans over me, kissing the top of my head. He smells like shampoo and fresh mint from his toothpaste. "Let me know if you need anything."

He flicks off the light. The door clicks behind him.

The sound of cars passing on the street filters through my window. Next door, a couple is arguing about a video game they're playing. Around me is Maddox's life. The cocoon he's built for himself. There are no clocks in this room. There's a small desk in the corner with his laptop. A framed diploma or award of some kind on his wall. A mug full of pencils and pens and a silver letter opener. A lamp shaped like a tree. Little things that make up a life. A life he's lived without me. A life I have no part of. All of us, Dad, me, Maddox, maybe even Jamie, somewhere—our own rooms, our own separate lives, our own framed shit on the wall.

I'm rising from the bed. Pushing open the door. I see Maddox on the couch, reading, his glasses on.

"You all right?"

I crawl on top of him slowly so as not to hurt myself. He doesn't stop me, just says my name once. "Jeanie." It's a command to my limbs to stay where they are. For me to stay inside myself. My body listens.

I kiss him on the mouth, and it feels warm and familiar. Is this wrong? I think. Am I using sex again? Same as I always have? But this feels different. It's Maddox. Maddox's lips on mine. Maddox's hands on my waist. Something warm is building in my stomach. I pull the blankets over me and press my body into his.

"You ready this time?" I ask.

"Jeanie, your shoulder."

"Don't be such a pussy," I say.

He doesn't laugh. He stares at me. Then pushes me flat against the bed.

"Ouch," I grunt.

"Shit, I'm so sorry."

I laugh and he shakes his head.

"Damn you, Jeanie King." Then he kisses me, hard, as if to punish me. I pull off his shirt and he tugs at my pants. The feeling inside me is growing, heating, filling my stomach. Everything is moving forward now, chugging like a train. There's no more talking. Just small noises. The shush of fabric. An intake of breath. The warm slide of skin. The creak of the bed. My shoulder is beginning to hurt, but I don't care. Maddox is moving above me, his eyes fixed on mine. The feeling has grown and is growing still. Hotter. It almost hurts. It does hurt. There's too much. It's a dam ready to burst. Maybe my stitches are ready to break. I'm tearing at the seams everywhere. Maddox moves faster, and I move with him. I close my eyes, see a golden, glowing light. The dam is beginning to crack. I can almost hear the sound. An imperceptible groan as everything builds.

"Jeanie." He says my name in a single syllable.

The dam breaks.
And I break with it.

Maddox takes a cab with me to the airport in the morning.
We're mostly quiet in the car, calm and resolute in our happiness. He reaches across the seat and holds my hand. I want to
resist at first, but I let him. I've never been a hand holder. Hand
holding feels much more intimate than sex. But I don't mind
right now. I feel so happy in this moment, I almost feel guilty
for it. I watch the buildings pass by, cars honking, the cab
driver humming some indecipherable tune. Maddox's hand in
mine. I like being with him. I like the way I feel around him.
And then it hits me: I like that I'm getting on a plane and leaving him, too. I know it's not normal. Of course it's not. I'm
not normal. What did I think? One conversation with my dad
and everything would be peaches? It's not. I'm not. I'm glad
that I'm leaving because it makes a relationship impossible.
I'm glad that a plane is about to take me to another continent
because it means he won't have a chance to leave me, or I
won't have a chance to break his heart. We reconciled, Maddox and I, we made love. And that has to be the end of our
story. How could it be anything else? My happiness is waning
with the realization. I don't know what to do about it. I don't
think there's anything to be done.

He kisses me before I enter the security line.

"Jeanie," he says. "I want come visit you. Would that be
all right?"

I lean forward and kiss him again. "I think I love you,"
I tell him. The words escape easily even though they don't
make sense. Do I really know him anymore? Is he the same
boy I knew all those years ago? The same boy I kissed in
high school? Yes, and no. He's a man now, someone different,

someone removed from those other versions of himself. But I love all of them. "I think I've always sort of loved you."

His smile is wide and heartbreaking. "I love you, too," he says, brushing a strand of my hair away from my face.

"And I'm not ready for this," I say.

He tries to keep the smile, but it wavers, flickering like a glitching image.

"I don't know if I'll ever be ready for this," I say.

His smile has changed now. He's already accepting what's happening. He's always been like that. Always one step ahead of things. Or, rather, outside of the natural progression of the world, as if nothing is actually happening *to* him, just around him, and he's perfectly fine with that. "You're not the type to wear slippers," he says.

"What?"

"You said the type of people who date are the ones who own slippers."

I laugh. A small flitting thing that dies in the air as soon as it leaves my lips. "I did say that."

"Can I come visit you anyway?" he asks. "As friends?"

I shake my head.

"Jeanie—"

"I can't," I say. And I really can't. I'm like two people, one who wants to say yes with all her heart, and the other who resolutely won't allow me to move forward. The other is stronger, larger, has guns in her pockets. I can't move past her.

"Can I call you?"

I bite my lip. I nod, but it's reluctant, and he sees the reluctance. Maybe he won't call because of it.

There are tears in his eyes, and they break my heart. I know he wants to fight this just as I know he wants to respect it, and me. He's a good man. He always was. That's part of the problem, I suppose. In the end, he's the type of person who could never fully understand people like me. He can't bring himself to look at the dark underside of the world. And if he did, he'd see the tiny speck of gray at the corner and think, *hey, what a beautiful shade of gray*. How could someone like him ever be with or understand someone like me? And that's what a relationship is about, isn't it? An attempt at understanding another human being, to look into each other's eyes and say, "I get you." He could never get me. And I love him for it. That's part of the conundrum. I love him because he's incapable of understanding me. And I can't love him for the exact same reason.

"Thanks for everything, Maddox." I try to use his name the same way he uses mine. I want to ground him into my memory. Trap him, selfishly. Seal him away forever.

He wraps me in his arms and already things have changed. He can't kiss me now. Can't brush the hair from my face. All he has left is a hug. I squeeze him back.

"Get that shoulder better, okay?"

"Okay," I say.

"We need you whole."

"I wish," I say.

"Bye, Jeanie."

I make my way quickly to the security line. I turn around once and see that he's still there. He waves and I wave back. I don't know when he leaves. I don't look back again.

PART IV
Oxford

CHAPTER 1

My house is waiting for me. It's the exact same as I left it, but it feels different. The ticking of the clocks doesn't sound the same. Josephine avoids me as if she's punishing me for being gone so long. That night I get way too drunk. I have trouble lighting my cigarette as I stand in the small garden out back. Josephine stalks the bushes. I think a fox has been vexing her.

I've gotten a text from Manda: *Heading to the hospital. I think this is it! OUCH!* She's having the baby. I text back as enthusiastically as I can. Somehow, knowing she's more than just a wall away from me makes me feel lonely.

Maddox texts a few times as well. Generic things.

Make it home safe?

How's the shoulder?

Was so good to see you.

Before bed, I see one more text from him.

My sheets smell like you. I wonder if he's drunk. I wonder if he'll regret sending that one in the morning. I don't respond.

Instead, I wrap the sentence around me like water. Close my eyes. Can you drown yourself in words?

⬤

I'm standing in front of William Gardner's front door. He lives in a semidetached Victorian house at the end of a quiet, posh street. He's not at home. It's three thirty on a Tuesday. He's in his office waiting for me. But his wife is home. I can practically feel her presence in the house. A soft wind is blowing, making the red and yellow leaves on the maple trees dance. A few snap off and glide away, free until they drop to the ground.

I knock on the door. Four knocks because I like to stand out from the generic three-knock people.

It takes a minute—because she's not expecting anyone, because she has to put herself together—but when the door snaps open, she's got her makeup on and is wearing a pretty pink shirt with the front tucked into blue jeans: the french tuck. Manda showed it to me once, back when her belly allowed her to tuck shirts in. Mrs. Gardner is pretty, aging well, with bright blonde hair and only a few manageable wrinkles around her eyes.

"Hi!" She sounds friendly, smiling like she'd been expecting me. "Jeanie, right?" She remembers me. It's kind of her. "So good to see you."

"Hi, Holly," I say, feeling slightly scandalous, like I'm a child that should be more formal with her. "Could we talk for a minute?" I ask.

"Oh, sure," she says. "But William is at the office." I realize then that she doesn't know he's been seeing me—not just the sex part but the therapy, too. Of course she doesn't. He's probably kept it a secret from everyone. He used a pseudonym in his paper. He can't be seen to have been treating a former student of his. He'd be fired.

"Actually, I'd like to talk to you."

"Oh, of course, yes, please, come on in." She nearly stumbles on the rug as she opens the door wider for me. Is that panic in her eyes? Has her posture gone rigid? I can feel the curiosity burning off her like gasoline on fire. We've met only twice, once at the college and once at a party for the psychology department staff and select students. I remember the way she held on to William that night. I remember her eyes on me. I remember thinking, *God, she knows*. And I'd been right. Of course she knew. Maybe I'm not even the first.

I look around their home as if it's my first time being there. It's big and beautiful inside, newly renovated with an open kitchen plan, five bedrooms, a study, and a cloakroom. Outside are a sunken patio and a garden surrounded by a redbrick wall. It must've cost a couple million pounds, but William makes a good salary and Holly comes from old money, so they can afford it.

"Tea?" she asks, like it's compulsory.

"Sure," I say in the same manner. That's what you do in England. *Would you like some tea?* Answer: *Sure*. Also acceptable: *Yes please*, or *that'd be lovely, thanks*.

She leads me to the kitchen. Everything is bright, monochromatic. White countertops and white cupboards illuminated by the celestial shine of overhead pot lights. I turn around to see the stairway leading to the second floor where the master bedroom is. I can picture William leading me up those stairs by the hand, laughing. William's hand in my hair. On my back. Skin on skin. Hot breath. Pounding hearts. Empty house.

Holly makes the tea and I sit at the kitchen table in silence. The granite countertops have been pristinely cleaned as if she'd been expecting company all this time. "You've been all right, Jeanie?" she asks as the kettle slowly comes to a boil. I can see what she's really asking: *What are you doing here?* She pours the tea and hands me my cup. Her hands are shaking slightly.

"Yes, thank you," I say.

"Careful, it's hot," she says, as if I wouldn't know that already. We sit for a moment, each holding the handle of our teacups, blowing carefully at the top of the liquid. Our eyes meet and I think I see something in her gaze. A pleading behind her thick mascaraed eyelashes. She's begging me to leave, not to do what I've come here for. I don't know how much time I have. I don't know what William will do when he realizes I'm not coming.

"So," she says, "William has been—"

"I've been having an affair with your husband," I say, setting my cup down on the granite countertop.

Holly's jaw snaps shut. An audible sound. *Click.* Steam rises from her tea like fingers reaching for her throat. "What?" Her voice is shaking now.

"You probably know it already. I don't know. Maybe you don't. But it's been going on for years. I want it to stop. I want it all to be over, so I'm telling you. You deserve to know."

She looks down at her tea, probably grateful to have something in her hand to distract her from what I'm saying.

"I'm so sorry, and I don't know what else to say. I'd like to blame him entirely, but that's not the truth. I pushed things to where they are. Even though I was a student, I knew what I was doing, just like he did. I'm not a victim." As I say it, I realize that I don't know if it's entirely true. Partially, maybe. But I do know that I need to vilify myself. I need to let her know that she is the one being wronged, no one else. She sets her tea down carefully on the counter beside mine. Our two cups sit side by side, steaming together like it's a shared hobby of theirs.

I don't see the slap coming. Perhaps I should have. But it happens so fast. Her hand reaches out toward my face, and the sound it makes when it connects is harsh and impressive in the silent emptiness of the house. My head jerks to the side and I'm shocked by the sudden violence of it. I don't reach to retaliate. I deserve this pain, and she deserves this moment. But I can't stop my eyes from watering, the humming sting on my red face. I nod to let her know I deserve as much.

"I—" I start, but she lifts her hand to slap me again. This time I pull away and it stops her. "Sorry," I say, though I'm not apologizing about William, I'm apologizing for flinching, for taking her moment of fury away from her. I sit up straight, lift my head, angle my cheek just slightly toward her as an offering. She notices what I'm doing, understands, and I can see her body deflate, though her eyes are red and her bottom lip is shaking. She can't do it. I want to tell her it's okay. Go ahead. I deserve it. But the moment has passed. If I'd wailed and apologized, blubbered and recanted, she'd have kept hitting me, maybe worse. But, instead, I've stood my ground, offered her recompense in the only way I know how, and now she can't take it. Perhaps that's worse. Perhaps I should blubber and beg so she can keep hitting me.

"Get out of my house," she says, voice breaking, the wall she'd held around her so pristinely tumbling down. I stand and walk toward the door. I can feel her behind me, can hear her footsteps. I wonder if she's about to attack me again, strike from behind. She doesn't.

Just as I'm reaching for the door, it pops open. William is standing in the doorway. He's got an intense look on his face; it makes his blue eyes sharp as diamonds. He's appealing as ever and I'm—I realize—as fucked up as ever. I should have had more time. He shouldn't have made it back home so quickly. But here he is, silhouetted against the brisk late-fall day. The sunshine breaks into strands of gold as it splits through the trees lining the small cul-de-sac. If ever I were to believe in God, it's in this moment, with the three of us standing around the doorway, eyes darting one to the other, my cheek reddening, Holly's eyes watering, William's mouth moving wordlessly. God is real. Real in his cruelties. Hallelujah and Amen.

"Hi, Jeanie," he says eventually.

Holly laughs, a wild sound like a crazy person's. I've never understood her more; I bet in another life we could've been friends.

"What's going on?" he asks, but he knows. He's been waiting for this moment for years. We all have. Silently anticipating, each secretly hoping for this, none of us willing to bring it to fruition.

"I think you two should talk," I say as I duck past him.

"Jeanie," he says, but I'm moving down the driveway. I can hear their intense, whispered voices behind me. Even now, they're unable to properly scream at each other. I'm almost to the street when I hear a door slam, footsteps behind me. "Jeanie!" he calls again.

I stop, turn around slowly. William is running toward me, his face serious, not angry, but intense. "Stop, please," he says, though I've already stopped. I can hear a bus pass by on Banbury Road. People are loading on, unloading. I wonder where they're heading. Maybe a tour of one of the colleges. Maybe to the museum to take in some marble sculptures of Greek heads. I envy each and every one of them.

"It's over, William. I can't see you anymore."

"But the therapy. Our work together. We've made such great strides. You can't . . ." He stops because he realizes what he's admitted to. It was never about me, not really. That was a perk. It was always about his work, his research, his standing with the university and in the world of psychology. His relationship with me doesn't matter, his relationship with Holly doesn't matter, he's all that matters, it's all about him and his own perception of himself in the academic world, everything else is second. I feel sick. Sick that I've been a part of this for so long. It has been an on-and-off thing for something like fifteen years now. Both of us decide to end it every other year before picking it back up soon after. We were too intricately tied now. Too used to each other and this demented part of our lives. I feel sick for Holly. And sick that this is the closest thing to a real relationship I think I've ever had. Or maybe I'm kidding myself. This *was* a real relationship all along. It's not that I shy away from relationships at all. The problem is, I only seek out ones that I know are doomed to fail. I remember nights when I convinced myself that I loved him. But really, I loved the idea of him. The relationship that I didn't have to commit to.

I remember one night he drove me out to the country. We sat on the hood of his car like high schoolers and he held my hand. We didn't have sex that night and for the first time, I'd let myself believe that he actually cared about me. But even then, he was using me, using me as an escape from his real life, from Holly and the pressures of his job. I think I knew this all along but was unwilling to admit it, unable to break myself from it. But I was using him in a way, too, wasn't I? I was using him to not feel so lonely all the time. To feel like I had some sort of power over my life.

I turn and start walking again.

"Jeanie, dammit, wait."

I don't. I keep heading down the sidewalk toward Banbury Road.

"You know why I chose you?" he says. And I suppose *chose* is the right word. He was the sexy professor, he could have chosen anyone, exploited anyone's troubled past for sexual and economic gain. Dr. Gardner—a real and true gardener, reaching out his hands to snap the stem from his most favorite flower.

"It wasn't your history with your dad."

I keep walking. I don't want to hear any more. He follows.

"No, it had nothing to do with him, not really. It was Jamie. It was always Jamie."

"Fuck off," I say. I'm growing desperate now. I walk even faster. I'm very nearly running, willing him to stop talking.

"It's amazing what you've done, really. What you've created. I mean, sometimes he adopts characteristics that you wish you had, other times you give him your weaknesses. It's fascinating, really."

"Shut up," I say, not bothering to turn around, not willing to run yet. My bus isn't here anyway.

"It's not quite false memory syndrome, and it's not quite schizophrenia, either. I think it's something entirely different. Some form of disassociation. This is what makes you so fascinating, Jeanie. This is what makes you so singular. You can't walk away from this, not yet."

I stop walking. My heart is racing. My breath is caught in my throat. My limbs are beginning to abandon me.

"Fuck off," I say again, but the words are weak, half-hearted. They're all I can manage. He can tell that I'm fading. I want him to wrap his arms around me. I want him to tell me it's okay, everything is going to be all right. I want to bury a knife in his neck.

"Jamie's not real," he says. He doesn't need to say it, but he does. The words fall off his tongue and land on me like heavy stones. I remember a scene in *The Crucible*, where a character is interrogated as they stack rock slabs, one on top of the other, onto his chest until his rib cage collapses under the weight. That's how I feel. I can't breathe.

"You've known, of course. You've always known. You've been aware of the fact but unable to distance yourself from it."

"That's not true," I say. "Why are you saying this?"

"Your family knew, too. But they were warned not to confront you about your psychosis, though they didn't always abide by that, did they? Your father said something to you, didn't he? Your aunt as well."

"No, she didn't." My voice is weak, bloodless.

"She did, Jeanie. You told me yourself. My God, your selective memory is outstanding. Jeanie, you're the most interesting woman I've ever met." That look on his face again. I'm a prize to him. A piece to be collected. An achievement, a degree to frame and hang on his wall.

"Jamie's dead," I say like the sentence proves my point. How can someone who doesn't exist be dead?

"You got rid of him when your dad left. Jamie had become a barrier you kept between you and your father. When your dad left, the barrier broke. You couldn't keep him up. That's my theory, anyway. In a sense, I suppose, your father really did take him from you."

It's not true. None of it. It can't be. I can hear Jamie's voice in my head that night. The last night before they disappeared. "Jeanie, you're . . ."

Only it wasn't his voice, was it? It was my dad's, standing in the doorway, about to leave me. "Jeanie," he'd said, "you're the best part of me." The rope that tugs at my insides breaks. An audible snapping. A cracking inside my chest.

"It's okay," William says. "I can fix you." They're the exact words I want to hear and he knows it. Fix me. Make me normal. Remove the slithering, worming, burrowing thing inside me that makes me the way I am.

I look him in the eye, take a deep breath. Somewhere, a magpie is laughing in an evergreen bough. *Fix* you? the magpie thinks, laughing, laughing. "I hope," I say, the words slow and careful, "that, someday, you make your wife unbearably happy."

He looks both confused and hurt at the same time. One day the words will sink in, and I hope to God he drowns in them. *Yes, words can drown you.*

I turn one last time and reach the street. There's a young couple waiting at the bus stop, laughing at some shared joke, some intimate connection. Perhaps because of them, William doesn't follow.

When the bus arrives, the doors open and the couple gets on. I stand there, staring at the vehicle—all the people inside. The step between the sidewalk and the bus seems insurmountable. How have I done this a million times without falling on my face? How can I manage that step when my limbs aren't attached to my body? I'm practically shaking.

"On or off, miss?" the driver says.

I don't say anything. Eventually he's forced to drive away. I walk the long way home.

I don't know how it's possible to hold two opposing memories in my mind, but somehow, I've managed. The dichotomy of Jamie's existence and his lack of existence. But it's the truth. I can both put my hand on a Bible and swear he was real and at the same time know he wasn't. I can see it all. Dad and I in the cabin. Maddox and I at the beach. Dad's hand smacking the back of my head when I missed a shot. Bruises on my arms and neck. Dad and I screaming at the lightning. Crying beneath the bed by myself. Writing letters: *Dear Jamie. Dear Jamie. Dear Jeanie.*

Mom after the crash, reaching toward me, not Jamie.

"Are you okay?" I can hear her voice still. We're sitting in

the ruined vehicle. The car is crushing her body. Elk are flee-
ing in the distance. My limbs floating. "Jeanie."

"I'm fine," I said. "Is Dad going to come home now?" I
asked, my voice shaking. I wanted everything to go back to
normal. I wanted to go home. I wanted Dad to throw me in
the air. For Mom to read me a story before bed.

"Yes, baby, he'll be home."

I can see her reaching for me then, turning as far as she
could to touch me, but her body couldn't make it the whole
way. She wasn't going for Jamie; she was trying to comfort
me. And I could have touched her. I could have lifted my hand
and grabbed hers. But I was so scared, terrified that if I lifted
my arm, it would float again and keep floating away from me.
I couldn't move. God help me, but I couldn't. I think that's
the moment when Jamie went from being a figment of my
imagination to a deep-seated psychosis. If she was reaching
for him, then I didn't have to feel bad that I didn't reach out,
that I didn't touch her one last time.

"Are you okay, Mom?" I asked, still unable to move.

"I'm fine, sweetheart, we're fine," she said, twisting, twisting. Her hand so close. "Everything is going to be just fine."
Her head fell forward, her eyes open like she was looking for
something on the floor.

I tried to wake her up afterward. I remember I was screaming for her when the truck driver found us. But after he'd
pulled us both from the car, laying my mom's broken body
carefully on the grass, I pointed back at the ruined vehicle.
"Get Jamie!" I yelled at him. "Go get Jamie!"

Sylvia Plath: *I shut my eyes and all the world drops dead . . .*
(I think I made you up inside my head.)

Now, walking down the street toward my house, I can see
Jamie. I know it's all in my mind, but I'm breathless with
the relief of seeing him. He's standing on the corner, waiting
for me. He's not as old as he would be now, nor is he quite

the young boy I'd imagined with me in Washington. But he's clear and real as anything. Blond hair, blue eyes, beautiful in a way that I'm not—in a way that Mom was. I wrap my arms around him. Kiss him on the cheek because I know I'll miss him terribly. I rest my head on my brother's shoulder. He tells me everything is going to be all right.

He smells like the ocean.

CHAPTER 2

Maddox has texted and called. I've ignored him. His latest text reads, *I hope this means something to you,* and he's included a link to an article. I open the link and read the headline. "Man Wanted for over Fifteen Years Turns Himself In." I read the article as if in a daze. See the grizzled picture of the man I'd just seen days ago. He's in police custody. He's been arrested. He's awaiting his trial.

"Holy shit," I say. He actually turned himself in. Why? I can't stop staring at my phone, at the picture of Dad. This shouldn't make me so happy. This shouldn't change anything.

It does.

He won't say what made him finally go to police after over fifteen years living in isolation, the article reads. I'm not glad he's going to jail. I'm not rejoicing in his misery. I'm the only one who knows what it means that he's given himself up. Only I can see the reconciliation in his actions. The plea for forgiveness. The absurd act of love.

"About time," I say, smiling.

Instead of responding to the article, I text Maddox, *You said you read Dr. Gardner's paper, right?*

Yes, he responds, right away.

Then you know about Jamie.

The dancing ellipses appear at the bottom of my screen to show that he's typing. *Yes. It's all true?*

I almost want to laugh. He's asking if I'm crazy, I guess. *Yes*, I type.

Do you want to talk about it?

No. I just want you to know . . . I stop. What do I want him to know? Something important. Maybe I want to know if somehow Dr. Gardner is wrong. Maybe there's been a mistake. Maybe if I ask Maddox about Jamie, he'll tell me of course he's real. He'll give me his new phone number and address.

But none of that is true and I know it. *We are our memories,* William says. But what if my memories are wrong? What does that make me? I feel embarrassed, humiliated that Maddox knows this thing about me, this flaw in the internal mechanism that makes me who I am. He's known for a while now. And yet he said nothing about it. That almost makes it worse—his silence. It takes me a while to write, but eventually I manage: *I care about you. But I can't be with you. Not like I am.*

What if I can help? he asks. His words are too close to Dr. Gardner's: "I can fix you."

You can't.

I'd like to.

I know, I write. The ellipses dance then fall. Dance then fall. There's nothing else for him to say and he knows it. Dance then fall. Dance then fall like waves on an ocean. Seagulls screaming overhead.

Two kids on the beach. The smell of french fries. I close my eyes. See us there still. A firework flashing. An imprint of light.

☀

I'm knocking on another door. One, two, three, four.

Donald, Manda's husband, opens it. "Oh, hi, Jeanie, how are you?"

"I'm fine," I say. "How are you guys doing?"

"Tired," he says, looking as exhausted as if he were the one who gave birth. "You know how it is."

I shake my head. "Actually, I've no idea."

"Yeah, well, right. But, you know, you can imagine."

"Sure," I say.

He stares at me for a second longer like he's forgotten why I'm standing there. Manda has been texting me, asking when I can come see the baby. Maybe he doesn't know. I've got a plate of lasagna in my hands that Deloris let me take home for Manda. Maybe Donald thinks I'm there just to drop it off.

"Is it a bad time?" I ask.

He shakes his head as if to clear it. "Right, no, come on in, please." He's disoriented. He's seen his wife split open like a bloody flower and push another human out of her body. The impossible violence of new life.

I enter the terraced house, which is laid out similarly to mine with its hallways and doors and small rooms. There aren't as many clocks, and there's more decoration. Fake plants, pictures of family, a painting of a forest in winter. I realize I've been in this house maybe only a few times in all the years I've lived next door. Manda was always the one to come over, seek me out. I feel bad about that now. I haven't been the best of friends.

"Here, I can take that," Donald says, taking the plate of lasagna from my hands. "Thank you," he says.

"No worries."

"She's just upstairs," he says.

I ascend the stairs, hand on the wall as if to steady myself.

I feel unmoored in this place. My own home is a wall away, and yet it may as well be miles. What do I do if she wants me to hold the baby? What do I say to her?

The door to her bedroom is partially open. I can hear a voice coming from inside. It's Manda. She's singing. Something about the sound fills my chest with liquid warmth. But it hurts.

I knock softly on the door and peek around.

"Jeanie," Manda says, smiling. Her voice is a little hoarse, but she looks genuinely pleased to see me. There's a bundle of blankets resting on her chest, wrapped tight. I can see the shape of the head, a dollop of black hair poking out one side.

"Is now a bad time?" I ask.

"No, no, of course not. Come on in."

The room is dim, with the curtains half-drawn to let in a sliver of sleepy sunlight. Everything about the room is calm and gentle. Pink blankets, a co-sleeper nestled beside the bed, outlet plugs already fastened into the walls as if the baby might crawl at any moment and stick her fingers in the little holes. Nesting, that's what they call it. What a bird does before laying eggs: preparing the nest, making everything comfortable and safe for the arrival of her offspring. I can picture Manda now, wings downy soft and wrapped gently around her child.

"How you feeling?" I ask.

"I'm wonderful," she says. I want to laugh but don't. Donald is *tired*. Manda is *wonderful*. "I think my vagina is ruined, though. I'm afraid to look."

"Maybe it's best not to for now."

Manda's hand is moving up and down, patting the bundle in front of her.

"Did it hurt?" I ask, knowing it's probably a stupid question.

"Oh yes," she says. "At least, I think so. It's sort of a blur.

And once I met her, I forgot about the pain. I know that sounds mad."

"No, it doesn't," I say, both because it's the right thing to say and because it's true. Manda wouldn't know mad if it bit her in the ass.

"You wanna hold her?" she asks.

My palms go instantly sweaty. "No, I better not."

"Go on, you'll be all right." She's already sitting up, straining ab muscles that haven't yet stitched themselves back together.

This is the moment I'd been scared of. How do you tell someone that you don't want to hold their baby? That you can't. That there's something inside you that won't let you, another version of yourself stopping you from doing what you know would be fine. That you don't trust your own limbs not to float away from your body. *It's not your baby,* I want to say, *it's me.*

She's sitting up now, gently lifting the bundle of blankets toward me. "Here you go, then." And it's the expectant look on her face, the trust and joy, her cheeks puffy and warm, that breaks the barrier inside me, at least for a split second. And in that second, I see my arms reach out and accept the child.

"Oh God," I say. The blankets are soft. I can feel the baby's limbs twisting around inside, and it surprises me. It's as if I expected her to be immobile, docile as a doll.

"There you are," Manda says as I pull the child into my chest. "You're a natural."

The baby is warm and smells sweet, like sour milk. Her face is squished, like a raisin. She yawns and it stretches every part of her skin. Her mouth goes bloodless white. It's the most amazing thing I've ever seen. A set of fingers rests outside her blanket as if she's holding the fabric to her chest. Her eyes are closed.

"She sleeps all the time," Manda is saying.

I press a single finger into her forehead, feel the soft, velvety skin give way. It's soupy and pliable and my finger leaves a tiny pale mark that slowly disappears.

"Donald says she looks like him, but I mean, how can you tell, right? She's days old. She looks like a baby."

I begin to rock back and forth. I feel like I'm enacting a scene I've seen in a movie. Mother holds baby. Mother rocks baby. This is what you're supposed to do, right? Oddly enough, it feels natural.

"She's perfect," I say. "What's her name?"

"I texted you," Manda says. "It's Hope."

Hope. Of course it is.

Donald calls up from downstairs, asking if we want tea.

"Sure," we both say in unison.

I begin to imagine this child's life. The useless things her parents will buy for her. Manda combing her long hair, pulling it into braids. Her first words. Her first bites of solid food. Her first steps. Her first bike ride. Her first time behind the wheel of a car. Her first love. My God, she will be so loved. I can feel that love like a warm bath spilling from Manda. This child, Hope, has the whole world in front of her. As long as there is that love, she will have everything she needs in life. The love of a mother heals all wounds. The love of my mother always did.

I know I'm about to cry only seconds before I see the teardrop fall from my face and onto the baby's cheek.

"I'm just gonna close my eyes for a minute, if you don't mind," Manda says. From downstairs, Donald is asking if we care for milk or sugar.

I don't lift my gaze from Hope. I watch her small movements, her face as she makes her little noises, the way her spine bends one way, then settles into another. Did I move like this when my mom held me for the first time? Did she picture this moment as she reached for me in that car all those years ago? I'm crying like a baby. Sobbing silently. A ball in my chest is slowly dissipating with each tear. I'm soaking her blankets. My legs feel weak. I find a rocking chair in the corner of the room and sit.

I rock back and forth while mother and baby sleep, crying as if the hole in my chest, or the baby in my arms, has finally ripped my heart wide open.

❧

"So what do you want to get out of this?" my psychologist asks. Her name is Dr. Baker. She has graying hair that frames her face in gentle curls.

I miss my mom, I want to say, but I can't bring my voice to form the words. *I miss my brother, too.* I know how absurd it is. I know it's all in my head. And yet I miss him like something that has been ripped from me, something ethereal but essential—like I can no longer feel a phantom limb that was never real to begin with. I can still picture him, hear his footsteps beside me as he followed me down the path to the beach. He wasn't real. *He wasn't real.* "I think I'm crazy," I say.

"*Crazy* is a term society invented to help it compartmentalize mental illnesses it doesn't understand," she says, her words confident, powerful. I like her already. "Nothing about what happened to you, Jeanie, is okay. It's completely *sane* to have such a visceral response."

"I think," I say, "maybe . . . I don't know. Maybe I need some meds."

She looks up from her notepad, smiling at me like a loving grandmother. "Let's talk, shall we?"

I nod, tears already welling in my eyes, coming so easy now that the wall has been broken. *I've* been broken.

In the corner of the room, a large analog clock makes a lovely snapping noise, marking the passage of each second.

The day is bright as I make my way to the dinner shop. The air is cold, but the sun is in its last phase of warmth before it gives way to the winter frost. People move around me, going about their days, smiling, or keeping their heads down as we pass each other on the sidewalk. The pavement feels solid beneath my feet. I'm looking forward to my shift. Looking forward to the smell of clean countertops and the barely perceptible frosty scent of frozen foods. I'm looking forward to seeing Deloris, asking how things are with her boyfriend.

I pass a small clothing store on my way and see a display in the window. A mannequin with a soft pink robe and matching pink slippers. I stop and look at her plastic feet. The slippers are fluffy and ridiculous—something I wouldn't wear in a million years. I take out my phone, snap a picture, and before I can think it through, I send it to Maddox with the caption *Someday*. It's probably a mistake. But I can't help myself. I wonder if he remembers.

I put my phone in my pocket and keep walking. When I pass by the music shop, I stop again. I stare into the store at the piano sitting by the window. The sun reflects off the glass in blinding ribbons. The little bell overhead jingles like water over small stones as I step inside.

I see the Scottish store owner—Billie, I think it was—standing by the counter. He's talking to a young girl who's holding a viola in her hands. He sees me, gives me a friendly wave.

I make my way slowly toward the piano, place a hand on the glossy surface of its body. It's a Blüthner grand. My heart is thrumming in my chest.

I sit down on the black varnished stool—uncushioned, uncomfortable, but familiar. I look briefly at Billie. He's watching me but still talking to the girl with the viola. I turn back to the piano. *Gershwin's Rhapsody in Blue. Rachmaninoff's Piano Concerto no. 2. Beethoven's Sonata Pathétique.* I can hear them all still, humming inside my veins. My hands rise expertly in front of me as if being lifted by spherical pockets of air. Slow and convex. I feel my phone vibrate in my pocket as I place my fingers delicately upon the ebony and ivory keys. I take a deep breath.

Then I begin to play.

ACKNOWLEDGMENTS

I owe so many people my gratitude. Without them, this book wouldn't exist.

To Michelle Brower, who picked me and my novel up from a dark place, dusted us both off, and made us shiny again. I couldn't ask for a better partner in this business. To the wonderful Caitlin Landuyt for her early enthusiasm and brilliant edits. To Edward Kastenmeier and the whole team at Anchor Books for their belief, passion, and hard work on behalf of my book. To Blake Crouch for helping steer me in the right direction when I was at a cross-roads. To Mark Haskell Smith, Jill Essbaum, Tod Goldberg, and the whole UCR Palm Desert MFA crew for the continued support.

Thanks to my early readers, Julie Block, Dr. Mary Turri, and Tara Block, whose encouragement and insights gave me the confidence I needed. To my dad and Adrian for the constant support and advice. To the Block sisters for supplying me with a place to disappear and write.

To my whole family for being my biggest, first, and best fans. To my kids for the daily inspiration. And to my wife for pushing me off that cliff when I needed it most.

ABOUT THE AUTHOR

Tyrell Johnson is a writer and editor with an MFA from the University of California, Riverside. His debut novel, *The Wolves of Winter*, was an Indie Next List pick, an *Entertainment Weekly* must-have novel, a *Vogue* winter reading selection, and an instant national bestseller in Canada. Originally from Bellingham, Washington, he currently lives in Kelowna, British Columbia.